The Rival

Also by Maisey Yates

Secrets from a Happy Marriage
Confessions from the Quilting Circle
The Lost and Found Girl

Four Corners Ranch

Unbridled Cowboy
Merry Christmas Cowboy
Cowboy Wild
The Rough Rider
The Holiday Heartbreaker
The Troublemaker

Gold Valley

Smooth-Talking Cowboy
Untamed Cowboy
Good Time Cowboy
A Tall, Dark Cowboy Christmas
Unbroken Cowboy
Cowboy to the Core
Lone Wolf Cowboy
Cowboy Christmas Redemption
The Bad Boy of Redemption Ranch
The Hero of Hope Springs
The Last Christmas Cowboy
The Heartbreaker of Echo Pass
Rodeo Christmas at Evergreen Ranch
The True Cowboy of Sunset Ridge

For more books by Maisey Yates,
visit maiseyyates.com.

MAISEY YATES

The Rival

CANARY STREET PRESS

CANARY
STREET
PRESS™

ISBN-13: 978-1-335-00627-1

The Rival

Copyright © 2024 by Maisey Yates

For questions and comments about the quality of this book,
please contact us at CustomerService@Harlequin.com.

TM is a trademark of Harlequin Enterprises ULC.

Canary Street Press
22 Adelaide St. West, 41st Floor
Toronto, Ontario M5H 4E3, Canada
CanaryStPress.com

Printed in U.S.A.

For Megan, Jackie and Nicole
for your invaluable support while I wrote this one.
You're the best friends anyone could ask for.

CHAPTER ONE

IF THERE WAS one thing Levi Granger knew, it was that he was never—not ever—getting into bed with someone from Four Corners.

They were, in his opinion, a ranching Death Star. Their choke hold on the region was why he'd formed the Huckleberry County Ranching Association five years ago. Four Corners had resources many of them could only dream of, and Levi had never been comfortable with one group having so much power. So he'd decided to do his part to try to balance that out.

Maybe, just maybe, it was partly because he had an old-school axe to grind with the Four Corners folks. But that wasn't his driving motivation. Being petty could only get you so far, and it certainly couldn't earn you the respect of your peers, which he'd done.

His voice was now one of the most influential in the community apart from the Four Corners people, and he took pride in that. And if it was partly because of his prior experience with Four Corners, fine.

It only meant he knew better now.

He'd been there and done that, in a business deal gone horribly wrong, and he'd learned his lesson. He wasn't going to sign himself over to them, to their collective, no matter how nice and clear-cut the deal seemed.

No matter how persuasive of a presentation they gave tonight.

Levi Granger was no longer a man who could be persuaded.

"Do you think that they'll do a ritual?"

Levi looked down at his little sister, who was full-on gawking as they walked into the barn that served as a meeting place for Four Corners Ranch.

"Obviously not," he grunted. "They only pray to Beelzebub when none of the uncleansed are around."

"So this is more like recruitment. A promise of enlightenment, and once you actually sign up, then the blood drinking begins."

He chuckled softly. It did something to ease the tension that he had felt creep up into his shoulders the minute that he had driven onto the property.

He hadn't been on the Four Corners property in more than a decade, and having to come back just made him mad. It served as a memory of all kinds of things. Things he preferred to not think about. Particularly difficult times in his life that he didn't like to dwell on.

Camilla, on the other hand, had no such baggage when it came to Four Corners, and had been desperately curious to come onto the property and get an inside look.

He understood.

For those who weren't part of the Four Corners collective—either as an employee or as one of the founding families—it remained a mystery. A ranching monolith out here in the middle of nowhere, in Pyrite Falls, Oregon.

They were far bigger than any other operation out here. Hell, they were the biggest family ranching operation in the state. A group of four families whose land totaled forty thousand acres all up.

They supported one another financially, they made decisions as a team, and they basically made it almost impossible to earn a living as a rancher in the surrounding area.

Not without being creative, at least.

The town had been invited to this meeting because now the Sullivan family—who Levi had personal beef with, the conflict kind, not the literal kind—wanted to create a new road access onto the Four Corners property that would make a road that bypassed Pyrite Falls altogether and bring people straight to the farm store that they were making at Sullivan's Point.

The small ranching collective that Levi ran, a response to Four Corners, was against it.

As was the town council.

And he had been chosen to voice the dissent today at the meeting.

He knew how this kind of thing went. Typically, the Four Corners people did whatever they wanted to in isolation, but when they asked for outside community approval, they expected townsfolk to fall in line. They expected the townsfolk to agree with them because they had money and a certain amount of influence in the community. Because many people sent their kids to school at the little schoolhouse on the property, many people worked for them or had family who did.

Levi stood apart. A rancher who wasn't afraid to go after them, head-on.

Because he already knew what a disaster it was to try to work with them. And he wouldn't be doing it again.

So he had been the natural choice to get up and speak his mind.

He didn't have his speech written down. He had it in his head.

In his heart.

He knew exactly what needed to be said, and he wasn't afraid to say it.

They waded through the crowd, and he and his sister Camilla took their seats in the front row, on the far left.

The Four Corners people were on the right.

At the front were Denver, Landry, Justice and Daughtry King. Then there were Wolf, Sawyer and Elsie Garrett.

The McCloud family, which consisted of Taggart, Angus, Hunter, Lachlan and Brody.

And then there were the Sullivan sisters.

God knew he couldn't tell them apart. Redheaded, all of them, and in floral dresses. There was one that was holding a baby, and sitting next to Angus McCloud. He'd heard through the grapevine that the McClouds and Sullivans had married up to one another. He knew that the oldest one was Fia, and she was probably the one seated at the far end with a neutral expression on her face. She had the look of an oldest child—he should know. There was another staring off into space, twisting her hair around her finger.

And there was a third, with her red hair tamed fiercely into braids, and very large glasses perched on the end of her nose. She was wearing a baggy set of overalls, the kind that he had never understood, because they made you question whether or not you were looking at a woman or a toddler—and she had a notebook on her lap. She was scribbling furiously on the pages, and looking around the room, pushing her glasses up her nose, before looking down again.

She had sharp features, and she reminded him a bit of an ermine.

And in turn, reminded him a bit of her father.

Brian Sullivan was a man that Levi wished he had never met.

He had screwed Levi over every which way, and had dragged his name through the mud on top of it. It might've all happened fifteen years ago, but he didn't care.

It was as fresh for him now as it had been back then, when he'd fully realized just how much he'd been duped.

It had been a shit show, and he was still recovering from it.

He looked again at the one in the braids.

He should probably know who they were. He had been to their house a time or two back in the day. But they'd all been little girls. And they bore no resemblance to the children he had known then.

"Wooow," said Camilla, to his right. "There's a lot of beefcake in here."

He grimaced. "Could you not?"

"I *could* not," said Camilla. "But I'm enjoying myself."

"Well, I doubt that Landry King is going to get up and put on a show for you. More likely he's going to get up and talk bullshit."

"You really hate all of them, don't you?"

"Of course I do. They're basically the big evil Death Star of ranching. Why the hell would I like any of them?"

"I don't know. Because maybe they're nice people,

and maybe you have beers with them sometimes down at the bar."

He shifted in his seat. "I do not."

"You're so *rigid*," said Camilla.

"I am. And I don't give a flying fuck about what you think about that."

"Charming."

"I don't exist to charm you, Cam. Whatever you might think."

They took their seats, and it was Landry King who got up and gave an intro, presiding over the meeting and giving a rundown of the things that would be covered. The first order of business was the road.

"Quinn Sullivan will be speaking first," said Landry. "Giving projected community impact and a detailed plan for what exactly is being asked here."

"Quinn. Come on up."

It was the ferret one. With her big glasses and her braids.

She walked up to the front of the room, and looked out at all the people sitting in the folding chairs.

Levi crossed his arms over his chest and glared at her. "Hello," she said. "I'm very glad that you could all make it tonight, because as you know, being a part of the community is something that's very important to those of us at Four Corners. I consider it a keystone of my values as a Sullivan, to care deeply about this town. Four Corners has been here since before Pyrite Falls was ever an incorporated community. And as it has built, and grown, my innate feeling of responsibility for it has only increased. What we are asking is that at the fork in the highway, we build a new bit of road access to Four Corners. There would be a bit of new pavement involved, and a change to the intersection there. Everything else would be done on our property. That road would take people on a direct route to Sullivan's Point, and to the new farm store that we plan to open. At the store we will be selling the produce that we grow at Sullivan's Point, some of the beef produced by the Garretts and the Kings. There will also be baked goods provided by myself and my sisters, and we will have a section for other local produce and products. We would love the idea of carrying art created by some local people, and would love to supplement our food supply, and maybe even premade meals, with things provided by you. What we hope is that this will be a financially valuable piece to the community."

She smiled, looking as if she was very pleased with herself, and the mic drop that she had just done. "I have run the numbers exhaustively, taking all of my education that I've acquired in agribusiness and applying it to this. I simply do not see how it can fail."

Everyone clapped, though he could see that people were exchanging dubious glances on the non–Four Corners side. They were just too polite to full-on freeze her out.

Levi, on the other hand, was not hindered by politeness of any kind.

"Thank you, Quinn," said Landry. "Next we'll hear from Levi Granger, who is speaking on behalf of the Huckleberry County Ranching Association. Go right ahead, Levi."

Levi stood and made his way slowly up to the front. He did not have a notebook. He didn't need one.

He looked out at the crowd for a moment, at each and every one.

Levi didn't have stage fright. He didn't get nervous speaking in front of people.

Because he didn't care what they thought about him. He'd been through hell and back when it came to public opinion, and many other things, and he had emerged out the other side a man who simply didn't give a shit what anyone thought.

All that mattered was integrity. The preservation of the land, and of his ranch.

And that was what bolstered him now.

"But it can fail," he said. "Maybe not for the people of Four Corners, but for the people of Pyrite Falls. Already, we are held hostage by the size of this ranching facility. John, what's going to happen to your store, when they build up their little hipster paradise that they've pitched? What's going to happen to Becky's Diner when Four Corners is producing all of this food?" That produced a ripple of discontent in the crowd.

"They're already their own little town right in the middle of us," he continued. "We already know how hard it is to compete when it comes to producing beef. We don't have a big pool of money and hundreds of employees helping us out. We don't have endless acres of land. They've claimed most of it. And while the rest of us have to endure the hardships of waxing and waning prices, accessibility and products, they're always able to cover the issues that each other has. If beef is lagging, the McClouds' equestrian money covers it, and on it goes. We're on our own. They look out for each other. They don't look out for us. A road that bypasses the main street of town to allow people to directly access the store that competes with many existing businesses is not in our best interest. It is not now, and it never will be. And no amount of allowing people to use their shelves to sell a jar of local honey, or featuring a clay pot that they tossed in the corner of their store," he said, directing this part right at Quinn Sullivan's over-large glasses, "is going to compensate for lost income."

"That's not fair," said Quinn, standing up and pushing her glasses up her nose. "We do care about the town. I *said* that. It was in my speech."

"Yeah, politicians say a lot of things, too. That doesn't mean it isn't horseshit. And it doesn't mean that what you said is true, either. And I'm gonna call it out. That's just you trying to make it sound as if you've given half a thought to what might affect the people around you. But you haven't gone deep enough. What about John's?" He pointed to the store owner sitting there in the third row.

The store stocked basic food staples, fishing and hunting supplies, gardening equipment and other miscellany. It was the only one-stop shop for miles, and if the farm store was aiming to stock food, it wouldn't be that anymore.

He looked around. "Yeah," he said. "What about me? You used to sell pies in my store, and some of your produce. The farmers market out front brought business to me, and what's going to happen when I don't have that anymore?"

"John," said Quinn, looking over at him. "We do care about that. And we're not going to carry things like pre-packaged products and processed foods…"

"All right, so you're just happy to have my store be the low-rent store. Need a Pop-Tart, go to John's. Need a fresh meal, head to Four Corners."

That sent murmurs out through the crowd.

"No. But when it comes to your store, we do provide the produce," said Quinn. "I fail to see how we are required to sell them in a particular venue that benefits somebody else. It isn't as if we're taking a product we didn't make and selling it—"

"But be honest," said Levi. "Who is helping finance your growing operation? Because I doubt it's as lucrative as the Kings. Or the Garretts, for that matter. Hell, I bet even the McClouds' horses pull in more money."

It was Gus McCloud who stood up then. "And our operation brings new people into the town all the time. We create tourism revenue that would otherwise not exist. Framing our ranch as a drain on the community is a pretty weak-ass narrative."

"Fair point," said Levi. "I do fancy myself a fair man, by the way, so it matters to me that we approach this in a fair way. But the decision of the Huckleberry County Ranching Association is to voice our opposition against new road access to Four Corners. It is our position that bypassing the town will put an undue burden on the businesses here, and give an unfair advantage to the Sullivan family, and to the greater Four Corners collective. We will be encouraging the county to deny the permits, and to reject the change. If the county should like to go ahead with it, we will continue opposition in other ways."

"Maybe you don't understand," said Quinn, facing him full-on with the full force of that ferret energy, and he swore if she had a scruff it would've been standing on end. "This is for the benefit of the community. People know that they can come here for this produce. It will be a destination store."

"A destination which allows people to bypass all of Pyrite Falls. Why would we agree to that?"

"There is another way," said Quinn. "They'll drive right through Pyrite Falls as long as you allow people to use the road that goes through your land, Levi Granger. That would be the most direct way to access the Sullivan's Point farm store from the highway."

"No," he said.

"What?"

"I said no. It's my land, and you don't need to be treading on it. Bottom line."

"But...but... You're being unreasonable," she said.

"I don't think I am. I think I'm being perfectly reasonable. I am here voicing the opinions of a collective, Ms. Sullivan. It's not personal." Except with all those sparkly green eyes pointed at him, it felt damned personal. And he couldn't deny, the memory of working with the Sullivans in the past made his gut burn now.

"You...you..."

"You had your turn to speak already," he said. "You ceded the floor. I am not done. This would have an impact that is difficult to project onto a community that is already struggling. These last few years have been hard. The financial burden of trying to keep small businesses going when movement and numbers were down has been incredibly difficult. We lost cows because we weren't able to travel to the USDA weigh stations. We are still trying to dig out from under all of these issues. And it isn't getting easier. In periods of financial instability, Four Corners is able to bolster itself in a way that the rest of us cannot, and we must look to our own interests. We vote against."

"It isn't actually up to a vote," said Quinn.

"You have to get the permits," said Levi. "And many people that are party to approving the permits are here, and I hope that they take into consideration the potential impact upon the community."

"I hope they do," said Quinn. "Because clearly there is a logic gap happening in your head. More people means more money."

"A logic gap?" he asked. "Is that college words for *you're stupid*?"

She turned pink. "I didn't say that," said Quinn. "But if you exemplify it…"

A roar went through the room, and arguments began to break out all over.

Over in her seat, his sister looked like she wished she had a bucket of popcorn.

She had always been far too into drama for her own good.

"Order," said Sawyer Garrett, standing up and making his way to the stage. "Thank you for coming and voicing your concern, Levi," said Sawyer, his expression cool. But Levi could see that Sawyer wasn't actually appreciative of Levi's presence. "It's up to the county now."

"Yes, it is," said Levi. "I trust that they'll make the right decision."

"Now that the meeting is through," Sawyer said, "everyone—" he looked over at Levi "—everyone is welcome to stay for a bonfire and some food. We are a community, even if we disagree sometimes. And if we can't come together over food and music, then what is the point of any of it? So I hope that all of you, regardless of where you stand on this issue, will stay."

Levi looked over at Quinn Sullivan, who was scowling, and he had a feeling that she was hoping if he did stay he choked on a chicken bone.

Fine. He didn't like her, either.

But he'd said his piece, and he was not staying for a barbecue.

"Come on, Cam. Let's go."

"I want to stay," she said, looking around with wide eyes.

"You can't," he said. "Because Quinn Sullivan is probably fixing to get her shotgun and dispatch me."

"Well, as long as there's a ritual sacrifice after, I think it's worth staying for."

"Speak for yourself when it's your own ritual sacrifice on the table."

"Please," she said.

"I'll take you down to Mapleton for pizza and ice cream."

"Okay," she said. "That sounds good."

They departed the meeting quickly, not speaking to anyone as they did.

"Actually, it's a good thing that we are going out," said Camilla. "I've been needing to talk to you about something."

"What?"

She wrinkled her nose and looked away. "I'm thinking about dropping out of school."

"What?"

"Well… It's hard. And I don't like being away from home. And I am an absolute weirdo there."

"It's only been a year, Camilla. Give it time."

"You need help, Levi. I've seen the office. It's an absolute disaster, without me there helping you with the paperwork…"

"I'm fine," he said, anger spiking in his blood. "Never talk about leaving school because you think you need to do something for me. Camilla, I didn't work this hard to get you where you want to have you leave school. But you need to be at school. You want to be a lawyer, Cam, and that means that you need school, and law school…"

"Maybe I changed my mind. The city is all well and good as a daydream, but what am I actually going to do there? And what's the point?"

"The point is that Mom and Dad are dead. And in their place I worked so hard to make sure that you all didn't lack for anything because you didn't have your parents. Dylan joined the military, and I've never been that thrilled with that, but it's what he wanted, so it's what he's doing. Jessie always wanted to work the ranch. And now she has a ranch of her own with Damien. And she's happy. You deserve that. That full dream."

"But back when I decided to go to school, Jessie hadn't left you. I thought that she was going to stay and…"

"I didn't want her to. I don't want any of you to be tethered to this place, to this ranch, because of me."

Lord Almighty.

As if this whole thing with the Sullivans hadn't riled him up enough, his sister was talking about leaving school. He couldn't have that.

It was not her dream.

And he really needed Camilla to keep going after her dreams.

He definitely wasn't having her give them up for him.

"It's okay, Levi. I won't make any decisions just yet."

"There are no decisions to be made. You got into school, you're going to school. That's it. That's final. And at the end of spring break, you're going back."

Quinn Sullivan better mind her own business, because Levi had his own problems, and he was in no kind of mood.

CHAPTER TWO

"WHAT AN ARROGANT BASTARD," Quinn said, still stomping about three days after the meeting.

He was making her angry, and no one liked her when she was angry. Least of all her. She mostly kept it under control these days, until she was in the safety of their home at Sullivan's Point, but Levi had tested that. And she was still absolutely feral now.

He was just… He was so…and then he…!

Ughhhhh.

Levi Granger was a whole problem. He had been a problem since Quinn was fourteen and had first seen him wearing a tight black T-shirt and painted-on jeans, hanging around Sullivan's Point just after he'd taken over his family ranch.

He'd been around quite a bit for a while, and sure, the whole thing with her dad had gone south. But everything with her dad had gone south. She was just as wounded by her dad as anyone else. And it had absolutely nothing—nothing!—to do with their plans for the farm store.

She'd run every scenario. She'd looked at this from every angle.

Making the changes that would bypass town was good because it would create a direct route. It was good because it wouldn't require an easement—only permits.

The easement option would be ideal in that it would carry the traffic through town and possibly bring business to everyone, but that meant getting Levi to allow them to use his land directly.

She hadn't realized both options would end up involving him.

A complication she hadn't considered, and Quinn considered almost every complication almost every single time.

Quinn Sullivan was book-smart and she was proud of it. She thought of it in those terms because most of the people in Pyrite Falls were often proud to declare that they were street-smart instead. Quinn had never felt that one should be forced to choose between different kinds of intelligence. Be well-rounded, she had always thought. And while it couldn't be claimed that she was *overly* street-smart, she had been away to college. A rarity both in her family and within the broader scope of Four Corners.

Because Four Corners was the kind of place where you grew up knowing exactly what you'd do when you grew up. The nature of the job was handed down from parent to child—at least it was ideally.

Where you would work the land until you were buried beneath it.

And while Quinn could see the appeal of a legacy, and of working land, she'd still wanted to *know*.

Why she should work it. How to work it best. Other methods one could use.

Both she and her sister Rory had been more interested in outside education than either Fia or Alaina had ever seemed to be. But while Rory had opted to go to school in neighboring Mapleton, to get a more traditional education, Quinn had wanted to go to the one-room schoolhouse on Four Corners land, because she wanted to be connected to the land in everything she did.

The ranch itself had been established by four families back in the late 1800s. Technically, it was four different branches, but it was operated as a cooperative. There was Garrett's Watch, McCloud's Landing, King's Crest and Sullivan's Point. Each named for the families who had first settled them and who continued to run them today.

And while Quinn felt that the wisdom handed down from her father—before he had left—and her mother—not that she had been big on the ranch itself—was valuable, she had decided to go away and get a degree in agribusiness. Because she believed so firmly in all the smarts.

It was why she considered herself a great candidate to deal with the current situation.

Sullivan's Point was the portion of Four Corners that Quinn ran with her sisters. Their parents had left all the responsibility of the place to them when they were very young.

Quinn's oldest sister, Fia, had figured out inventive ways to keep the place running. By and large, they leased the ranch land while they tended a very large garden filled with fruits and vegetables, which they had turned into a very profitable business. They'd just taken some houses that had historically been used to house ranch hands and turned them into short- and long-term rentals, which were now being managed by her sister Rory.

They did canning and baking and sold things fresh

at a roadside stand, at farmers markets and the store in town. But the latest bid for expansion was the farm store that they were building right on their property.

Of course, the sticking point to getting the farm store open was making sure there was an access road from the main highway. But in order to get an access road directly into that side of Sullivan's Point, and avoid sending people down miles of dirt road to get right to the heart of their store, they were going to need to strike an agreement with the neighboring rancher.

And the problem with that was the neighboring rancher was…Levi.

Levi was a whole thing. Difficult, some might say.

Well, the Sullivans, Garretts, McClouds and Kings found all neighboring ranchers to be somewhat difficult. That was the problem when you were the biggest dog in town. People often took your mere existence as an invitation for a fight.

"Yes, you've remarked on his being an arrogant bastard," Rory mused. "Four or five times now, in fact."

"Well, it's true." Quinn scowled at her own reflection in the mirror.

"Do you not think…?" Quinn looked over at her sister, who had rolled onto her back on the bed, a book clutched to her chest. "Do you not think that maybe he has a point?"

"No, Rory, I don't think he has a point. We are not trying to hurt the town. If anything, we're going to help the town. I put in all kinds of projections. If a certain number of extra people come out to visit our store, it's not taking anything from John just because they decide not to go to a store that they wouldn't have gone to anyway. They're different demographics, and the whole thing is a straw man."

"Do tell."

"It's a straw man because the whole thing isn't actually a thing. It's simply a fake boogeyman erected to distract from—"

"I do know what a straw man is," said Rory. "But thank you."

"I didn't say that you *didn't* know what it was," said Quinn.

"No, you just sounded like it. You have a way of coming across as a bit superior, Quinn."

Quinn and Rory had grown closer in the last couple of years, but even though they were next to each other in age, they hadn't really been close growing up.

Their home had been tumultuous. Fia and their mother had been at each other's throats all the time, to the point where Fia had even run away for a while at the peak of it all.

Quinn had responded to the unrest with hostility. Toward everyone. And that had made it hard for Rory—or anyone—to know her. She'd put her head down and tried to cozy up to her dad, get him to be proud of her, because the drama inside the house had been too much to bear.

Rory, who had always been softer-spoken, more anxious, had responded by retreating. She'd befriended Lydia Payne, and they'd gone to school in Mapleton together, and she'd spent tons of time with Lydia's family. Dinner with them, sleepovers. Quinn didn't blame her, really.

Then Rory had gone off to college…and come right back. She had only made it through one semester, and she hadn't wanted to talk about whatever had happened. Quinn had been on the verge of going off to college herself and had been determined to stick it out instead of coming home because she'd wimped out. Not that she'd said that to Rory.

But it was part of their whole…schism. They just weren't the same person, not even close. Still, since they'd both been back at the ranch, they'd leveled out a bit. Rory had found a place managing the rentals while Quinn took a managerial role in the overall financials, and that had brought the two of them a little closer. It was nice because Quinn had struggled to make friends on the ranch. Well, she struggled to make them in general.

"I don't mean to act superior. But it's just that in this, I actually know what I'm talking about. I know what I'm doing. I'm frustrated that some big…lunkhead of a rancher gets to come in and just say he doesn't want to do it, and because he speaks with a certain amount of conviction, people listen. If anybody actually cared, they would know that I'm just right."

"You always think you're right," Rory pointed out.

"No, Rory," said Quinn. "I only have a fight if I think I'm right. If I know I'm right. I don't think that this is going to hurt the community in any regard, and if we are carrying merchandise from other artisans, then it's actually going to increase business for them. Because I believe that our store will be a destination for people up to an hour away, and there are other business models for this kind of thing that could support that. And like I said, those people wouldn't have been coming to go to John's anyway. He by and large supplies people on their way to the coast, people who live even more rural than we do and people who live around here. Because everybody occasionally needs a bike pump, a very specific kind of screw and an inner tube to float down the river. But that is the kind of stuff he has, and it isn't the same customer."

"You should've said that at the meeting."

Quinn growled. "I was *mad*. Anyway, if he's so worried about the community, he should be worried about us. One more year of posting in the red and we're at risk of having to sell off chunks of acreage to the other families."

"They'll never actually enforce that."

"You think, and you hope. But they could."

"Where exactly are you going?" Rory asked, as Quinn finished putting on some blush and eyeliner, and regarded herself in the mirror.

She didn't often wear makeup, but this seemed like it called for it.

"I'm going down to Smokey's Tavern to see if I can find any of the cowboys that were at the meeting the other day. Because I am going to say it. I'm going to make the point. There should be guys from the ranch and collective down there, and it would be a good opportunity for me to do a little bit of outreach."

Rory looked at her skeptically. "I should go with you."

"Why?"

"No offense. Like really, no offense, but you are... you are..."

"Just say it, Rory."

"You can be a little pointy. And sometimes you poke people. Even when you don't mean to."

That made Quinn feel just...upset. She never *tried* to poke anybody. She just said what needed to be said.

And often, she felt she had facts and logic on her side, and people seemed to get weird about that. Like maybe she should find a way to soften the truth they didn't want to hear, and she had never known how to do that. It had been a long-standing bit of annoyance for her.

"What?" Rory asked, staring at Quinn.

"I'm just trying to figure out what I'm supposed to be doing," Quinn said. "Like how do you soften something like this? Am I supposed to say *nice hat, you're wrong*?"

Rory threw her head back and laughed. She flung her book to the side. "You know, it wouldn't hurt, Quinn. It wouldn't. Let's go together."

Rory's curly hair was loose and flowing, and her sister always looked effortlessly feminine and beautiful. She knew Rory had felt awkward in school—well, Rory had been awkward in school. Freckled, bespectacled, braces on her teeth, all limbs, but she was anything but awkward now. She was wearing a light yellow dress that only went down to midthigh, and Quinn knew a moment of envy for just how easy it was for Rory to be soft.

Quinn had never known how to be soft.

It had caused her a whole lot of problems in her life, but those problems weren't exactly instructive on how to fix them.

Quinn had done her best to take her more complicated features and use them to her advantage. It was one reason going to school had been so important to her. If she could approach things from a logical, educated standpoint, it often was distancing, and made things not seem personal. In fact, Quinn found it helpful.

"Come on—let's go," Rory said, grabbing hold of Quinn's arm.

Quinn looked at herself one more time. She had put

her hair into two little buns, and had traded out her glasses for contacts. She had on a velvet choker and a wide-collared floral dress, and she thought she was doing the '90s justice, and really that she looked quite pretty, if she said so herself.

She knew that men liked pretty. And soft.

So she was going to attempt that. Quinn had no real desire to be soft. It only got you hurt. But sometimes it could be useful, so she needed to give it a try.

Quinn was book-smart. But she could admit, she was often not people-smart. She tried, but she was results oriented, and sometimes the smoothness of the process felt negotiable. Damn the torpedoes, et cetera.

But perhaps if she was dressed soft, she would sound soft.

And if all else failed, she would just have Rory talk to them about romance novels. That was about the softest thing that could ever occur.

Rory was nothing if not supersoft.

Quinn had been soft once upon a time. If there was one thing she admired about Rory, it was how she'd retained that. Of course, as far as Quinn could tell, it also made Rory anxious and overly concerned about things Quinn just preferred not to care about.

She used to care about all kinds of things. And then she'd whittled it down. She cared about her sisters, the ranch and her own goals. The end. It was the best way to be. The best way to keep herself from getting hurt.

They piled into Quinn's car and drove the ten minutes off the Four Corners property to Smokey's.

That was why they needed road access. The gravel road that led all the way to Sullivan's Point as it stood was a very, very long drive that would cover a car in fine dust, and also, it was the road they used for daily, practical things. The road they used for their horses, for their tractors, and they really couldn't have traffic from the public cluttering it all up. Well, they could, and if they had to, they would open the store using the main road, but she had a feeling it would severely hinder the amount of business that they got.

"I can hear you thinking. You might find it helpful to dial back some of the intensity," said Rory, as they pulled into Smokey's parking lot.

"I don't know how to do that," said Quinn.

"I get that," said Rory. "I do. But…you could try."

"Sure," said Quinn.

Except she didn't even know how to try. Honestly. She just didn't know.

If she did, she would do it. If she knew how to be honey, so that she could catch all the flies, she would've transformed herself into something sticky and syrupy long ago.

They filed into Smokey's, and Quinn froze at the door. She wasn't used to having so many men…look at her.

At Four Corners, they were like wallpaper. Practically invisible. But at the bar, they were a little bit less… known, and she could see that they appeared to be two eligible women who weren't normally *around*.

Quinn wished that she cared.

The problem was that at an extremely formative age she'd developed a crush on…

It didn't matter. She wasn't going to think about that insufferable bastard.

He was a problem. Not a crush.

She had been so childish back then. A giant open wound wandering around feeling all the feelings. No more.

All that mattered was crushes were not a thing for her *now*, and maybe it was partly because some of her heart and soul had been tied up in one a long time ago when she'd never gotten it back. No one had ever felt half as compelling, half as interesting.

Half as big of a pain in the ass.

But she wasn't going to think about that, because she wasn't going to think about him.

She noticed that Rory looked disinterested in all the attention they were getting, and she thought that was strange, since Rory was a true romantic, and she would've thought that Rory would be thrilled to have a man pay her some attention.

"This is not how it goes in a romance novel," said Rory, as if she already knew what Quinn was thinking.

"What?"

Rory shrugged. "I mean, that's not true. Sometimes a romance novel starts with a one-night stand in a bar, but the connection is electric. And I feel no electricity. So if you're wondering why I'm not excited about this…"

"Oh, Rory," said Quinn. "I don't care about romance. All I care about is lobbying for road access. And so away we go."

They marched deeper into the bar, and Quinn recognized some men from the ranching collective and made her way there quickly. "Hello," she said. "I'm Quinn Sullivan. You may remember me from the meeting the other day. I just wanted to talk to you about…"

"Put away your religious tracts," said a lazy, laconic

voice from across the bar. She didn't have to look to know who it was.

The goose bumps on her arms gave it away.

"This has nothing to do with religion," said Quinn.

"I don't know. You sure seem to have that kind of bright-eyed fervor."

Quinn couldn't decide if that was a compliment or not. She decided it wasn't.

"Mr. Granger..."

"Miss Sullivan," he said. "I am busy."

He gestured toward a blonde sitting on his left. Quinn honestly hadn't noticed her.

And she felt...

She didn't like what she felt *at all*.

It wasn't her fault that Levi Granger was the best-looking man she'd ever seen in her life. It wasn't.

She could remember very clearly a time when Levi had come to the ranch to talk to her dad about something.

The soybeans, she assumed.

She had been fourteen. She had seen Levi before, but for some reason that time it had been like seeing him for the first time.

It had burned itself into her psyche, into her consciousness. It had changed everything. Everything she had ever dreamed about, fantasized about... Not that she really had fantasies at that point. But she had really thought that a smooth-faced boy from one of the popular dance bands was cute, and also the Fox from Robin Hood. And all of it had been vague and disconnected from anything real. And then suddenly it had all slammed into her, visceral and far too big for her body to contain.

She had always been a creature of feeling. She always had a temper, and then as an extension of that, she had always been very excited when she was excited, and happy when she was happy.

And so, the moment she had seen Levi she had been immediately, viscerally, passionately in lust.

She had at least been smart enough to know that it wasn't love.

But just very suddenly there was no one and nothing else that would ever do for her. His square jaw, dark hair, blue eyes and solid frame had lit her on fire. And it hadn't mattered that he was twenty-five; in fact, it had been the appeal of him.

All of the men at Four Corners were *familiar*. And more than that, the ones she went to school with were *boys*.

Levi had been a man.

She had grown out of that, mostly. She didn't flutter anymore when she saw him because she didn't flutter in general. She had been to college in the intervening years, and she had met a great many men, none of whom had felt compelling to her.

So she simply *hadn't*, and if the holdover of remembering the visceral impact Levi had had on her body had influenced that, then fine. She had used it as a talisman.

Convenient when she was hundreds of miles away from him, less convenient when she was only a mere few inches from him. He was the biggest barrier to her current goal, and he had another woman on his arm.

"You were the one who spoke to me," she said.

"Because I see what you're up to. And I'm here to tell you, it's not going to work. I happen to know for a fact that your permits are going in for review tomorrow, and it isn't going to go your way."

"You can't…you can't possibly know that," she said.

"I possibly *can*. My case was made, and it was made well, and you're simply going to have to deal with that, Miss Sullivan."

"I…I will not."

"You don't have another choice."

"Can we please…?" She did her best to gather her temper, because she didn't do explosive fits of temper any more than she did vulnerable these days. "Could we speak outside for a moment?"

"Why?" He leaned back, resting his hand on the woman's lower back. "There's no reason you can't say what you have to say right here."

"I feel that we may bore the lady."

The woman looked between the two of them. "I'm not bored," she said, smiling, and for some reason, Quinn found that she wanted to punch the other woman in the teeth.

"Well, it's proprietary," Quinn sniffed.

"Proprietary," he said, drawing out each syllable. "Now, that is a big word."

"Levi…"

"Quinn." He said her name like she was a child.

"Please, come outside."

He took his time answering, like he actually had to mull the question of going outside. She could not understand it. He either wanted to go outside or he didn't. Okay, he said that he didn't. But she did. And so there.

"All right. We'll go outside. I can turn you down out there just as easily."

She led the charge just outside the door of Smokey's, and stood beneath the yellow light, her arms crossed.

"I don't think that you're giving this full consideration. I told you, there's a *gap*."

"Please," he said. "Explain it to me. Slowly."

She could not tell if he was being serious or not. "We would be bringing in extra people," she said. "People who wouldn't be going to John's anyway." She spoke each syllable of what she had already gone over with Rory slowly and laboriously. "It's obvious that our way is the best way."

"It's not obvious to me," he said, his expression unreadable.

She could not fathom if he was this obtuse, or if he was playing the part to perfection.

"It should be," she said. "I respect and understand that you have spent your life working your land, Levi, but I have actually had formal education on this very thing. I am much more qualified to make commentary on whether or not this is a viable—"

"Again," he said slowly. "Viable for *you*."

"No, for everybody," she said. "You don't understand because you don't have the appropriate knowledge to make the decision."

"Say it," he said. "Go ahead and say it, Quinn."

"You're being stupid," she said.

The minute the words left her mouth, she felt awful. Mean. She felt that instant regret that had always come when she'd lost her temper and she hated it. He had… pushed her, and he had a way of getting under her skin. He always had.

He asked her to say it, because he was acting like she thought it, and even if she did think it…

"Good. I'm glad that you were able to be honest. And of course you're right," he said. "You're at Four Corners, after all, and I'm just a struggling rancher. What do I know about anything? It must make you so angry, given the fact you are so much smarter than me, that I won."

"You did not win," she said, her voice low.

He looked around. "I think I did. They're not going to approve your permits, Quinn. You're not going to get access. You're going to be at a disadvantage, and you're going to know what it's like to actually have to struggle to make a living. All that schooling, and still just scraping by. Almost as if ranching is hard fucking work."

How dare he imply she didn't know that? "I will figure this out. I will."

"Good. See that it has nothing to do with me."

He turned and started to leave, and she reached out and grabbed his forearm. And the minute she wrapped her fingers around him, the minute she made contact with his skin, she wanted to jump back and howl.

"I…" Their eyes clashed, and she felt desire tight in her gut, pull its way all through her body. Why was it like this? Why was he like this?

"I'm not going to give up," she said.

"Good for you," he said. "Good for you."

"Don't leave," she said.

"Miss Sullivan," he said, a slow grin spreading across his face. "I came out here to get laid tonight, and that pretty blonde in there is going to do the honors. So unless you're volunteering to fill the position, I suggest you let me back to my business."

Her whole face felt like it was on fire. Like it had been sprayed with hair spray, and someone had lit a match on it. She felt exposed and horrified, because she didn't actually think that he would want to take her to bed, but she had the horrible feeling that perhaps he saw that at one point in her life she had wished that he would take her.

They'd barely ever spoken to one another. He was a lot older than her, and she'd always been too embarrassed to ever approach him at the moments when they had been in the same vicinity. He had been a fantasy, nothing more. She had known, always, that he wasn't actually something she was going to have in reality.

But… But. Old longings died very, very hard.

Even when the person was infuriating.

"I am not volunteering," she said, absolutely certain that she was the color of a beetroot.

"Well, then. I bid you good-night."

And he left her standing there feeling utterly defeated, and she howled, kicking the side of Smokey's, and then hopping up and down when her foot hurt.

She covered her face with her hands. She didn't know why she felt things this deeply. It had always been something that…

She used to follow her dad all around the ranch, talking, laughing. Weeping when a sheep had a lamb that died, raging when the chickens got killed by a fox. She'd felt everything, always. Until he'd left. Until all of her feelings had been whittled into a sharp point. Until the only thing driving her had been rage. And then once she'd reached the dead end of all that anger, she'd decided that she had to protect herself. Her goals. She just didn't want to be hurt again, and she didn't want to hurt other people, either.

She'd leaned in to her education. It felt like protection. Like a shield protecting her from the things outside of herself, and the feelings in herself.

It was just simpler that way. And the truth was, she

couldn't just…turn her feelings off. She wished. But her anger had protected her, until it had become uncontrolled. And inside… Yeah, inside it was still her go-to. A release that didn't leave her hurting.

Though it did sometimes leave her feeling sorry.

Which she didn't like, either.

The door opened, and Rory appeared.

"What happened?"

Rage boiled inside her.

"He's just impossible. I legitimately can't tell if he's actually dumb, or if he's…"

"It doesn't matter. You don't need to get Levi Granger on your side."

She sighed. "Unfortunately, Rory, I think that I do. Because I'm pretty sure that if I don't… I'm pretty sure that if I don't I'm not going to be able to get anybody on my side, and if I can't get anybody on my side…we might as well give up now."

One thing Quinn couldn't do was give up. So that meant that she wasn't done. Maybe Rory was right, though. Maybe Levi wasn't the place to start.

She would go back in, and she would talk to other people. And then she would go down to the county herself tomorrow. She would make sure this happened. She was determined. And when Quinn Sullivan was determined, God help anything that got in her way.

CHAPTER THREE

"SEE YOU AT the end of the day, Cam," Levi said as he headed out the door, into the early, pink morning.

He felt…angry, sure, and filled with restless energy. He hadn't gotten laid last night. He'd been really looking forward to it, too, because it had been a while.

Sex for him was more of a rare indulgence than he would like, but he was busy, and he didn't bring women back to his house. A holdover from when his siblings were young.

Even though he more or less had an empty nest now, he hadn't quite made the switch mentally.

Quinn Sullivan…

He would like to think it had nothing to do with her. Nothing to do with the fact that her red hair and freckles felt burned into him.

Nothing to do with the fact that she enraged him, but had exhilarated him a little bit, too.

The blonde had just seemed bland by comparison by the time he got back in.

That fight had run his blood temperature up far too hot.

She'd called him *stupid*. She outright had.

And that was the thing that made him angriest.

When people underestimated him. Thought he was an idiot…

Yeah. Well. He'd done some things that were dumb. That was the simple truth.

Brian Sullivan had made sure that Levi knew that he had only been able to take advantage of him because Levi had been careless. Because he wasn't as smart.

And he could see that same arrogance in the man's daughter. She thought that because she'd gone to school she was smarter than him.

He shook his head and got in his truck, driving over to the barn where the horses were.

A couple of his hands were on the grounds already, and he nodded, tipping his hat to both of them as he got out of his truck to head over to his horse Jasper's stall.

He did his best to run his spread with the kind of courtesy and kindness that he valued. He did his best to prove that he had a place here, and a right to be a rancher, and it didn't matter that Four Corners, the Death Star, was only a few paces away. His place was a good place to work.

He couldn't pay the wages they did over at Four Corners, but the men he had working for him were loyal. They believed in what he was doing, and eventually, he would be able to pay better.

That was another problem of existing next to such a giant spread.

They paid well. They had their own school for the children of the people who worked there. Many of the people who worked there also had places to bunk. They were just so big they were able to offer the kinds of benefits that Levi could only dream of offering his employees.

Hell. It didn't matter. He loved what he had. And it

had taken years for him to dig out from under the soybean fiasco.

His reputation had been shot to hell because of it.

He could still remember…

The day that Brian Sullivan had shown up on his doorstep with this plan.

He'd said that he heard Levi was in some trouble, particularly since his parents had died, and that he was at his wit's end figuring out how to work the land and what exactly to do with it.

Levi had been so desperate for help. For someone to come alongside him and…

He'd had to drop everything and care for his siblings. He'd had no real support for himself and this had felt like a gift.

The truth was, as wonderful as Levi's father had been, he was not a businessman. And most of the land was sitting in disuse. There had not been a lot of money for…anything. The house they lived in was modest at best, and there were many things in it that needed repair, and Levi didn't even know where to begin. He needed money. Money to take care of the kids, and time. Time to cook the meals and…

He was grieving all over again, having just lost his mother a few years before, and he just hadn't known what else to do but to sit down with Brian Sullivan and listen to his plan.

It can't fail…

Yeah. He'd heard that again recently. *It can't fail.*

And from Brian's perspective, Levi supposed it hadn't failed.

He had been able to broker a deal with a giant factory farm to cover Levi's land with soybeans. Levi had made some money on it, just enough, but it had tied up his land and prevented him from building anything new. And when he discovered that Brian was pocketing a massive amount of what had been on offer from the company...

Well. Brian had informed him it was Levi's own fault.

He hadn't read the fine print.

You're like your daddy, Levi. You're never going to be an entrepreneur. You have to work for people like me, who know things.

Those words still lived beneath Levi's skin. In his blood.

And *fuck that*. In the years since the soybean deal had ended, he had built himself a thriving operation. Against all odds, frankly, because, again, it was difficult to succeed here, but he'd found his niche.

And he was proud of it. He was damned proud of it. Of everything he'd accomplished, everything he'd done.

He got on Jasper's back, and he rode. Down the road, and up into one of the high pastures, just riding. Trying to do something to defuse the rage that was boiling in his body.

He had *succeeded*.

In spite of what teachers had said he'd do. In spite of what Brian Sullivan had said.

It had been hard and he'd worked harder and he'd made it.

Camilla had once given him a magnet for the fridge that said, "No one can make you feel inferior without your consent."

He'd laughed it off like it was silly, and not something he needed, but it had become something that he had actually held on to. Deeply.

He had been vulnerable, and in a difficult space, and so Brian Sullivan had been able to take advantage of him. Additionally, he had been able to make Levi feel inferior. And Levi had accepted that back then. Because he'd felt inferior.

He didn't anymore.

He'd brought the ranch out of that time and into strength. He'd raised his siblings and launched them into the world.

And Quinn Sullivan didn't have the power to make him feel inferior.

He rode his horse hard and took in the view, the rolling mountains with sharp-tipped pines reaching up toward the sky. The intense blue of it all, the green.

The Four Corners crew didn't have more of a right to this place just because their ancestors had come and managed to get themselves a huge plot of land.

He had a right to be here. This was his. His blood was in this dirt.

His parents were buried here. It was his.

And he would fight for that. And he would fight for this community.

And Quinn Sullivan and her high-and-mighty ways were not going to sway him.

And they weren't going to make him feel inferior, either.

Because he was different now, secure now.

He would never go back to how he'd been.

FIA CAME OUT of the kitchen onto the front porch, where Rory and Quinn were right in the grass, pinning clothes up onto the clothesline, and kicking chickens out from under their feet.

"The county called," she said.

"And?" Rory asked.

Quinn only leaned in, trepidation freezing her words so she couldn't think, let alone speak.

Fia let out a long, slow breath. "They denied the permits."

"Fia…"

And she saw Fia was dangerously close to crying, which was not something she had ever seen from her older sister.

Her older sister was strong. She had to be. She had led them all these years, since their dad had left and their mom had moved away.

When Fia was a teenager, she'd been volatile. But later Quinn realized it was because she'd been the one who was so much more aware of how their parents were falling apart. She'd been angry and it was understandable. She'd fought with their mother like she'd hated her.

After she'd come back from running away she'd changed. She hadn't bothered to fight with their mother anymore. It was like she'd come back with a decision made. From then on Fia had treated the ranch and the house like hers. She treated them like hers.

Like she'd known their parents would abandon them and she'd needed to make the conscious choice to stay and care for it and them.

Right now she looked absolutely defeated, despairing. Quinn hated that. From the bottom of her heart she felt like they owed Fia for all she'd done for them. She wanted to fix this for her. Desperately.

"I don't know what we're going to do now," Fia said,

shrugging. "We built the whole thing, we're almost ready to go, but if we have to make everybody drive down this dirt road... Most people are going to decide it isn't worth the hassle."

"But they can get here," said Rory. "And maybe we can make it so amazing that it actually just seems like an adventure. Like you have to go deep into the wilderness to go to this little store in rural Oregon. Almost as if you're traveling through an enchanted wood."

"That's ridiculous," said Fia.

"It's the kind of ridiculous that would probably end up getting a million views on the internet," said Rory.

But Rory was always way more dream than reality. The sort of person who thought buying a lottery ticket might be a viable retirement plan, and Quinn and Fia were a lot more grounded. Which was truly painful in moments like this.

"We have one more option," said Quinn, feeling absolutely filled with indignation and purpose.

And that all-encompassing, ever-expanding sense of *something* she felt whenever she thought of him.

"It's not an option, Quinn," Fia said, "and you know that. He was the chief objector to us getting that extra road access..."

"Because it was going to bypass the town. But going through his property will not bypass the town. It solves the problem. Barring us from using that road would just be petty."

Unfortunately, she had the feeling that Levi Granger was petty.

"Quinn..." Rory shook her head. "We might just have to acknowledge that we're in a little bit over our heads."

"I will *not* acknowledge that," said Quinn. "Because this makes sense. It's logical, and we aren't wrong. He's wrong."

They needed this. If they couldn't get this up and running, they really were going to be the dead tree branch of Four Corners. They might as well lease out 100 percent of their land to the Kings, and Sullivan's Point would lose its identity altogether.

And her dad would be right.

About her. About what she could accomplish.

She couldn't have that.

"I don't know," said Fia. "I feel defeated. We tried to do this the right way, we tried to take the community into consideration, but it has been an uphill battle the whole time. The Kings were against us... We don't even have the full support of Four Corners. They're indulging us. Don't think I can't feel that. They never thought it was going to succeed, not really. We aren't the same as them. We aren't men, we don't have cattle, we don't have horses. They don't respect what we do."

"That's not true," said Rory. "They're not all that way."

Fia wiped a tear from her cheek. "I know. This was just... It's my dream and I..."

"And you'll have it," said Quinn, fiercely. "Everything that you've done for us, all the sacrifices that you've made, none of it is going to be in vain, Fia. I swear to you. I swear. I am not going to let you lose your dream."

"That's really sweet, Quinn, but I don't know that there's any way around it."

"There is," said Quinn. "I'm going to prove to Levi

Granger that I'm right. I'm going to…I'm going to offer him something."

"What?"

"It has to benefit him, too, right? This whole thing? So I'll find something that he needs. I will make sure that it's something I can give him."

"I don't know about that," said Fia slowly.

"I do," said Quinn. "I do, and I will make sure that we win. I promise."

Because in spite of everything, Quinn had always been a dreamer. Or maybe more accurately, a planner.

And what she set her mind to, she accomplished.

It was the one good thing she had gotten from her dad.

Her dad had left. He hadn't been faithful, he hadn't been true. He hadn't really loved this place.

But Quinn *did*. And she was going to do right by it, and by Fia and Rory and Alaina. She was going to fix this. If Levi Granger was the only obstacle to getting what she wanted…she was going to plow right on through him.

Regardless of how broad his shoulders were.

"What are you going to do?"

"Well, tomorrow, I am going to go to his house, and I'm going to make him an offer."

"And you think that's going to work?"

"It has to."

There was no other option.

CHAPTER FOUR

QUINN WAS DETERMINED and a little bit breathless by the time she was on the road to Levi's house the next day. It was weird.

It was an eight-mile drive up the dirt road from Sullivan's Point to the main road, and around a long, smooth curve. And there was Levi Granger's property, and yet she never went there.

Ever.

And heading that direction now filled her with the kind of adrenaline she usually only experienced when she was in a rage.

Quinn was not a fighter. Well. Quinn wasn't a *fist* fighter—*anymore*. Quinn was happy to fight with words, however. More than happy.

She hoped that it wouldn't be necessary in this particular instance. But she'd hoped that from the beginning, and now here she was.

Hoping to negotiate. Ready to fight.

Except Levi was so problematic. Putting it mildly.

But she was armed with a plan. A plan she'd cobbled together last night in a feverish fit of desperation. She thought it was a very good plan, actually. In exchange for him allowing them to forge the road from the highway through his property to the farm store, she would offer him her advice. She had a degree in agribusiness, and she knew full well that Levi had no such thing. In fact, she'd spent the night digging through info on him and had come up with some she hadn't had before.

"Digging through info" meant calling Colleen Brady, her mother's old friend, and asking for anything she knew. Colleen always knew a lot. Apparently, Levi hadn't even finished high school.

She knew he'd been running the ranch here since his parents had died—eighteen years. He knew the land, and she didn't doubt it. But she had a feeling there was a lot he didn't know about structuring a business, about organization and about a great many other things she'd studied. In truth, she could help him.

She was fairly excited by the prospect. Maybe *excited* was the wrong word, but she felt supercharged, so there was that. Because she loved a challenge. In her mind, that was the point of her education. She had gone afar, and now she could bring what she had learned back home. It was perfect. She drove up the long dirt driveway that led to Levi Granger's homestead.

She had never actually been to his homestead.

Why would she have been? He had to be ten…maybe eleven years older than her.

Okay, she knew exactly how much older than her he was. That was the side effect of her little… *Crush* sounded extreme.

She'd become attached to the shape of his face. And the width of his shoulders.

But to say "crush" implied an emotional attachment, and that she didn't have. No.

She was way too…academic for that.

However, fourteen-year-old Quinn was very interested in his…homestead. And current Quinn had easier access to her fourteen-year-old self than she might like.

Usually, she kept her emotions pretty tightly policed, related to all that previous…rage that she had. And she'd learned to channel it all for good.

She needed to channel her anger now. Minimize it.

She couldn't see Levi as a villain.

She had to try to change her mindset so that she could see him as a potential ally. Because she needed him.

She needed him to need her, too.

There was no grand ranch sign signifying that she was on Granger land, not like the big sign that greeted all visitors to Four Corners. Just a narrow, dusty road lined with pine trees.

She rounded a corner, and a small dwelling came into view. All ramshackle wooden shingles on the roof and rough-hewn planks of wood.

It was little more than a shack.

That was a shock. She hadn't quite envisaged…this.

She hadn't realized things were quite so hard. And they had such a terrible story—the whole family did—and it made her heart contract with concern. He must need advice. Because the ranch could not be profitable if this was what he lived in.

Then, from around behind the dwelling, she saw movement.

And there he was.

Broad-shouldered and wearing a red-checked flannel shirt unbuttoned all the way down, he had a black cowboy hat on his head—a sight that was commonplace to her, so why she noticed at all, she'd never be able to say.

He was holding an axe.

He set a log on top of a large tree stump, held the axe high above his head and brought it down mercilessly upon the upended log. He sent the pieces flying. He picked up another bit of wood and began to set up all over again, and she couldn't help but notice the practice in his movements. The fluidity. His muscles. And…what might've even been a tattoo on his ribs. She blinked rapidly.

She got out of the car and shut the door.

"If you used an awl it might be easier."

He stopped, midmotion. He had a dark beard and hair, blue eyes. And she felt like they were looking straight through her. Worse, and weirder, she felt pinned to the spot. Like her shoes had been glued right there to the dirt, and she couldn't move.

She'd seen him just two days before. She couldn't figure out why she was frozen now.

He'd made her mad two days ago.

And for the first time in recent memory, angry felt like the safer option.

Why was she…fluttery now?

She had to get unfluttery really quickly.

"Excuse me?"

"Just… If you used an awl…"

He stood still for a moment, appraising her in a way that made her feel like he was seeing deeper than her skin. The silence made her unbearably uncomfortable, and she was about to say something else, when he spoke. "Miss Sullivan?"

"Yes?"

"Did you think that I needed pointers on how to cut wood?"

"I thought you might like it to be easier."

His mouth twisted upward into an approximation of a smile and he made a hard, grunting sound that may have been a laugh. "Ma'am, I prefer things to be harder. I like life to be a punishment, actually. So that I never slip into a false sense of security and believe it might treat me kindly. It hasn't yet. I don't like to be caught unaware."

Quinn always knew what to say. Speaking was a natural gift. She opened her mouth, and words poured out. But she had no idea what to say to that. "I see." She paused for a beat.

"I'm not sure you do."

And that was it. No questions about her, no nothing. It was like trying to get blood out of a stone. But that was fine. Quinn knew how to fill a silence.

"I feel that we got off on the wrong foot."

He simply stared at her.

"And I would like to see if we can find…a right foot."

He looked down, then back up at her. "I have a right foot all on my own, but thank you."

"That isn't what I was talking about. I'm almost certain you know that."

"Almost. Okay."

She cleared her throat. "I came here to talk to you about a business proposition."

He looked up and she felt compelled to follow his gaze. There was nothing there but the tops of the evergreens.

Finally he looked back at her. "A business proposition. How interesting." He did not sound interested. In fact, all he did was set up another piece of wood, raise that blasted axe of his and bring it down hard onto the log, splitting it as effortlessly as he had done the first two.

She pressed on.

"The permits got denied."

"I'm shocked to hear that."

He was obviously, patently, not.

"You aren't. You told me they would be."

"Ah, so you were shocked to hear that. Even though you did hear it from me."

Irritation crept up her spine. "Yes. That is true."

"So what exactly do you mean by coming here and telling me you have a business proposition?"

"You're our last hope, Levi."

"You'd have been better off if Obi-Wan Kenobi were your only hope, Quinn. Sorry to tell you." He turned away, like he was dismissing her.

"Levi," she said. "Please hear me out."

He turned back toward her. The way that he moved, the way he paced himself. His words, everything else… It threw her off. The other night, he'd been angry. This morning was even worse.

He was dismissive.

If he didn't want to listen, her options were so perilously limited.

"We need you," she said. "If we could use your road as an access to the store, it would solve everything. People would still drive through town before turning to Four Corners. The distance on the dirt road would be shorter. People would just come in from the other side of town."

"And you don't have any other plan?"

She shook her head. "No."

In that same manner as before, it was like he missed a beat before speaking. "Sounds like poor planning."

"We had a good plan, but you, the town, disagreed with it."

"You have enough land you could have put the store nearer to the road."

"We each have our own plot," she said, running over the tail end of his sentence. "The Kings were hardly going to let us build a facility in the middle of their land. We're a cooperative, but that only goes so far."

He plunked the axe head down on the ground, his hand gripping the handle hard. "Fair enough." He lifted the axe and turned it slowly. "I do fancy that I am a fair man, Miss Sullivan. But you really thought you could plan all of this on the assumption that I and the whole town would be all right with it?"

"Yes. Well, no. It isn't that we simply *assumed*... We really did think the permits would be a formality. We were paying for the road and we didn't foresee there being any issues. But there were issues."

"Yes, there were."

"So now we need to come up with something else, and that involves you."

He said nothing, but somehow the slight lift of one dark brow spoke in loud volumes.

She cleared her throat and continued. "I have a degree in agribusiness. And there are some things that I could recommend to you that you can improve here on your homestead."

He lifted the axe up off the ground and turned it so the blade was facing him. He brushed his thumb over the sharp edge, then looked over at her. "Because you think I need it?"

"Yes. I mean... I'm sorry about what I said the other night."

He smiled, slow and unkind. Her heart was thundering now, but with excitement. This was the part she'd been waiting for. "I would love to do a review of the place and give you pointers on what you could do."

"What's your area of expertise?"

"*Everything.* From the business end, profits and different types of crops. I know so much about how to organize, how to maximize land use, how to ensure you have the right paperwork, streamlining and, well… everything." The words flowed effortlessly, because she was an expert. Because she knew—exactly—what she was talking about. Exactly what she was doing, and it felt great.

This was what education got you.

Pennies well spent.

"You know so much about *streamlining and everything*, but you have to ask me if I can provide you with an easement for road access?"

"Our land is the way that it is. And the county surveyed it the way they did, and reached the conclusion they did. And that's the thing. With ranching, you're going to run into the realities of where exactly your ranch is set. But that doesn't mean you can't refine things."

"Is that so?" He leaned back on his heels and she suddenly became very conscious of the difference in their height.

Quinn was not a tall woman. She was the smallest of all her sisters, and she'd compensated for that by being—what some would call—unreasonably determined. She was willing to grit out any situation that came her way, willing to fight and push and scrap if need be.

As an adult she'd discovered she could use her brain instead of actually scrapping with anyone. But that same baseline determination was what had gotten her through...everything. Most especially getting scholarships and leaving Pyrite Falls and Four Corners for the first time and going to California for school.

She'd worked so hard. To fit in. To get the best grades. To learn what she needed to. Because her goal had been to bring it back home to Sullivan's Point and help her sisters. Especially Fia, who had taken such great care of them after their parents had gone.

So it didn't matter if he was tall, and unyielding and far too slow to speak, and a whole lot of other things besides. She was Quinn Sullivan, and she knew her business.

"It is so. And I would like to have the opportunity to speak to you in depth about your needs."

He looked her over. Slowly. Very slowly. And with that a burning sensation started in her stomach and bloomed ever outward.

She was aware—so aware—that she was pale and he could probably see it.

She hoped desperately he couldn't see it.

"Miss Sullivan," he said. "That is a pretty terrible plan."

She hadn't expected *that*. "Why is it terrible?"

"Well," he said, picking up another log. "I don't need anything." He brought the axe down on it with a crack. "Not even an awl."

"But everyone needs something."

He just looked at her. Utterly unreadable.

"Nope."

"That's it? You're just saying no? That's it?"

He straightened. "I've been running this place pretty damn good for the last eighteen years, and I expect I'll run it just as well in the years to come. Also, I don't see myself joining up with Four Corners folk. There are some mistakes you make only once."

She knew he'd done a deal with her dad, and she knew he hadn't been happy with it, but this had nothing at all to do with that. That was ancient history.

"I'm not my dad," she said.

He stared at her, far too cutting. "I don't simply take people at their word. Not these days."

"I'll show you," she said, because she couldn't bear the idea of just…failing. She didn't fail. She never failed, especially when she was right, and she was right. They just needed the use of his road for some traffic to be able to get to their store, and in exchange she would help with whatever he needed.

It was reasonable, and it would be good for *everyone*.

He was being ridiculous and he was wrong and she would make him see that.

"I'll prove myself if that's what you need. I'll be back. With a binder."

He laughed then, loud and hard, and the sound echoed up through the pines around them, and she hated him just a little bit. "Make sure to include lots of pictures or I might not understand. After all, you're the one with the degree. I'm just a rancher."

And then Levi Granger walked away and left her positively awash in outrage and thwarted purpose and some throbbing heat that she just didn't want to dwell on.

One thing was certain.

Quinn Sullivan would never remain thwarted, not for long.

She had book smarts. And she was going to use them.

LEVI GRANGER HAD better things to think about than the small woman who had invaded his space today. If there was one thing he couldn't stand, it was a know-it-all. A know-it-all that wasn't him, anyway.

He knew this land so well, when he closed his eyes at night he could walk himself through it.

He knew this land so well, it was branded onto his soul. And some uppity collegiate with freckles on her nose and hair the color of a cooked carrot didn't have anything to teach him about it just because she had a certificate that said she understood.

You couldn't understand this work by reading about it.

You had to have dirt under your nails and calluses on your hands. You had to have blood soaked into the dirt and sweat soaked into every fence post.

He had inherited this place at eighteen. He'd made his mistakes. One rash mistake he'd paid for, for years on end, and he'd learned. You didn't make deals in haste.

But this... This was a deal he wasn't going to make. Not with a Four Corners person, and most especially not with a Sullivan.

That road she wanted to have people—strangers—driving on wound around the mountain, and to a quiet spot with a big oak tree. Under that tree, his parents were buried. Well, it was where their ashes were, anyway. And it was where he sat and talked to them, even now.

There was no way in hell he was allowing an influx

of people onto that road, no matter how fast Quinn Sullivan tried to talk her way into it.

But she wasn't his problem. Not now.

He had much bigger issues, like what Camilla had told him over pizza the other night. It was unexpected, and he was unhappy about it. She hadn't worked so hard to get into school just to come back because she was worried about him. He had thought that maybe it wasn't the best idea for her to come for spring break, and he'd been right about that. Because she had taken a look at the state of the house and him, and decided that he wasn't coping with an empty nest.

And no amount of him telling her he had been waiting for an empty nest for the past fifteen years had done any good.

His sister was the baby. And she meant well.

They *all* meant well.

Jessie *meant* well…and she was off with Damien now, his best friend turned brother-in-law, and that had been up there on the most shocking things that had happened to him in his life.

Dylan had joined the military—Lord Almighty, Levi would never be okay with that—and was deployed again.

Camilla shouldn't be considering coming home. Not when she had a whole life, a whole future out there for herself.

But it was the strangest thing. The way that you could take care of three people for that many years, and somehow, the minute they get grown they think they have to *take care of you*.

Levi never wanted to have kids. He had raised plenty enough of them already. And anyway, he figured he didn't need to have any, because this was what it was like. You finally got them out of your house, and they came back, and they acted like they knew more than you.

That did remind him of Quinn Sullivan. Making suggestions on how he might cut a log. The girl didn't look like she was strong enough to lift an axe. She had looked petite and fragile today. Wearing a floral dress with her strawberry-colored hair blowing in the breeze. He would've laughed at her if he weren't so nice.

Okay, he had laughed at her, but just the once.

But she was ridiculous.

And he wasn't all that nice.

He walked up the side of the mountain, the most direct path to the main house. He could have driven, and he could've taken a path, but Levi liked to do things direct.

The new house had been finished just a few years ago. The final stage in his parents' dream that they hadn't been able to see come to fruition. When they'd died, they'd all been living in that cabin down by the highway, because there had been a bigger house under construction for them. It had taken years for it to get finished without them. Insurance money had helped see it through—that and the deal he'd struck at eighteen that had been...well, it hadn't been the best decision, but it had gotten them through and it was up now anyway. Well, all that and dogged determination on Levi's part. But that house had never been intended to be the final one. They'd had another set of plans, and really just out of a desire to see their dreams finished, Levi had gone and built that next one. Even though he lived in it mostly alone now.

And the house wasn't the only thing that needed finishing. Because Camilla needed to go out and get on with her life. Then things would feel finished.

Finally.

When he pushed the door open, his sister was literally on her hands and knees in the entryway scrubbing at a muddy boot print.

"What are you doing?"

"This place is a mess. Levi, you don't do well when you don't have people that you're responsible for."

"Excuse me. I don't think you get to tell me what I'm doing well."

"I call it like I see it." She pushed a mop of blond hair out of her face and looked at him with furious blue eyes that reminded him far too much of his own. She was stubborn. And he knew he couldn't come at her from the front. That was the thing with them. They proved that there was a fair amount of nature inherent in a person's behavior. Because the Grangers were stubborn. All of them. Down to their cores.

"Well, did you see fit to call that I might need some lunch?"

"You have food in the fridge."

"So you're only taking care of me to the degree that you want to."

"Yes," she said.

"Have mercy. Child, you have to go back to school."

"Levi…"

"Has it occurred to you that I might actually want some time alone?"

"It actually did. But I expected to come back and see that you were…I don't know…doing something. You did so much for us, Levi. You do so much for us. And

I thought that maybe once all the kids were out of the house you might…move toward having a life."

He had no idea what his sister was talking about. He got up every day and he worked the land. There was no other life. No other life that he wanted, no other life that he had ever dreamed of. And all right, the case could be made for the fact that he simply didn't have dreams. But when you were a seventeen-year-old kid who lost both parents to separate tragedies in less than a year, you kind of quit having dreams. You just focused on what you could do. On raising the kids that were left behind. That was what he'd done. He'd made the land his own, and he had used it to sustain them.

There wasn't more. Not for him. And he was fine with that.

"You don't know what all I do with my time."

"You haven't done anything with it except work in the time that I've been back home."

"Maybe I have a different life when you aren't here."

There was *some* truth to that. He wasn't exactly having a thriving sex life in full view of his siblings.

That, he did on his own time.

But he assumed she didn't mean that, either.

He was happy to pretend she didn't have a sex life, and he imagined that was mutual.

"You need someone to take care of you." She sounded like a little hen. Cluck cluck cluck.

What was with women who had to be more than ten years younger than him thinking they knew better than him today?

And he thought of the little redhead that had appeared in his driveway earlier. "I'm fine, Camilla."

"Are you really?"

"Yes, I am."

She frowned. "What about all your records? Are you set to do taxes this year?"

"I'm hiring someone. And anyway, I can handle that on my own."

He knew well enough now to know to hire out when he needed it. He was good at working the land. Paperwork? Well. Part of being in charge was knowing your strengths. He knew his. They weren't paperwork, and that was fine.

"I worry about you," she pushed.

"Well, don't. I'm a grown adult, and I took care of you for your whole snot-nosed life."

"You're the epitome of an isolated mountain man. You haven't shaved. The contents of your fridge—while plentiful—are not healthy. You basically live the life of a hermit. I don't want that for you."

He looked at his sister, the world feeling tilted. He had spent so many years worrying about her. And he was grousing about her acting like she suddenly knew more than him, but there was more than that. She was worried. Worried in the way that he worried about her. While she was away, he was concerned about every-thing. Boys taking advantage of her at parties, putting something in her drink. Her feeling stressed about her grades. Her having issues with friends. It was a con-stant turn of concern. But the idea that she was actu-ally worrying about him while she was supposed to be taking care of herself… "Yeah. I…I am. I'm actually… Camilla, I want you to go back to school and not worry about me, in part because I'm in the middle of chang-ing some things."

"You are?"

And he thought about Quinn again, and the fact that she needed him. And Lord help him, he didn't want to get involved with a Sullivan in any regard.

But since the Sullivan had involved herself with him...

Maybe he could use that.

He could consider it back pay from the Sullivan family.

"Yeah. I have some new plans on the horizon. Someone coming in to help manage some things. Don't even worry about it."

All he needed was for Quinn to show off that binder and get Camilla on her way.

And then he could get her out of his hair.

That did not mean he was agreeing to the easement, though.

He'd already lost some of the land's integrity because of a hasty choice he'd made at eighteen to trust the wrong person. He wasn't making the same mistake again.

CHAPTER FIVE

"I WOULD LIKE to vote to increase the budget for the easement endeavor."

Her sister Fia looked up at her, as did Rory.

"You need a budget increase to get Levi Granger to agree to an easement?" Fia asked, tilting her head, her red hair sliding over her shoulder in a shimmering wave. "I mean, it's better than you needing heavy artillery, I guess."

"Negotiations are young, Fia. Who's to say where it will end up?" Quinn said. "But for now, I need a laminator. I need to go buy one."

Fia frowned. "How much is a laminator?"

"Around thirty dollars."

"You don't need to *request* thirty dollars," Fia said.

"Yes, I do. Because we need to make sure that our business expenses all come out of the correct account and are accounted for."

"You're exhausting," said Rory.

"Thank you. At this point it's better than being *exhausted*, because we have work to do." And what she did not say was that Rory and her featherheaded approach to everything was equally exhausting to Quinn.

A person needed to be exacting; at least, in her experience that was the case. Rory was too much of a romantic to deal with budgets and receipts. Fia was a little bit more like Quinn was. Practical, measured.

Though, in Quinn's opinion, Fia could also be a little bit too head-in-the-clouds when it came to an idea she really, really wanted to make work—practically be damned.

It wasn't common, but though she knew her sister would deny it, Fia was a dreamer, fundamentally.

Quinn didn't dream. She'd learned not to a long time ago. She'd once been dreamy. She'd fantasized about life when she was a grown-up, when she'd be old enough to kiss Levi Granger and show him she was a woman. Then maybe she'd leave for a while and become successful. She'd go to cities and live in an apartment for a while.

Levi would come for her eventually, of course.

But that was all before. Before her dad had left and her family ranch had begun to crumble, and she'd realized dreams could only ever be dreams because you couldn't see the future.

Fantasies got you nowhere.

Planning, on the other hand…

She had her boots on the ground, and she had enthusiasm, which she knew that sometimes people mistook for optimism, or for some kind of unrealistic viewpoint, but that wasn't it at all.

Quinn was *researched*, and that allowed her to be enthusiastic. Quinn knew what she was about; she had the education, she had the understanding.

It was how she had gotten to college in the first place. She had been older when she'd gone. She had assembled the appropriate documentation, she had gotten a collection of scholarships, had gotten recommendation letters, had done prerequisites and online classes. She had known the path to get herself there. She hadn't simply sat around dreaming about it.

When Quinn was sixteen, she had realized that her anger was going to kill her.

She had gotten into a fistfight with a boy at the one-room schoolhouse. And perhaps he could be faulted for hitting a lady. But the lady had hit him first.

She had just been so angry when their dad left.

She had been driven by it.

As if it was a motor propelling her around the ranch. Like a little Tasmanian devil. But in the end, it wasn't sustainable, and it hadn't gotten her anything.

Fia was the one who'd sat her down and lectured her after Quinn'd punched a kid at school, who had then in turn punched her back and left her with a split lip that Fia'd had to treat. As she'd dabbed the wound with a medicine-soaked cotton ball, she'd lectured her.

You're so smart, Quinn. But I don't know what happened to the sweet, sensitive kid who used to cry when a robin fell out of its nest. Now you're just acting like you can punish Dad by being awful to the people around you, and you won't get anywhere doing that.

Fia had been right. At that point their mom had been there, but not really. She'd been emotionally wholly checked out. And maybe that had contributed to Quinn being even angrier. She'd had this strong need to prove she wasn't her mother by not dissolving.

She'd needed to put mileage between herself and the kid who'd chased her dad barefoot down the driveway with tears streaming down her face as she'd begged him not to leave.

Anger had felt safer than that.

But she didn't want all of her goals to implode because of her dad. She'd remembered who she'd wanted to be. She'd pulled herself back.

Quinn had replaced anger with logic. And with drive. When she found herself being powered by the drive to succeed, all of that energy became productive.

It was so much better than being angry.

"Soooo... I take it he didn't say yes," said Fia.

"No. He didn't. *Yet*."

She tried not to think of the derisive way that he had looked at her. The dismissal on his face. He was just... He was so obnoxious.

He hadn't listened to a single thing she said, and she had training, she knew what she was talking about. He was just so...

He was a *man*.

That was the problem.

Men, in her experience, were inherently self-centered and prone to thinking they had thought of absolutely every eventuality, when in reality they just wanted their way.

And he was a whole, particular thing that she couldn't put her finger on. He had refused to move with her rhythm. Usually her energy invigorated other people.

It was like he was a black hole where her enthusiasm went to die.

Or worse, where it went to turn into electricity that rocketed through her body like lightning and couldn't be contained or controlled.

She had persevered, though, and she would be back, stronger than ever.

"I told him that I would be back tomorrow with a binder, so tonight I need to make a binder. I need to go point by point on what he could be doing differently at his operation, which I grant is going to be difficult because I don't know very much about his operation, so I have to make sure that I cover all my bases."

"And your bases will be…laminated?" Fia asked.

Fia was making fun of her. But Quinn didn't care. Fia wasn't the one who was trying to conquer the black hole.

"Yes, Fia. It's called making a professional impression. I'm trying to convince him he needs input from me, so I have to look like someone he can take seriously."

"Have you ever been told that you're a bit intense?" said Rory.

"Have you ever been told that you have the intensity of a feather pillow?"

Rory smiled. "No. But I like that."

"He is *impossible*," said Quinn.

He'd been so dismissive and so rude. And there he was, chopping wood in front of what was essentially a shanty, and given what she knew of his ranch, he should be living a lot better than that.

He was the only supplier of Wagyu beef in the immediate area, and the product sold for an absolute premium. Unless he was severely mismanaging things, he should be doing quite well, and yet she'd seen the house.

"Well, maybe you should enlist Alaina," Fia said. "Impossible men have become her specialty."

Their youngest sister, Alaina, had a baby, and was married to Gus McCloud, which meant she was in very close proximity to all the McCloud brothers.

Alaina'd had a bit of a rocky road to happiness, but now she seemed pretty well giddy with it.

And yeah, the McCloud men, who she was now surrounded by, were notoriously hardheaded and difficult. Her husband most of all.

"He's not the same kind of difficult as Gus," she said, trying to figure out how to articulate the Levi of it all. "He's...he's arrogant, first of all. Gus is not arrogant."

"You don't think so?" Rory asked.

She thought about her brother-in-law, who was scarred and a bit gruff, but ultimately one of the most caring men she'd ever met. Alaina was mouthy and had a quick-burning temper. Gus couldn't be arrogant, not when dealing with Alaina.

"No," said Quinn. "I don't think so."

"Hmm." Rory picked up her phone and brought up a video call.

Alaina, all red curly hair and smiles, answered. She was holding their nephew on her hip. "Hey," she said.

"I have a question for you," said Rory. "Is Gus arrogant? Quinn doesn't think so."

Alaina howled with laughter. "Yes. He's the biggest, most arrogant bastard on the planet."

"Hey." They heard a man's voice off to the side and Alaina quickly flashed the phone over toward him.

"This is irrelevant," said Quinn. "I don't care about Gus."

"That's hurtful," Gus said just from outside the frame.

"That's not what I mean," she said to her brother-in-law, and she could feel all the impossible heat she associated only with Levi flooding her. "I just mean that I'm trying to deal with Levi Granger, and I think he's more arrogant than Gus."

"Oh, yeah," said Gus. "Levi Granger is an asshole."

"See," said Quinn. "Levi Granger is an asshole." For some reason, that sat wrong with her, and made her feel bad, too, but she did not recant. "And it is a noted, documented fact. But I'm not going to let him make me angry. I'm going to make a binder instead."

"Sorry," said Fia, dipping her head toward the phone. "You got involved in a sister dispute."

"Do I need to come over there?" Alaina asked.

She was about an eight-minute drive away, living on McCloud's Landing, a few miles away on the interconnected dirt roads that ran between the ranches.

"No. This is all about Quinn requesting money to buy a laminator."

Alaina laughed. "A *laminator*. That's what this is about? Aren't those like twenty bucks? Let it never be said the Sullivan sisters couldn't make a mountain out of a molehill. I'll talk to you tomorrow." Alaina hung up.

"Well, thank you for that," said Quinn. "I didn't need to involve the whole family."

"Yes. We can drive over to Mapleton and get a laminator."

"All of us?"

"All of us," said Fia.

Which was how she found herself bundled up into her sister's turquoise truck, and headed the hour out of Pyrite Falls into Mapleton, the closest town that actually had some decent-sized services.

Pyrite Falls itself was less the town and more a strip of buildings. With Smokey's Tavern, John's grocery store and Becky's diner, the place was very small.

The public school was in Mapleton, and the children of the families that worked at Four Corners had the option to send the kids to the one-room schoolhouse on the property to be schooled that way. That was where Quinn had gone to school.

All of them had, in fact.

It really was the most extreme small-town life. Pyrite Falls was tiny, and Four Corners was a small town unto itself.

It had been really different, going down to California for school. Even in the Central Valley, which wasn't exactly a budding metropolis, it had been a big change.

But Quinn had kept focused. Her head hadn't been turned by any of the fancy things in the city. She was back to herself then. She knew who she was and what she wanted.

She'd wanted a degree to help her add another shield. More protection. Something to help her feel good enough, because she hadn't known what else might do that.

She hadn't gone down there to date, though she had often felt a little bit left out when the people around her went and had fun. But she had gotten there on scholarship, and she was determined to do the best she could.

She got her agribusiness degree, and she was ready now. It didn't matter that she hadn't done the social-life thing in college; it wasn't what she had done college for.

She was exceptionally good at keeping focused on a goal.

That sort of energy was adjacent to rage, after all.

It just required that you bit down on something hard, and refused to let go.

They rolled into Mapleton, and she looked around, trying to see if there were any new businesses on Main Street. It had been a little while since she had come into town, and tourist season was a great time of year to go.

People often came to stay in the vacation rentals. There was a resort off in the mountains, and it attracted quite a lot of people.

It wasn't the same kind of tourist town as somewhere more picturesque like Copper Ridge, but it had its share of people who enjoyed coming and visiting.

There was a new clothing boutique, and she knew that, without even asking, Fia would stop them there.

Her sisters *did* have an affinity for dresses.

But the first thing they did was stop at a store that had office supplies, and she got not only a laminator, but also a very large binder with flowers on the outside of it.

She made sure that Fia and Rory voted yes on every purchase, and technically, it was all still right within the bonds of their family business, because they would've been a majority and outvoted Alaina even if she would've said no. But Alaina would not have said no.

Anyway, it didn't matter.

They stopped then and got a couple of new dresses, and then went to one of the local coffeehouses, where they got iced, flavored espresso drinks.

"Now, this was a good day," said Fia.

"How soon do you think we'll be able to get the farm store opened?" asked Rory.

"It squarely depends on Levi. If we have to figure out how to get the road dug in all the way from the main drag, it's going to be costly and create a huge delay. I mean, obviously we can open and put out signs and hope that people want to drive eight miles down a dirt road, but that's going to be a bit of an uphill battle." Fia took another sip of her drink. "And it's a battle that will probably cost us so much, the store will fail before it ever begins."

"You've done a good job," said Rory. "Whatever happens, Fia. You've done a great job."

Fia would never say it, but Quinn believed it to be

true. The Sullivans had had it hard. They were also re-
silient. They were the only family on the ranch made
up entirely of women.

The McClouds were all boys, the Kings and the
Garretts mixed. The Sullivans had had to be creative
once their dad had left. There weren't a plethora of
sons to lift hay bales and do manual labor. They'd always had to lease out their fields and hire foremen.
They had to focus on their own strengths and hone
them. They produced a massive amount of hazelnuts,
vegetables, fruits. They baked, they made preserves.

Their dad's abandonment and their mother's subsequent dissolving had forced the girls to band together.
When Quinn had managed to get her anger under control, she'd begun really homing in on ways to make the
ranch more profitable. With Rory's head for management, Fia's coolheaded leadership, Alaina's tenacity and
Quinn's hyperfocus on all things agribusiness related,
they'd built themselves a profitable spread.

They made money not only on the ranch land, but
also on their other skills.

It had never been Alaina's passion, but it was the
rest of theirs. And it was one reason that Quinn had
felt inspired to go to college. What Fia had done was
figure out how to work smarter, and harder along with
it, and she had turned Sullivan's Point into a huge success. But it had taken creativity and hard work. It had
taken her forging new ground. Their father had done
beef, just like the Garretts, just like the Kings. Fia was
the one who had decided to take a risk and get into
fruits and vegetables. Nuts. She was the one who had
decided to lease the land. In Quinn's opinion, Fia was
the most creative businessperson in the entire collec-

tive, and Quinn looked up to her mightily for it. Not just that, the amount of emotional support that Fia had given to the rest of them over the years. It wasn't easy being the oldest in a dysfunctional family. Everyone else at Four Corners proved that. Sawyer, Gus, Denver… They were all a mess.

But Fia had done it.

"Thank you," said Fia. "But we'll see. If this all goes to hell, you may be cursing me rather than thanking me."

"The others will have our back," said Rory.

Four Corners was run as a collective. The other ranches had invested money into the farm store endeavor, because it was what they did. They invested in each other's ventures. They had done it for the McClouds when they had opened up their equestrian therapy facility, which was proving to be not only extremely helpful, but also successful. They had done it for the Kings when they had wanted to expand their pastureland. They had done it for the Garretts when they'd needed to do the same.

They would bail each other out, always. Because it was what they did.

Fia's eyes narrowed. *"Maybe."*

"Is this about Landry King?"

"No," said Fia. "Because not everything is about Landry King."

"But you hate him," Rory said, tilting her cup back and crunching an ice cube. "You know. In that way a woman hates a hot man, and wishes to be stranded alone in a cabin with him on a mountainside with *only one bed* to work out all the raw tension."

Rory was addicted to romance novels. She tended to view things through an overly romantic lens. Quinn also believed Rory to be a virgin. Which meant that everything she said was big talk about nothing that she knew anything about.

That was, of course, another hazard of growing up in a place this small.

You either got into insane entanglements with people that would be in your life ever after—which was what she assumed had happened with Landry and Fia, and definitely what had happened with Alaina and Gus—or there really just wasn't a whole lot out there.

Which was what Quinn and Rory suffered from.

"Please stop," said Fia. "I do not want that. But I also don't think that he would actually... He wouldn't do anything to hurt the ranch. Okay. But it is going to take a leap for those men to think that this is something worth investing in. They understand what they understand. Meat and horses and masculine grunting."

"Do you think they don't respect you because you're a woman?" Quinn asked.

She had never really gotten that vibe off any of them. But Fia dealt more with the other families. Because they were essentially the founding members of the collective. Fia, Gus, Denver and Sawyer.

"Not *intentionally*. But look, they're a pack of alpha males, and I'm an alpha female. We don't always mesh, we don't always see eye to eye, and I think that they have an ingrained sensibility that is different from mine. So yeah, sometimes I do feel like I'm in an uphill battle because I see things differently than they do."

"You should have me go to talk to them sometimes. Now that I've had all the schooling..."

Fia looked at her like she was young and naive, and that made Quinn feel a little violent. So she curled her toes in her shoes. "I don't think that they're going to put a lot of stock in that. You having something that they don't have."

It had never occurred to her that they might think that way. She had an education; that made her *qualified* to speak on it.

"That would be stupid," said Quinn. She opened the top of her drink and took out an ice cube, crunching on it the same way that Rory had.

"I hate to be the one to break this to you, Quinn, but sometimes men are stupid," Fia said. "No matter how nice your binder is."

"Well, I'm going to prove to you that I can do this. That it was all worth it. Me being away for four years. I'm going to show you that this is going to come together. You can trust me."

"I do trust you, Quinn. It's Levi Granger I don't trust."

CHAPTER SIX

LEVI WAS BEGINNING to wonder if Quinn Sullivan was actually going to return with the binder as she'd promised she would.

He wondered, too—if that were the case—if he would be able to get rid of Camilla by simply telling her that he had somebody managing the financials and flashing the binder. He actually *could* hire somebody. But he liked to take his time to mull stuff like this over.

He could ask around, find out who Damien used. Though, Levi would still need to meet whoever Damien suggested personally. He didn't do business with faceless fat cats. Not anymore.

Damien was his best friend, who had become very successful running a winery, and the guy really was a business savant.

Levi wasn't a slouch. His Wagyu beef operation had required a whole lot of certifications and other things that he had initially thought would be impossible.

But he would never admit that something felt impossible. He was physically incapable of it. He had known he could do the work—he just wasn't sure that he could show it in the paperwork. But Damien had been a big help with that and, Damien being Damien, had never made him feel like it was a negative that he had needed his input.

It also made sense, though, because Damien had more experience with certifications and the like.

He never really needed to talk about the actual reasons he needed the assistance.

And they didn't much get into the negative history of the ranch.

He wondered how much Quinn knew about the deal he'd made with her dad.

It was clear that she thought she was a clever little genius because of all that schooling.

School, in his estimation, was nothing but privilege. Had nothing to do with how smart you were. Just whether or not you could get there. Fine for some if they could jump through all the hoops they needed to in high school to get scholarships. Fine for some if their mommy and daddy were alive and could pay for it. And even if not alive to pay for it, just alive so they could be the adults, rather than him having to do it.

His were in the grave, and he hadn't gone to school because he had been busy taking care of his siblings and, before that, his mother while her health declined.

Anyway, sitting down, staring at papers all day, it was all bullshit anyway. The words jumped around and the letters turned themselves every which way. It was such a pain in the ass to sit there and try to read a page of shit he didn't even care about while the ranch was going to hell or his mother needed something. It just didn't make sense.

Of course, there had been times that all that had jumped up and bit him in the ass, but he dealt with it. He made mistakes, being young and inexperienced, and he covered it.

He didn't need somebody like Quinn Sullivan showing up and acting like she knew better than him just because she'd gone to school and he didn't even have a high school diploma.

Of course, very few people knew that. His siblings didn't know that. There wasn't any reason to talk about it.

Not that he cared. It just didn't come up.

But he went back down the driveway around the same time she had shown up yesterday, and parked his truck next to the old cabin. Just in case.

Then there she was. When she parked her car and got out of the driver side, she was clutching a big, flowered binder to her chest that he swore was nearly as big as she was.

He only looked at her. He'd gotten the feeling when she'd been here last that his silence, and his pace, was off-putting to her.

He was going to use that. Use the fact that he liked to chew on his words a minute before he spoke, whereas she spit words out like they were tacks she needed to expel as quickly as possible.

"Here I am," she said. She stared at him. Clearly, she expected him to say something. So he didn't. "I said that I would come back, and I have. Is there somewhere that we can sit?"

He looked around, then looked at the cabin and back to her.

"Oh, no, ma'am," he said. "The inside of my house is not fit for a lady like yourself."

She frowned at him. For some reason, he noticed that she was wearing white ankle socks. White tennis shoes. He didn't know why he noticed that detail. And he also didn't know why his immediate thought was that the socks were cute.

He looked back up at her face. Covered in freckles, her nose wrinkling slightly. Like a mad little bunny rabbit. "I'm not sure that I… A lady such as myself? I work on a ranch, Mr. Granger."

He was amused he'd managed to get her to call him that.

He'd known her since she was knee-high to a prairie dog.

Well, *known* was a strong word.

But they'd grown up in a town the size of a vole's tit, plus he'd had business with her family once upon a time. And still, he'd managed to set the tone and get her acting all formal.

"Miss Sullivan," he said, drawing it out to the point of a drawl. "I just hate to be inhospitable, but I don't want you seeing the state of things." He was a liar. But he was having fun with it.

He realized she wasn't just thrown off by him taking his time to speak. She thought he was *dumb*. She thought she knew more than him. So let her twist about a little bit, and he might as well play into it.

"Well…" She wandered over to the stump that he had been cutting on yesterday, and put one white tennis shoe–clad foot right up on it.

Her dress rode dangerously high up on her pale thigh—and she was too damned young for him—but he wasn't made of stone, so he did notice. Then she put the binder down on her thigh and opened it up, supporting the other side on her forearm. "This is the first page. I'm going to show you the different ways that you can use your acreage to increase profits."

He only looked at her. And he could see her mounting discomfort, and took great joy in it.

She started talking, running right over the silence, and he was regretful to find out that she actually did know some things. He wondered how much of it was intel from the old deal he'd done with her dad.

He'd been a dumb kid when he'd signed that lease. Ten years with his land tied up growing soybeans for a factory-farming outfit at a terrible rate, thanks to all the cash Brian Sullivan was skimming from the deal.

But he'd read the contract wrong, and he'd agreed to longer terms, a greater loss of control and a smaller profit than he'd thought, and he'd reaped—no pun intended— what he'd sown for years after.

He'd been planning all that time, ready to jump into the beef industry and take control back, and in the last six years he'd done that and been successful. He'd started making up for the lost years, had made enough to send Camilla to college.

But there was more he could do, that much he knew.

She was talking about seasonality and the way to keep things rotating.

"Now," she said, "I know you mostly do beef. Wagyu. I looked it up. Because, of course, in order to put this together I had to know as much about your operation as possible."

He nodded. "Right."

For all that she had done her research, she still somehow believed he lived down here. That this was the house. Of course. And she was making assumptions on his management, because if he had Wagyu, and he still wasn't turning a very big profit...

"And you're probably thinking, all the available fields would be best used for more grazing land."

"I am?" he asked, keeping his tone blank.

"Yes," she said. "Because that's how cattle ranchers often think. But no. Not necessarily. It just depends on how quickly you want to increase the amount of cattle that you have. My money would be on diversification. Because every segment of the industry is volatile. So while you can certainly specialize, I think you might be better off growing a staple crop."

"I've done that," he said, keeping his expression flat.

Her face went red. "Oh. Right. Of course. I just…"

"You're not looking as well researched as I was led to believe."

"Well." She started flipping pages madly. "Let's get into your tax structure."

He looked at the page, all full of tables and numbers, and he blinked hard and looked away. "Listen. You seem very smart. But smart isn't the be-all and end-all. Not *this* kind of smart. Have you ever actually done work on a cattle ranch?"

"No. But I know about the particulars of running it as a business. The valuation, and the amount of work you have to go through to get different certifications, the USDA weigh stations…"

"Great. So, if you read about flying a plane, do you think you can actually get in the cockpit and pilot a plane?"

For the first time she looked a little bit uncertain.

"How about this?" she said, suddenly. "You take the binder and look it over." She dumped it into his hands and he regarded it with as much trust as he might allocate to a live snake. "Tomorrow, I'll come back to the ranch and I'll put in a day's work."

"Excuse me?"

"If you want to see whether or not I have something to offer you, if you want me to prove myself, that's just fine by me. I'll come tomorrow and report for work, and you can see what you think of the information I've compiled into the binder. Then after that you'll see I do have something to offer you and you'll be more amenable to the easement."

More *amenable* to the easement. She hadn't really asked what he wanted or why at all. She was talking herself in circles like an overactive ferret chattering at her own tail.

And why not let her? She was smart, so very smart, and why not let her get hog-tied by her own brilliance?

"I start work at six o'clock sharp, Miss Sullivan."

"I'll be here. What sort of shoes should I wear?"

He looked back down at the cute little white sneakers and the cute little socks. "Not those."

"Work boots. I assume," she said.

"If you assumed, then why did you ask?"

"Because I know well enough to try and be prepared. I'm not an idiot."

He felt strongly that this was up for debate.

"Sure. Work boots. Not some fancy little JCPenney cowgirl boots."

And then she looked like she might actually implode. Which was gratifying as hell.

"You know I actually *live* on a ranch, right? I have stood ankle height in horse shit on more than one occasion."

He arched a brow. "Then you ought to be cleaning the stalls out a little more often."

She frowned. Deeply. "You know what I mean."

He crossed his arms and leaned heavily against the side of the cabin. "I don't know that I do. Perhaps you should be a little more exacting in your language. I would have thought that your fancy book-learning institution might've taught you that. Ma'am."

She narrowed her eyes. "Are you being intentionally provocative?"

"No. At least, I don't think so. Because that's a college word, so I'd have to figure the exact meaning."

He had intended to lean in to her assumption that he was a dumbass, though he had a feeling he might be overplaying that hand.

The truth was, pretty much to spite the world he had done his level best to educate himself however he could. Audiobooks were a particular boon. The fact that you could *listen* to all kinds of information had been life-changing to him. There were still issues, for sure. But people always underestimated him. He knew the land, and he could find out what he needed to know.

And he had sure as hell worked on making sure he had a vocabulary that could knock someone on their ass if necessary.

Quinn Sullivan was begging to be knocked on her ass.

"Somehow I don't believe you."

He lifted a shoulder. "That's too bad. It's not up to you to believe me or disbelieve me. Remember, I'm the one with the road."

Her cheeks turned as red as her hair.

He'd made her mad. Damned mad.

And he liked it.

"I'm fine. Thank you. I will be back here in work boots tomorrow."

"I leave at six, sharp. Bring your own coffee. I don't share. Oh, yeah… And the house is up the road a piece." He smiled. He couldn't help it. "I was messing with you."

"You were… Excuse me?"

"This isn't my house. Drive up the road a couple more miles tomorrow. You'll see it."

And he took that binder with him, all tucked up under his arm, and he left her there, satisfied he'd taken her down quite a few notches.

CHAPTER SEVEN

By the time she got up the next morning, she was stamping about the kitchen in work boots. She was in a fury. He was the worst. He was *absolutely the worst*.

And he was making fun of her. With his angular jaw and large hands and…and…

And.

Did he think she was a greenhorn?

She had grown up on a ranch. He knew that!

She'd been mucking stalls, feeding horses, fixing fences and managing the pastures since she was in Velcro shoes.

And no, they didn't currently do the kind of ranch work that he did, but they had made this place profitable. She had managed to get herself to school, where she had learned all about the economics of this kind of thing, about the legalities, managing a business, and whether Mr. Free Citizen of Pyrite Falls wanted to admit that those things mattered, they did. They absolutely did.

So there.

She started the coffee maker, which was designed to fit a thermos right underneath the spout. With bleary eyes, she shoved it beneath and pushed the on button. Then she turned to get some cream out of the fridge, and heard a splattering noise.

She turned around to see that she had put the thermos beneath the spout, upside down. And the coffee was running out over the bottom of the container.

With absolutely no deference given to whether or not her sisters were sleeping in their upstairs bedrooms in their adorably eclectic farmhouse, Quinn let out a howl of rage.

A moment later, Fia appeared at the top of the stairs. "Are you fighting a dragon down here?"

"Philosophically," Quinn said, having shut the machine off and hurriedly begun cleaning up the mess. "Yes."

She reset everything and put the thermos beneath, this time checking to see if it was right side up. "I often think it's utterly unfair that a person has to make coffee before they've had coffee."

"One of those true injustices in the world, I agree," said Fia, crossing her arms beneath her breasts and leaning against the wall. "Did you need some help?"

"I don't need help. I'm going to work at Levi Granger's ranch this morning. Because *apparently* I have to prove to him that I know what I'm doing."

"You're off to a great start," said Fia, looking around the kitchen.

"Don't oppose me, Fia," she said testily. "I've had enough of it."

"I'm not *opposing* you. I am *teasing* you."

It felt the same to Quinn. And she was far too raw for any of it.

"He's infuriating," said Quinn.

"I'm sure that he is," Fia said, and Quinn felt she sounded patronizing.

"Do you know Levi?" It was possible that Fia knew

him in a different context, but the idea made Quinn feel scratchy.

Fia shook her head. "No. He's way too much older than me for us to have known each other socially back in the day. Anyway. You know I don't...go out or anything."

"Yeah. I do."

She had long assumed it was because Landry King had broken Fia's heart. And yet Fia didn't seem like a romantic. But then, she had often thought perhaps that was why, as well.

Rory was a ridiculous romantic. She had dreams of being swept off her feet.

Quinn had no such dreams. Quinn just hadn't decided yet if she wanted any kind of romantic entanglement.

It seemed like a hassle, from her perspective.

Watching the dissolution of her parents' marriage had been disheartening.

And really, her dad leaving had put a big dent in her ability to trust anything with a penis. How could you ever get back to trusting somebody that you had known your entire life when they proved that they were...not at all who you thought. How could you ever look at anyone the same way again?

Quinn hadn't been able to. It was one reason she'd been so angry.

Her dad hadn't just left them; he'd taken with him Quinn's entire view of the world.

Nothing had ever been the same.

But right now, Fia's expression just looked so...sad. It made Quinn wonder. It made her wonder if she knew her sister at all.

"Fia…"

"There's nothing to talk about, Quinn. And certainly nothing that requires a summit at five thirty in the morning. I don't know anything about Levi Granger other than the fact that he has a reputation for being stubborn. He does not have a reputation for being dangerous in any way, though, so I imagine that you'll be fine. Unless he is a very stealthy murderer of young women that he puts to work on his ranch."

Quinn wrinkled her nose. "Well, let's hope not."

Fia smiled, but it didn't reach her eyes. "Listen. It doesn't matter if you think you know someone or not. You can't always trust them. Just… I haven't heard anything bad about him, but I want you to be careful."

"Be careful, of what?"

"Just the same speech I gave you in college. Watch your drink and all of that."

"He's a neighbor."

"That doesn't mean anything. We don't really know him."

"I don't think I'm in any danger from him. Though, he did not respond well to the binder."

"I'm not sure that I would've responded well to the binder, either." Fia moved forward and patted her on the arm. "In all seriousness, he's been in the community long enough that if there was anything untoward about him, we would know. But I love you, and break a leg. Well, no. Don't do that. That doesn't really work when you're talking ranch work. Because you actually might break a leg."

"I will *not*, Fia. I know how to do farm chores."

"Do you?"

"Yes. This is what I do. This is my area of study."

"What kind of ranch work do we do?" Fia asked, sweetly.

"I know how to ride a horse. I know how to muck stalls. I know how to buck hay."

"When have you bucked hay?"

"I *have*," she insisted.

The look her sister gave her was so skeptical it nearly lit the fuse on Quinn's explosive temper. But she didn't indulge in that. Not anymore. "Like *physically*, you have done the work?" Fia asked.

Quinn took a heavy, calming breath. "Yes. I think. I mean, I remember being out when the hands were doing it a couple of years ago."

"You're tiny," said Fia. "Very cute, but pocket-sized women are sort of impractical for heavy lifting. Believe me, it is also my burden to bear." She smiled. "But we're very good at getting things out of hard-to-reach places."

"Well, I'll let him know if he has anything that has fallen into a tight crevice, I can try my hand at it. Literally. And I'm leaving now." She grabbed her thermos and headed out the door, getting into her car and making her way down the dirt road that led to the main highway.

Things were already bustling on the ranch. This was the time when ranchers got up to do things. That was another perk of being a Sullivan, she had to admit. Unless it was a bread-baking day, they didn't keep quite the same early hours as the other families. They didn't really have to. Because their primary focus wasn't animals.

But there were already trucks on the roads, ranch hands moving between plots of land and getting a start to the day's work. By the time she got out to the main highway, there was even more traffic. The day started early for almost everyone that lived in Pyrite Falls, even if they weren't ranchers. Because they often had quite the commute to get to work.

It was a difficult life. But there was something kind of profound about it, because it was harder to make it here than not. It was a place you had to choose. You could fall into it, for certain. Inherit land. But it wouldn't simply sustain itself. You had to make it sustainable.

There was something poetic about that, at least to her.

She was pondering that when she turned onto the road that would carry her to Levi's house.

He had said that the house was farther up the road. But she had no real idea how far, or how she was supposed to gauge it.

She drove on, though, passing the little shanty he'd been chopping wood in front of both days when she had arrived.

Why hadn't he told her it wasn't the house?

He was sort of determined to mess with her. To prove that he was smarter than her.

Maybe that was it.

She thought about that for a moment. She wondered if it made him feel intimidated that she had gone to college.

Maybe. She was proud of her accomplishments. She had worked hard for them.

It just wasn't an assumption around here that people would go on to have higher education. It had been interesting to actually be at school. Many of the people that had been there had found it to be compulsory. Like moving on to the next grade in high school. Not a discussion at all, but an inevitability. It wasn't like that here. It never had been. Many people expected to go into some kind of trade. Many of the women expected to get married, to be a ranch wife.

But not Quinn. Even before her father had defected, that hadn't been her goal.

But after... Well, afterward it had become even more important to her that she got an education. That she made her own way.

Because she had seen what could happen to a woman when she made her entire world a man, and that man left.

Her mother had collapsed.

She had never been the same.

She'd been less hostile to Fia, so in that sense it was good. It was like her dad leaving had let all the air and anger out of the place. But at the same time... She just hadn't been her. She'd been like a shell of the woman she'd been. It was hard to be both grateful for it and mad about it, but Quinn managed.

Even now that her mom was living in Hawaii, basically in paradise, living her best life, she wasn't the same person she'd been before.

She would probably say she was happy. Away from the tiny town of Pyrite Falls, away from the grind of ranch life. Living on island time and enjoying dating around and lunching with friends.

Quinn had gone to visit her mother on a couple of different school breaks.

It was beautiful there.

And her mother seemed like a new person surrounded by all the sea. Even though it was good in many ways, Quinn had issues with it.

And Quinn didn't want to be changed by a man, even if that change took her to Hawaii.

Quinn wanted control.

To be in charge of her own destiny, and to heck with anybody that tried to meddle in it.

Including *Levi*.

Thinking the guy was hot didn't give him permission to get under her skin.

She wasn't a romantic.

Appreciating him in a visual sense didn't mean he got to control her emotions.

Maybe that was part of her problem. She had vanquished her anger just a little bit too well. Maybe she needed to call upon it, even if it was just to fuel her through today.

She couldn't really be mean to him, because he did have a point: she needed him.

But she could be intense. She was very good at that.

Then she rounded the corner in the winding gravel drive, and looked up and saw a massive house. Absolutely huge. With big, brightly lit windows, and what looked like a chandelier inside.

It was gorgeous. Rustic and modern all at once, and she wasn't quite sure how it managed to be both of those things, but it did.

That asshole.

He had been absolutely playing her.

She had driven up and thought that she could easily identify that he had a need based on how meager his living situation was, but his living situation wasn't meager at all. In fact, it made the Sullivans' farmhouse look like a dollhouse.

She got out of the car, clutching her coffee service

tightly in her hands, holding it just a bit too tightly, until her knuckles began to ache.

That absolute *bastard*.

But she did her best to breathe through the rage because being mean to him wasn't going to win her anything, and she didn't *do* uncontrolled rage. Not anymore.

Not even when someone was an uncontrolled, vile jerk…

And then the front door opened and he was standing there, wearing a flannel shirt, a black cowboy hat, blue jeans and…socks. He did not have his work boots on yet.

It disturbed her that even when angry with him, the impact of him, physically, was like getting hit by a truck. A very sexy truck.

"Come on in."

"I'm on time," she said, scampering up to the doorway.

"Sure are," he said, but somehow managed to sound calm and like she was wrong all at once.

"I *am*," she said, keeping her voice as smooth and placid as possible.

He looked at her, his expression maddeningly blank. "Yeah."

"You aren't ready to go."

"No. I'm not."

She squinted. "You said you were always ready to go at six sharp."

He nodded. "Yeah."

"And you aren't," she pointed out.

"You're the one who invited yourself along today, Miss Sullivan. I don't quite understand why you think it's up to you to give me a lecture on timekeeping."

That shut her up effectively. Because he was right. She'd pushed for this. She didn't feel bad in the sense that he'd made her feel mean. No, he'd made her feel like she'd made a grave tactical error. He was…maybe trying to annoy her? And she was letting him.

There was a big pile of shoes by the door, but his work boots were set next to a bench right there in the expansive entryway.

The kitchen that was behind him was huge, well-appointed with many modern conveniences.

She heard footsteps and startled, looking up at the staircase to the right, to see a little blonde wearing a white T-shirt and short shorts flitting down the stairs.

"Levi," she said. "I didn't know that you had company."

Well, Quinn felt like saying the exact same thing.

She felt…she felt like she'd been dipped in boiling oil. She was hot. And raw.

He was letting her see his morning-after…situation. Oh, *she hated men so much.*

Because of course he just had some woman in his house that he…

"I can wait outside," said Quinn.

"No need," said the blonde, waving her hand. "Are you…coming or going?"

Quinn frowned. "I'm… I just got here."

Did he have a revolving door? And this blonde woman was just *used* to it? She had the night shift, some other woman had the day shift?

Who in the world had that kind of time? Quinn had never managed to squeeze a love affair into her life, and Levi was juggling multiple women?

"Okay," said the woman, laughing. "That makes more

sense. I didn't think he had *that* big of a personality transplant since I was here last year. I'm Camilla. Levi's sister."

His *sister*. For a full ten seconds she was stunned, and she was...

Why had she assumed it was his lover? Even if she wasn't his sister, she could have been a committed girlfriend. Or even a wife. It wasn't like she knew everything about Levi.

So why had that been the go-to? And why had it bothered her so much?

Well, the truth was, she didn't trust men as a species because of her dad. Sad but true. The thing was, if someone you'd known all your life could turn out to be hiding secrets, then anyone could be.

Many *Dateline* episodes supported that theory.

So maybe her go-to was a bit more judgmental than it should be. But that was how she stayed safe. It wasn't personal to him. It was just her issues.

That was all.

She really didn't know enough about him. Well, she did know he had a sister. Sisters, in fact. And a brother. She knew *about* the Grangers. It was that thing where you talked about people but you didn't necessarily know all the details because it was from a hundred different sources. But everybody knew each other's biography in a small town.

Levi Granger had been taking care of this ranch since his parents died when he was a teenager.

He had younger siblings, and they'd been in his care, too.

Many people sighed with sympathy when they talked

about him, though in the next breath they often said that he was a difficult asshole.

It was funny, though, that she hadn't even thought about his siblings when she had come up here. Or really, his biography in general.

Her dad leaving, her mom leaving a few years after, those events had impacted her profoundly. It stood to reason that Levi would be even more affected by his parents dying. Maybe it wasn't entirely fair of her to judge him.

Well, she could judge him, she supposed; it was just that perhaps his behavior had a fair source.

She would remember that during the day when she was tempted to be irritated at him.

"I'm Quinn Sullivan," said Quinn. "I work at Four Corners next door."

"Oh, I remember you. From the meeting."

Which meant Camilla probably wasn't her biggest fan.

"So, what are you doing here?" Camilla asked.

Quinn straightened, trying to look official. "I'm consulting."

Levi cast a disdainful eye over her that seemed to say: *we'll see.* Then he looked up at Camilla. "You should go ahead and get packed, Cam. You need to get ready to head back to school."

"I do?"

"Yes, you do. I already showed you that I'm good."

"*She's* your consultant," said Camilla, looking shocked.

Quinn looked at him, and then looked at Camilla.

She had no idea where that had come from. Or what it meant.

"Yes," she said. "I'm his consultant. I have a degree

in agribusiness, and experience with admin and business at Sullivan's Point, and I've offered to put in some time here."

She could feel his rage getting hot and bright, and that made her feel...

Just. Damned. Fine.

She had one on him. His sister was worried about him. He wanted her to leave, and he'd already told a lie to get her to do it, and now Quinn was here.

If he wanted to, he could have said she was lying right away and he hadn't, which meant what he really wanted was for his sister to leave. And he was willing to do a lot to accomplish it.

"That's...great," Camilla said, smiling, even if slowly. "Levi, you really need somebody to help you get everything in order."

She could have crowed in her victory. "I *am* helping him with that. I'm getting a good look at the ranch today to kind of see what's going on, and to give more of a detailed overview."

"He showed me your binder. It was very comprehensive," said Camilla.

"Did he?" she asked, turning to look at Levi.

Levi's expression was frozen, his teeth gritted together. "Yes, I figured I'd show her the plan so she wasn't so worried."

"Because you were so enthused about the plan yesterday?"

"The binder itself felt convenient," he shot back.

Quinn nearly gasped, but didn't. She nearly bent down and picked up one of the shoes from the pile by the door and lobbed it at his head, but she didn't. Satisfaction had gone to rage in white-hot record time.

He'd been using her binder to placate Camilla, and he hadn't been planning on using her expertise at all. He was just using her.

That dirty rat bastard.

Oh, she was mad now. And in work boots. She should go step on his foot while he was only wearing socks.

She wouldn't, though, because she didn't do that anymore.

She was Zen.

She was calm.

She was the sea.

Filled with monsters. That wanted to eat his head off.

The intensity of what she felt around Levi was too much. Much too much. Always too much.

"As you can see," said Levi, "everything is under control." He went over to the bench and started to put his boots on, easy as you please, and not acting at all like he had been caught being a duplicitous son of a bitch.

"I worry about Levi," said Camilla. "I was thinking about dropping out so that I could come back and help manage the ranch."

Quinn didn't really hear all of it. What she heard was "dropping out."

"Don't drop out," said Quinn. "Your education is the most important thing. I graduated a couple of years ago, and I've never regretted it. You have to finish college. It's one thing that no one can ever take away from you. The things that you learn."

"I tried to tell her that," said Levi.

She stared at him, and this time it was her turn to be slow to speak.

"*You* tried to tell her that?" Quinn asked.

"Yeah," said Levi, putting his boot down heavily. "I did."

"It just doesn't seem like you..."

"Doesn't seem like what?" He looked at her with baiting eyes. She was smart enough to know there was a hook in there, and she didn't want to bite down on it.

But that didn't mean she had an easy time looking away.

She hadn't noticed that his eyes were blue. But they were. Dark like sapphires, but they weren't cool. Not really. Not when you looked deep enough. There was a spark there, and it looked dangerous.

He wasn't simple, either.

There was a constellation there. Emotion and thought and so many other things she'd never simply looked at another person and seen.

She felt rocked. Thrown off her axis.

Why did he do this to her?

Better still, why did it matter?

She felt like she was being pulled toward him, and that was enough to alarm her.

She took a step back.

"Nothing," she said. "Anyway. Don't we have work to do?"

"Just let me know what you need to get on your way, Cam," said Levi. "I'm just going to be out on the property. So, call me."

"Okay," said Camilla, looking between them. "If you insist."

"I do."

He grunted and jerked his head toward the door. "Okay, Dr. Quinn, let's go."

"I don't actually have a doctorate," she said.

"Yeah. But you're acting snotty, and have higher education, and it was a TV show."

She sniffed. "I don't remember it."

He gave her a sidelong glance. "How old are you?"

"I'm twenty-five."

He shook his head. "Lord Almighty."

"What?"

"Just get in my truck."

She climbed in the passenger side, nearly straining a muscle getting in. And she bit back a comment about the size of his truck and whether or not it was relative to egotistical damage as she did so. It was a nice truck. More evidence of the fact that he actually did quite well, obviously.

"What exactly are you *not* saying to me, ferret?" he asked.

"Are you just going to keep calling me names?"

"I was thinking about it. Because it's funny."

She wrinkled her nose. "I don't find it funny. Nor do I find it funny that you actually *do* need me, because clearly your sister was thinking about dropping out of college, and you were going to use my binder to try and convince her you had help when you didn't."

"Guilty as charged. What gave that away?"

"Your total lack of being receptive to me at all this morning coupled with Camilla's certainty that you'd hired someone as a done deal."

"I'm not going to apologize. You're the one who rocked up here like the sharp end of a stick, poking around in everything and inserting yourself where you had no business."

"I do have business. You came down to the meeting and you put us in an impossible position. I'm going to

defend my ranch and my livelihood. That's…obvious."
She gave him a sideways look. "And funny thing, you
actually seem to care about college."

"Wrong. What I care about is that Camilla doesn't
take options from herself because she feels like she
owes me in some way. I don't give a shit what she does.
She could work at the Wendy's a couple hours away or
be a rocket scientist—wouldn't change the way I feel
about her. What I do care about is whether or not she
misses out on her own dreams because of guilt. Especially out of guilt over me. That isn't what I want, and
it sure as hell wasn't the point in getting those assholes
raised."

"Oh, I…" Quinn's parents hadn't seemed to care at
all. She didn't quite know what to do with this very
certain…fire from him about wanting the people he'd
helped raise to be happy.

"My brother didn't go to college, and I'm proud as
hell of him."

"What does he do?" she asked.

"He's in the army." He laughed. "Not my first choice.
We've lost enough. We don't need to go losing any more,
and the military is dangerous, but I'm proud of him."

"Right. I get that." She felt a little bit…bad. Because
now he had mentioned his losses, and his role in taking
care of his siblings. Because now suddenly he wasn't
just a scowling caricature. Now he seemed more like
a real human being. "But either way, you were going
to use my research, my binder, to get your sister to do
what you wanted."

"She's worried, and it's silly. She's twenty. She needs
to finish school. She doesn't know what the hell she's
even talking about. She's nearly done with her second

year and she just needs to finish it out and stop being dramatic about it. I think she misses being home. I think it hasn't been the easiest change for her. But she's just got to finish. She's got to get through. She'll be glad she did when she does." He paused for a long moment. "Like you said. Nobody will be able to take it from her. And there's plenty of things that life can take from you, so you've got to hold on to what you can."

That resonated in her soul, and she hadn't expected that. For him to say something that felt…wise.

She shifted. "Don't you have another sister?"

"Yeah. Jessie. She doesn't live here anymore. She's out a couple hours away with her boyfriend. My best friend. The tool."

"Oh," said Quinn. "That must have been dramatic."

"Not really so much. He's a good guy. And he'll take good care of her."

Well, there, that was sort of an annoying, male thing to say. It made her feel a little more balanced to be irritated at him again. "Does she need to be taken care of?"

"No. Jessie can take care of herself. But I think every older brother wants his sister with a man who will take care of her instead of a man who might cause her harm."

She wasn't sure that man existed. "Good point. But I don't believe that you can count on other people to take care of you."

"Really?"

"No. You can't. Life is too uncertain. You can't pin anything on other people. You can't hold out hope that they are going to give you what you need. You have to be prepared to manage all your own stuff. It's the only way to go. The only way to be."

"Well, that's quite a perspective."

"One you don't agree with?"

He shook his head. "No. I agree to a point. Though, I have to say, my siblings became more important to me after my parents died. But the buck stops with *someone*. Someone was in charge. When you're the one in charge…you aren't really leanin' on anyone but yourself."

That made her unexpectedly uncomfortable, because in their family, Fia was the oldest. Quinn had gone and gotten the education stuff taken care of all on her own. They hadn't been able to count on their parents to help them, and yes, they did have each other for emotional support, and Quinn had done a lot to keep Sullivan's Point going, but it was different from taking care of your younger siblings.

"My sisters are important to me," said Quinn. "Don't get me wrong."

"But when push comes to shove, and you had to fight, you would expect to do it on your own."

She nodded. "Yes. In the end, that's what you have. You have to expect that. Nobody else can fight all your battles for you."

"And yet you *need* to have an agreement with me. So in that sense, you can't fight this battle on your own. You'd just be boxing in a corner."

Irritation ignited and she did her best to tamp it down.

"Also different," she said. "You've necessitated this… this thing. But I aim to make it a fair trade so we don't owe each other. I'm not trying to hustle you. I'm not asking for a favor."

"We'll see, Quinn Sullivan. We will see."

They drove on, until they reached the edge of the

field. And she found herself looking at how large and firm his hands looked on the wheel, then let her gaze drift to his jawline, square and rough, like maybe he hadn't shaved that morning.

"This is the field where we had a cover crop until recently. I'm reinforcing the fence line along here so we can expand some of the pastureland for the cows."

"I think you should plant hemp," she said.

He turned to her, his eyebrows lifted. "Do I look like a fucking hippie to you?"

"It's a very popular crop," she said, keeping her tone measured. "I'm not suggesting that you grow THC. In fact, that's oversaturated at this point. When it was legalized, the emerald gold rush was…"

"You know I live here, right? I saw it all happen the same as you."

She realized then she was paraphrasing a class she'd taken, and she felt slightly embarrassed. "I like to talk about this stuff. Sorry. Sometimes it turns into a monologue. I'm not suggesting you grow plants with THC. I'm suggesting hemp because worldwide there's a demand for items made from hemp fiber. There is high value in it."

"*No.* Thank you."

"What, like on principle?" she asked.

She hadn't taken him for being like that, but maybe she should have. He was stubborn and unteachable. His opinions on marijuana as a crop were firmly set in stereotypes and not in the modern era.

"It doesn't make sense to me," he said.

And she knew there were some battles she could wage and win, but she had to start from a better vantage point than this.

She held back a sigh. It hurt her to admit to herself that it actually did matter whether or not he was on board with what he was growing. He had to care or it wouldn't be sustainable. And genuinely it wouldn't do her or her sisters any favors if he was grudgingly offering them the use of the road, because it could cause issues later. "It is important that it make sense to you. It is your land, after all."

"That's the first thing you've said that we can agree on," he said.

"I'm actually not here to be an antagonist, Levi, whatever you seem to think."

"I don't think anything about your behavior, Miss Sullivan. You asked to be up here today, and while you're here, you're giving your opinions. You might recollect I didn't ask for them."

"Maybe not, but you told your sister I was consulting. So you might not want my opinions, but you kind of want me."

Silence bottomed out the conversation and she shifted, trying to ease her discomfort. She cleared her throat. "You're treating me like I'm trying to hurt you in some way, or like I'm a villain, and I'm not. I just want to come up with something that works for both of us."

He crossed his arms. "Come up with another suggestion for me, then."

"Well, I would approach this from a few different ways. I think because of the diet you have the cows on, you can use the manure as fertilizer. If you have excess, you can sell it. There's value there. Additionally to that, which is sustainable, you can plant... Christmas trees are an option. They are a very popular export in the state. Hazelnuts are one of the things that we grow at Sullivan's, but we don't have a plot as large as this field."

"That will take time," he said.

She nodded. "It will. But if you have time to invest, I would try something like that. They're easy crops. They are very agreeable to the region. Or you get llamas. Llamas also fare really well here."

"I don't want fucking llamas."

She looked at him, and she did not kick him. She felt like that was a win.

"Then Christmas trees," she said. "How about Christmas trees?"

"That sounds like some made-for-TV movie bullshit."

He just wasn't going to make this easy. And maybe she had no right to expect him to. Just maybe. But she wasn't an enemy and he was acting like she was. She really did just want to help. Or she wanted something mutually beneficial, and what she couldn't figure out was why he was being such a jerk about it.

He'd done that deal with her dad and that huge factory farm for all the fields and he couldn't do this with her? She knew it had soured a bit—her dad leaving had messed a lot of things up—but she wanted a *road*, not every inch of his land.

She was local. And she wouldn't be leaving. She'd be accountable.

"There are big companies that you can pay to have come harvest them," she said.

"I'm skeptical of making agreements with anything corporate."

"You can hire your own laborers, then. You can export them across the state, and even the country. You have to get a cycle going. Different sizes, different years, and yes, it is going to take time, but it's renewable, and an investment. In the future of the land."

He paused for a moment. "I like the idea of growing something native."

The rush of relief she felt over that little bit of near-relenting was disproportionate, she was certain. She felt it all the same. "I thought it might appeal to you. Well, I guess I didn't think that, but I hoped."

"This land has been in my family for generations, Ms. Sullivan. That means something to me. This place means something to me."

"I do understand that."

"All right. Let's get to fence fixing."

She was jarred by the abrupt change of subject. But she was ready.

"Okay. Let's fix the fence."

CHAPTER EIGHT

THE AFTERNOON SUN was high, and it was warm. He knew he was being mean by keeping her out this long without stopping for food. He did have water bottles in the truck, and he had made sure that she was hydrated. He didn't need her turning into a little ginger raisin on his watch.

He was beginning to get concerned that she might burn. She had brought a hat, but she was just so stinking pale.

He shouldn't care. And he shouldn't be transfixed by that near-translucent skin, or her freckles.

Dammit.

"Did you put on some sunblock?" he asked.

"Of course I did," she said. "I'm a redhead."

He could see that she was doing her best to not punch him in the face, and that it was a battle she had come close to losing on a few occasions.

The more of an ass he was, the more she tried to be calm, and that just seemed to make him want to push her harder.

"I'm not sure what I'm dealing with here," he said. "I felt like I needed to make sure. I don't want you broiling on my watch."

Her eyes glittered like green beetles. "I don't even need a college degree to know that I need to wear sunblock if I'm going to so much as even smell a ray of sunshine."

"Well, at least you have some kind of practical knowledge."

She looked up at him, staring hard. Her eyes were clear and green, and the freckles across her nose were arrayed in a scattershot pattern.

She was pissed.

And she really was very cute. Even in the work boots.

The work boots themselves weren't cute. It was just that she stomped around in them like she was a six-foot-six lumberjack, and there was something about that which he found sort of charming.

Even if he shouldn't.

As mad as she was at him now, she'd been furious at him this morning. And he wasn't all that thrilled that he'd been caught in his subterfuge. Nor was he very happy with himself that he'd entrenched in the lie that Quinn was consulting him about anything.

Because now Camilla had a name. And now Quinn knew his weak spot.

Though she had seemed more helpful than conniving on the drive over. They hadn't talked much while they worked on the fence.

He didn't know the Sullivans. That was the problem.

The people at Four Corners had a decent reputation, but the Pyrite Falls folks who weren't part of the outfit definitely viewed them with a mix of suspicion and respect. And, of course, they made fun of them. The Four Corners ranchers were a big-ass collective. They had a lot of power in the area, and as one of the few ranchers who *wasn't* part of that massive operation in this area, he felt a little uneasy about joining up with them in any way. Because if things went awry, they had each other, and what did he have?

He was paranoid. He had every right to be.

If a man didn't learn from his mistakes, then he was no kind of man.

He truly believed that.

So, he was learning from them. Because it was the only thing to do. And that meant being cautious when it came to making this deal.

He didn't know how much traffic it was going to bring through the land, and there were other variables. And he liked to be certain now.

"Okay," he said. "Let's stop and get some food."

"I'm fine," she said, looking all dirty, sweaty and determined.

"No. You need to get some food. I'm not letting you go pretending I'm some kind of tyrant."

Well. He *was* kind of a tyrant sometimes. But he didn't starve tiny women. That was a hard line, even for him.

"Let's go have lunch at Becky's."

"Oh, that's really not necessary," she said. "I'd be totally fine with some cheese or bread or…"

And the more she protested, the more he felt like digging in.

"I'm not having you drop dead on my land, Miss Sullivan. If you ever want to be let back here again, we're going to lunch now, and it's my treat."

"Well, thanks." She looked at him with a very bland expression on her face.

She was mad. Mad mad.

He was beginning to recognize that the blander she appeared, the more she was seething.

He urged her into the truck and drove across the field, back toward the road that would take them out to the main highway.

"So you've been in charge of the ranch since you were eighteen?" she pressed.

He turned out onto the highway and kept his eyes fixed on a pine tree at the first curve in the road. "Yep."

"That must've been really difficult."

He never talked about this. There was no point. He wasn't a big talker, never had been. He hadn't had a lot of friends growing up, or in his whole life. He'd had Damien, who had been there every step of the way, so there had never been anything to explain.

When it came to women…

He didn't do the talking thing.

He couldn't remember if anyone had ever asked him something like this before. Conversational, but digging into his past. Into him.

"Think you ought to get to know the devil a little better?" he asked.

"No. I just… I'm curious. When you did that deal with my dad, I was so young. I remember you coming by the house but of course we never…"

He looked over at her and she turned pink. Interesting.

"I never got to know you."

"Not surprising. You Four Corners people keep to your own. You're kind of snobby."

"No, we aren't," she said, and now she was pink because she was mad. "We are a huge community filled with people who love ranching and the land, and we have barn parties every month after our town hall meetings and…"

"For the people who work on your ranch. You're like a club that nobody else can get into. That's fine. But you have to know that you're a little bit…insulated. Plus, very few other places around here have your land and your earning capabilities. Land is the most valuable thing you can have."

"Well, it can be a little bit of an albatross, too, believe me. The work that we've had to do to make Sullivan's as profitable as everybody else's plot is pretty intense. It is a hell of a lot of work. We're all sisters. We had to get creative. Everybody has hired ranch hands—that isn't the thing. It's just that when it comes to the McClouds… You have five men who can contribute to the heavy lifting. That's just a whole lot of manpower that you aren't paying hourly. The Kings have four. The Garretts only have two, but still. We wanted something that we could do. Practically. We've been creative with leasing fields, with planting… And the farm store is part of that. It's diversification, which is good for the whole endeavor, but also for us specifically. We needed to provide something that only we could provide. You doing beef is a great example of that. You're a smaller operation and are focusing on premium product rather than simply producing volume."

That made him feel unexpectedly sympathetic to her. He hadn't thought about how the Four Corners crew might still have to negotiate things individually. He hadn't realized what it meant to be the Sullivan sisters. It reminded him a lot of the kinds of bargains he'd had to make in order for ranching to be profitable.

He didn't want to relate to her.

"Are you saying that the beef ranchers on Four Corners are just producing volume?" he asked.

"No. Not at all. They have great stuff. I am just saying that it's more accessible. And yours is premium."

He looked at her, lifting a brow. "Are you saying my beef is premium?"

Better to make a joke than feel empathy for her. Better to defuse the moment.

She opened her mouth, then closed it. Then opened it again. "I… You mean the cows, right?"

"What else could I have possibly meant?"

Her cheeks were pink, and he was fascinated by the way her freckles faded when she was pink. "Right. Okay. But my point stands. It isn't actually that unusual for people about town to not know you all."

She frowned, and he could see that she had never considered this. But then, he didn't see why she would. So many people worked at Four Corners Ranch. They must have over a hundred employees. They were a huge percentage of the population of the town. Many of them lived on the property. Kids went to school on the property. They must feel entrenched and enmeshed in the community. It was just that they, of course, so rarely left their own little pocket that they didn't ever look up and see all the strangers.

"Well, I just think that's an assumption," she said. "We would all be very open to socializing if anybody wanted to."

"You're a ranching gang," he said.

"I just don't agree." She was on the verge of sputtering. "I… It's not like I get along with everyone because I live there."

"Really?" he asked.

"No." She let out a harsh breath. "Look, the idea you're excluded because you aren't Four Corners people indicates you'd be included just because you are. And no. That isn't true. I didn't have friends growing up on the ranch. For years all I wanted to do was please my dad and then...well, later, my temper caused all kinds of...issues."

"Can't imagine why." He looked at her, and he tried not to feel sorry for the image her confession conjured up in his mind. Of young Quinn living on that ranch without any friends. "You rolled up onto my land and talked down to me, so I can see why maybe people find you an acquired taste."

"I did not *talk down to you*. I'm confident, Levi, and it is not my fault if men perceive confidence in women to be a threat." She snorted. "I mean, ask yourself if Sawyer or Denver or Gus have friends. They do. Are they any nicer than me?"

"I don't think Denver King has friends," he pointed out. "And anyway, did you meet my sister this morning? And I know you haven't met my sister Jessie, but believe me when I tell you, I am very comfortable with confident women. You, Miss Sullivan, were being kind of a dick."

She sputtered again, and he took great joy in that, even as they rolled into the main drag of Pyrite Falls, and he pulled directly into the small parking lot of the ramshackle wooden building that housed Becky's diner.

"I have been very nice!" she protested.

"Oh, really?"

He killed the engine and got out of the truck, and he heard the passenger door slam a few seconds later. She was huffing and stomping in those boots again. "I was not a... I was not a dick."

"Oh, you didn't take one look at me and what you assumed was my situation and me beneath you?"

"I did no such thing."

"Then how come you assumed that the cabin was my house?"

"It *appeared* to be."

"And if it were, would that make you better than me?" he pressed.

Because, again, it was better than feeling bad for her.

"No. There is no shame in…" She scrunched up her face and he thought she might be praying. Or she was doing some kind of breathing or counting exercise. "No. It isn't about being better. It's about seeing the resources that you had and wanting to make sure that you were doing the most with them that you could."

He could see that he had really riled her. He wanted to chase that because she had no right. No right at all to come onto his land, knowing nothing about him, about his life, and just deciding she knew best…

He couldn't stand that.

She could leave anytime. She didn't need to keep on trying this, and he didn't have to treat her nicely. She didn't have to be here.

You're feeding her lunch…

Because starving her was a bridge too far; he'd covered that already.

Also, caregiver habits died hard. He hadn't always wanted to care for his siblings, either. He'd literally raised Camilla from the time she was two. It had been hard. He hadn't enjoyed every moment of it.

He'd had to take their grief and walk them through it, while he stumbled through his own darkness blindly. He'd seen his brother through teenage heartbreak, when he'd never had time to experience his own. He'd walked his sisters through puberty, when he'd known sweet fuck-all about how to handle all that, but he'd learned.

Pads, tampons and Midol for cramps? He was a pro at providing whatever they needed.

He'd become their mom and their dad before he'd become a whole person himself.

He was good at caregiving. Sweet little else.

In some ways, they'd passed him up. Because he'd never really learned how to live life as a whole adult.

He'd felt like he was running with a gun to his back, for years. With someone snarling in his ear: *don't stop or everything falls apart.*

He'd never stopped to take a breath. He'd grieved while learning to run a ranch, while taking care of his siblings. He'd let go of any aspirations he'd had outside the ranch, any dream that wasn't what was right in front of him, because there had constantly been fires to put out. So you couldn't look ahead, not any further than the immediate path in front of you.

He'd wanted to be in the rodeo so damned bad. He'd had a gift for it. It was the thing that had sustained him while he was trapped in classrooms wishing he could be outdoors more than anything.

He'd have been good at it. Better than managing a ranching spread. But in the end, it hadn't been a choice. In the end, he'd had to give everything of himself over to that place.

And he could never, ever stop moving. Not to catch his breath. Not to shed a tear.

He didn't resent it—it was how life had gone. What could you do?

It had made him who he was.

He was a parent, in every way that mattered, and he couldn't just not…

He took care of people, even if angrily. It was kind of his brand.

"You think that you're smarter than me because you went to college," he said flat out, because he might as well make her say it.

"I think…" And she was squinting again and trying very hard not to confirm that, but the thing was, he was fairly certain it was true, and he was 100 percent right about her.

He waited a good while, and she didn't continue her sentence. "What is it you think, Miss Sullivan?" He kept his voice low and measured on purpose.

"I think," she started, "that I worked very hard to get myself to college because I valued it."

"And you think that somebody who didn't go didn't work hard?"

She sputtered. "No. I think perhaps we had a different value system."

"And what do you suppose my value system is? Beer and tits?"

"I didn't say that," she said, turning the color of a lush, ripe strawberry.

In a perfect world, those would in fact be his priorities. But his world had never been perfect. He'd prioritized taking care of his ranch and taking care of his family over anything that he might want to do.

That seemed to be what Quinn Sullivan didn't understand. It was all fine and good for some to be able to do whatever the hell they wanted. Not that he would've chosen that anyway. It was just different worlds. Different philosophies. They didn't see eye to eye, and they wouldn't.

But he was bound and determined to force her to admit that she was a snob. That she had judged him. He didn't really know why. Well. Yeah. He did. Because all fine for her to have the life she did, and pass judgment on his.

He was in danger of letting her become emblematic of a whole system he wanted to rail against. One he'd always been angry about, but was even angrier about it as time went on and he…

He'd had to be there for everyone else. No one had really been there for him.

Any fixing he'd done, he'd done on his own. And still, he got treated like he was less.

Wow. What a whiny-ass thing to think.

He didn't often indulge in self-pity, but for some reason, all this stuff with Quinn had a way of pushing him that direction.

They walked into the diner, and Sarah, the normal hostess, was standing there with a pen behind her ear and an apron tied around her thick waist.

"Hi there, Levi," she said. "Usual table?" She looked over at Quinn and frowned.

It was obvious to him that she had *thoughts* on his appearance with a Sullivan. But she wasn't going to speak them out loud.

Probably only because she didn't know Quinn well enough to do it.

She would normally have no compunction about scolding him.

He had not been insulated by a whole big ranch. He had been insulated by the town. When his parents died, there had been a whole lot of adults around these parts that had taken care with them. Took an interest in them. And nobody could carry the weight for Levi, but there had been support.

People had lent a hand. Women had come by with casseroles. Sarah among them.

"You having your usual?" she asked.

"Yeah," he said.

"Coke?"

He nodded at that, too.

She looked at Quinn expectantly. "I'm not... Can I see a menu?"

Sarah shook her head, but fished a menu out of the pocket of her apron. And while they walked over to the table, Quinn reviewed it quickly. "I'll have the Caesar salad. And iced tea?"

"You don't eat here very often?" he asked after they were seated.

"Is it that obvious?" she asked.

"Sarah, please get Quinn a Legend Burger. She doesn't want the Caesar salad."

"Excuse me?" Quinn asked, even as Sarah walked off without a word. "You don't get to decide what I want. Maybe I'm a vegetarian."

Well, that would be a hat trick. A little ranching expert who lived on the land producing the most beef in the area being a vegetarian.

"*Are* you?"

"No. But that's beside the point. What if I have a gluten allergy?" she asked.

Another hat trick, considering she and her sisters provided most of the baked goods for the area and he couldn't remember a preponderance of them being labeled as gluten free.

"*Do* you?" he asked.

"*No,*" she said. "But maybe I wanted a salad."

"I'm not saying that you didn't want a salad, but what I'm confident in is that you don't want *this* salad. It's a Caesar salad, but only in name. It is chunks of iceberg lettuce, thick pieces of purple cabbage, and it comes out of the bag that may or may not be as old as my kid sister. You don't want it."

She practically hissed like a mad cat. "It said Caesar salad."

"I am pretty sure they put ranch on it."

"You come here a lot, then," she grumbled.

"I do. And the Legend Burger is good. Do you even know what it is?"

She frowned. "No."

"It's named after Gideon Payne. You remember Gideon."

"Who doesn't? He set every football record for the county back in high school. I don't even care about football, or Mapleton High, and even I know that. They gave him a whole parade when he left to join the military. Plus, he's my sister Rory's best friend's older brother."

"Lord. That's a mouthful."

"It kind of is. But what is the burger, other than named after Gideon?"

"It has barbecue sauce and onion straws and it's excellent. The stew is also good. The pie is *damned* good. Don't get fancy. There are some things on that menu that shouldn't be there. It's to suggest variety. Don't mess with *variety* at a small-town roadside diner. Unless it's for some reason a weird special that is much lauded by the locals."

"I actually *do* live here," she said.

"But you don't eat *here*."

"No. But it's because we all do a lot of cooking. So we don't really have occasion to." She put her little nose in the air when she said that and he wondered if she had any idea how snooty she looked. He shouldn't be remotely charmed by it.

Much like the socks.

Those damned *socks*.

"So don't presume to be an expert," he said. "You think you're an expert on just about everything, don't you?"

"And you are pretty much bound and determined to twist everything to suit your narrative. The fact that I believe I'm an expert on *what I want to eat* is not arrogance, Levi Granger."

"The fact that you think you're a better expert on the menu than I am is, though."

She scrunched her nose and bit her lip, and her cheeks turned pink. Like she was trying to hold back words with all her might.

And he could see the *moment* she lost the battle.

"You are a hardheaded pig," she said.

He'd done it. He'd broken her.

"Wow," he said, drawing the word out. "So this is where our business partnership is going to go."

"We don't *have* a business partnership. Because you're asking me to jump through all these hoops for you and you've offered me nothing in return."

"You're pretty feisty."

"I am when I have to be."

She was fascinating. Feral and a bit mean, but she sure as hell tried to cover it. She inherently thought she was better than him, and she tried to cover that, too.

She reminded him of...

Not of him. Not totally. Except she seemed wounded. That was the truth of it. A feral animal tended to be yet more feral when it was injured.

He knew that well.

He should hate her, and he found himself more interested in poking at her than getting rid of her altogether, and maybe that was a side effect of having not had this kind of experience before.

He hooked up. But he had never been one to have a relationship. It just wasn't possible. Not with his life. He had to either be ready to get himself a ranch wife, or he just had to enjoy the pleasures of the flesh. He had never seen a way to have anything in between. Not while working the land and taking care of his siblings. And it had definitely crossed his mind that there would be something to getting himself a wife.

But then he just...couldn't. He could never get himself past that initial thought.

He just couldn't see depending on anyone. It was better, way better, to handle it all himself.

It just made more sense.

Because you couldn't depend on people. In that, he agreed with Quinn, but it was perhaps not exactly the same bent.

Things happened that were beyond people's control. Those structures that people counted on, that nuclear family, their parents...

For him, it had disintegrated. Not because his parents weren't good people. They had been.

His dad had been a great man. He had loved deeply. Too deeply.

When his wife had died, his heart had given out.

Levi would never be able to believe that the two things weren't connected. Broken-heart syndrome, he was sure of it.

The fact that he had a heart attack less than a year after his wife had passed...

It was a thing. He knew it was. Levi had watched his dad fade. Turn gray, his weight going down, every bit of responsibility he carried clearly costing him more.

Levi had started picking up more and more in that year. Trying to do some of the work his dad struggled to do. Wishing he could do something with the business end but being utterly baffled by it all. Knowing the finances were slipping and not knowing how to fix it.

One thing Levi had known was that he could never do that to himself.

It wasn't an issue for him at this point. He couldn't fathom having the time, energy or trust to begin to fall in love, and even if he *could*... Well, Levi wasn't here to die of a broken heart.

Better to never let your heart get that involved.

The truth was, he already had too many liabilities in his life. His brother joining the military...

That killed him. He never wanted him to know that he spent his waking hours in a state of anxiety when his brother was deployed, but it was the truth.

When Camilla had gone off to college, it had been the strangest thing. He'd been glad. It had been the moment he'd been waiting for.

When she'd gone, he'd felt a lot like he'd lost a limb.

And Jessie, who had been there all along, when she

had moved away with Damien, even that had been difficult. And he wanted her to have it. But that didn't make it easy.

He was, in many ways, a parent. It was all a bit much. He didn't need any more. And so, he had decided to forgo the ranch-wife route.

He'd raised his kids anyway, so to speak. He didn't want to do all that again, either.

He didn't want to create more people to love. More people he could lose.

He was great with chatting up women in a certain way. He didn't do it all that often. He was busy. He was a rancher, and he had to get up early. Plus, he had various siblings in and out of the house, and he had never believed in bringing women back where they could see.

Except the first time. A girl he knew from school had come by to visit and bring cookies, and she'd given him sympathy and a kiss, and one thing had led to another. It had been a godsend in some ways. Because right then it had felt like time was slipping through his fingers because God knew who might drop dead next.

He'd been filled with the need to go *quickly* then.

Sign a contract quickly with a factory farm.

Take the pity sex on offer when it turned up.

He didn't regret that. Because in the years after, sex had been scarce.

As the kids had gotten older and they were able to be alone into the wee hours of the morning, he'd taken his women to a motel after meeting them in a bar.

Now, with Camilla out of the house, he supposed he could...

He never did, though. Because it felt weird.

Motels were fine.

But yeah. Actual conversation with women, he wasn't all that well-versed in. She was…irritating. Compelling.

Once he had started getting her goat a little bit, he had really gone in for it. It was like he hadn't been able to help himself. But then, she was picking at a scab of his. So it seemed fair.

"Hey, Levi."

He turned and saw Dave Calhoun, and gave him a half wave.

"Hey, yourself."

"Granger."

He gave a half wave to Jaime Lopez as well, and to Jeff Carmichael, Alan Gutierrez and some other men he knew from the Huckleberry County Ranching Association.

"So everybody knows you," said Quinn.

"Yeah."

"I guess I take your point about the Four Corners folk. Because I don't know any of them."

"Listen, you just keep to your own. Granted, your own is big. You guys are basically half the town."

"Yes. But does *everybody* see it as us versus the rest of them?"

"Whether you want to believe it or not, it's not perspective so much as reality. Anybody in ranching has to compete with y'all. And it isn't easy. You have collective money that the rest of us don't have. You have ways of covering each other, helping each other, that we don't."

"If we're using an easement on your property, it seems like we need to maybe offer you a little bit more."

He frowned. "I have no desire to be absorbed into Four Corners."

"That isn't what I mean. I just mean that maybe you're

right. You should get some compensation. After all, land is important. And if we're using your land…"

"I am aware of how important land is."

He was land rich before he was anything else. Now. The contracts he'd signed that had kept his fields tied up for all those years had taken these last five years to begin to result in riches for him. He'd hog-tied himself back then, and he wouldn't do it again.

He'd also been the subject of suspicion for that deal. The factory-farm angle plus the Four Corners connection hadn't made him popular.

He didn't relish stepping back into that space.

She had no idea what she was saying when she made statements like that. No idea who she was lecturing.

"I worked hard for you today and I am willing to continue to work hard to show you that I'm genuine, and that I know what I'm talking about. And that even if I'm from Four Corners, our desire to ranch right does extend to our neighbors."

She looked down. "Does this have something to do with my dad?"

He snorted. "What do you know about all that?"

"Not everything. But you could tell me…"

"No need to discuss it." He didn't like talking about it. It still made him feel all the old feelings. The ones he never needed to revisit.

"Do you think I was thrilled that he left?" she asked. "I have my own issues with my dad. You aren't going to offend me. Or shock me."

He shook his head slowly. "I'm not interested in having the discussion."

"If you won't discuss it, then how do I understand?

My dad aside, what could Four Corners do, what could they have done, to make people trust us?"

Nothing. That was the truth. He'd been too mired in his own stuff to really give a shit about the giant ranching collective next door, and he wasn't overly concerned with them now. His niche was his, and it worked well for him.

But he'd worked hard to get here, and he had reservations about making changes again.

"I can work," she said. "I can give you a whole week's worth of work. I can give you whatever you need, but my sisters and I have worked so hard for this, and I don't want it to fail because our customers don't want to drive eight miles on a dirt road to get to the store, and I don't want to fail because a bunch of crusty men at the county think they know what's best. And I really, really don't want to fail because my dad doesn't have the same level of integrity I do."

"Maybe you should apply for work at the county," he said, and he was half-sincere.

"Conflict of interest, plus I have a job. It's at my ranch, on my land. You understand that—I know you do. This life chooses you. And I went out and I made myself as qualified as I could, but this is… This is escaping me. I learned all of these things and now I'm having to ask a bunch of men for permission for my business to succeed, and I hate it. So I'll work for you. I'll show up every day. I'll sort through your paperwork, do anything for your business I… I know I can help you and I know we can make this work, and I know I can make you trust me." She took a deep breath and kept on going. "You assumed the worst of me, and that isn't fair."

"Guilty by association, I admit it. But also, because

you think that you should be allowed to show up and flash your fancy degree and have my trust. That isn't reasonable, Quinn. The degree means something to *you*. It means nothing to me. I don't need a degree to run a ranch."

She looked down. "Then why…?"

"Here you go, honey," said Sarah, setting a burger down in front of each of them, along with their drinks and an extra basket of fries.

"Thank you," said Quinn, just as he nodded and said, "Thanks."

"Why do you need help with your paperwork, then? If you have it all together." She took a fry and stuck it in her mouth.

So she was opting to be a brat now that he'd refused to answer her questions. It seemed to be the Quinn Sullivan go-to.

"I don't care to do my paperwork. It stresses my sister out. She thinks that I leave it too late, and that it's not as organized as it could be. She's a control freak, and she's meddlesome. And that's all you really need to know about it. Camilla's anxiety about it is her issue. I said what I did to placate her. I didn't say it because I needed it."

"So you're saying there's no validity to her concerns?"

"None. Like you, I think she got a little taste of the broader world and thinks she knows better."

"You don't think another perspective might be helpful?"

"Not one I didn't ask for. And I didn't ask for yours, sweetheart."

"Okay, maybe I shouldn't have expected to show up and just have you respect me because I told you I went to college. It's clear to me that we don't speak the same language when it comes to education. However, you are being reductive. And you don't have the right to under-estimate me just because my credentials come from a school. And because I'm a woman. And small. Admit it, those things make you skeptical of me."

He looked at her. He didn't know how to explain to her that it wasn't her gender or her size.

It had something to do with those little white socks. And the white shoes.

So he just went ahead and decided to agree. Better to have her think that he was a misogynist than a weird sock fetishist. That wasn't even what it was. Probably. Maybe.

Hell.

"Yeah. I am," he said. She angrily took a bite of her hamburger. And he could see her attempting to not re-spond to how good it was. He felt the corner of his mouth lift up into a smirk. "I told you."

"Well, I didn't get to sample the Caesar salad."

"You're welcome."

They ate the rest of the meal in relative silence.

And when they were finished, he paid in spite of her protests.

"Why don't you call it a day," he said.

"No," she said, turning to look up at him. "I won't."

CHAPTER NINE

SHE DIDN'T KNOW what she was doing. Well. She did. She was digging in. She was digging in because he was being impossible. She was digging in because she didn't think it was fair that he got to make all these declarations. That he got to set the rules. That he got to underestimate her, and then set the bar so low that all she would have to do was step over it, and he would be able to be unimpressed, because it was *unimpressive*.

And if he was going to make assumptions about her based on her dad, and not even share the details with her, then she was going to dig in and make him see that she wasn't the same.

"Okay," he said. "Then let's keep working. Right through the heat of the day."

He drove the truck straight past her car, and on back to the field.

"I'm just fine," she said. "I have no problem putting in a full day's work, and I will put in a full day every day this week."

"You're stubborn, Quinn Sullivan, I'll give you that."

That felt like a compliment, whether he meant it to be one or not.

She knew she was stubborn. And she was proud of it. It was literally her whole personality. That she had been stubborn enough to become the person she was, and stubborn enough to persist in helping Sullivan's Point in the way that she knew it needed.

And when they were done working on the fence for the day, they went to the stalls, and she didn't even ask him any questions. She found all the tack she needed, and got her own horse, and rode with him through the different pastures to check on the cows.

Her grumpiness *did* abate when they looked at the cows, who were truly beautiful animals.

Wagyu beef was very particular, and had to be approved as such before you could call it that. The cows had to be raised to obtain a certain marbled content to the meat. It was very high in fat and extremely rich.

And the animals were glossy and thick and glorious.

This was what she loved about ranching. This was what she loved about the magic of working the land. That everything good and glorious that people ate and enjoyed came from it.

She was often thunderstruck by those sorts of realizations. That there had been a human being who had looked at the wheat in the field and said: *let's try it and mill it.*

Who had decided that it would pair nicely with yeast that would add air to it, and that they could make fluffy, chewy bread.

Humans who had looked at sheep in the fields and thought, *Why not try shearing its wool off, and then spinning that wool into a string, and then taking that string and looping it all different ways using sticks to make a fabric?*

The building blocks of life played out in these fields. And not just the things that were necessary for survival. But things that made being human a joy.

Milk and meat and cheese. Sour cream and heavy cream. Fruit and bread.

It all came from ranches. And farms. At least, the very best of it did.

She believed in the family farm. In the family ranch. They lived it; they exemplified it. Fresh and local.

It was her passion. And when she could clear out her anger, frustration, annoyance…when she could set aside all the issues from her childhood, she could just embrace the *passion*.

Because to her, it was what loving the land required.

She could see that reflected in Levi Granger's operation, as well.

He did good work. And it was sustainable. His animals were in good condition, and his land was well-kept.

Properly irrigated. It was true there wasn't a whole lot he could learn from her out here. It was going to have to be the paperwork. The paperwork, and the offer of a percentage of the profits of the farm store. She could see that now. But she was definitely going to have to talk to her sisters about that.

By the end of the day, everything hurt.

She was great at riding horses, but she didn't do it all that often. Her sister Alaina was a full-on horse girl, and she basically did everything on the back of a horse, but that just wasn't Quinn.

Quinn preferred to drive her truck around, or even an ATV.

She could hear her own thoughts about sustainability rolling up to mock her even as she thought that.

She did prize ecologically sound practices. It was just…more convenient. And it wasn't that she didn't like horses; it was just that she found them to be sweaty and occasionally inconvenient.

Just a little bit more of an endeavor than getting across the ranch sometimes needed. In her opinion. But that meant that she had some serious muscle soreness in places she didn't want it.

She had baited Levi, it was true, and he had taken that bait. The work had been hard.

She had done it, though. And she would be back tomorrow for more.

"Were you genuinely unaware that most people regard Four Corners with suspicion?"

She was a bit thrown off by the question. He had a way of doing that. Throwing off the conversation, the expected rhythm.

Her equilibrium.

"Yes. I thought that we… I thought that we had really built up a good rapport in the community."

"Think about everything you have, think about how much better the ranch functions, how much better you will live than most of the other people in the community."

"It's okay that some people own ranches and some…"

"Work on them. You have that idea, don't you? That some people are made to run businesses and other people are made to work at them."

Quinn frowned. "I don't really. I mean, when you put it like that, it sounds horrible."

"It's been said to me."

"It has?" she asked.

"Yes. I was told that I wasn't smart enough to go running a business."

"I'm sorry, Levi. That wasn't right. Whoever said that to you… It wasn't right."

He paused for a moment. "It was your dad."

Quinn stopped and turned to face him. "My dad said that to you?"

"You must know that the whole thing with your dad was kind of a big disaster."

"I know that my *dad* is a big disaster."

Levi laughed. "Well. That is one way of putting it."

He'd said he wouldn't talk about this, but now he was. She wasn't sure what she'd expected to hear, but not this. Not something so personal. She'd imagined his business dealings with her dad to be dry and, well, *business*.

She'd thought maybe she had the monopoly on feeling personally wounded, slighted and insulted by her father.

"If it makes you feel any better," she said softly, "my dad didn't exactly think that I was worth much, either."

He stared at her, and she felt like he could see far too much. "How is that possible? You exemplify all the things your dad said that he valued."

"I'm not sure whether or not that's a compliment."

"It's a statement of fact. You're smart, and you're determined. He always told me that those were important things."

"Well, he doesn't see them when he looks at me. What he saw was somebody who was flighty and irresponsible. Somebody who was led by their emotions, and created problems because of it. That's what he saw. So…I wouldn't necessarily take what he says to heart."

"Clearly I didn't, or I would never have started my own business."

She laughed. "Well, I didn't realize that you and I had a common enemy that we were doing things at."

"Doing things at? What does that mean?"

She shifted, feeling uncomfortable. Because she didn't talk about this. And she had the feeling in that sense they were on the same ground. Which was very odd.

They were supposed to be working together, though. Being forceful, angry Quinn certainly wasn't bringing him onto her side. Maybe this…common ground was a better place to start.

"I went to school, I succeeded, I got myself there—I did all that to spite him. Because he acted like I could never take all of my passion and turn it into something that looked like drive in the way that he recognized it. He thought that caring more about himself made him smarter. I know he thought that. He thought I had too much passion in me, for the right thing, not just for the bottom line. But I could never be that person. We were never close to the other families in Four Corners because my dad…"

"Yeah, I know. He opposed them on a lot of things. That's why he ended up doing the soybean deal with me. Because they wouldn't allow him to do it on Four Corners land. And I was too young to realize it was because there's a deep distrust of factory farming, and for good reason. For damned good reason."

"I know. And it wasn't something that had ever been done here before, so people didn't understand. But yes, he went around the Four Corners families, and he used you. And that really was a terrible thing for him to do. And then he made you feel bad, about things that he shouldn't have. And so now you've started a business, to spite him. And that seems fair."

He chuckled. "Yeah. I guess it is at him. All right," Levi said, wiping a bead of sweat from his brow. "It's time to knock off."

"How do you determine that?"

"What?" He looked at her like she was insane.

"I just mean how do you decide when to 'knock off'?" She did the best she could to pronounce the quotes, which was for sure a little bit rude but she hoped he would miss it. "As far as I can tell, we didn't really knuckle down and do any one project."

"Didn't... Listen, this isn't a corporation. This is a ranch. I do the vast majority of the work on my own. I have a couple of guys who work for me a few days a week, but more or less this is my responsibility. I move with the seasons. I move with the sun. I'm the boss. I do what works for me."

She made a musing noise. "Right. Well. It just seems to me like maybe if there was a more clear-cut system..."

"You get on my nerves and you aren't going to be working with me this week," he said, his voice hard, uncompromising. A challenge.

Why did she want to rise to his challenge so much? She had never in all her life looked at a brick wall and wanted to run into it quite so hard.

"And what exactly will you do if I show up without permission?"

He looked at her, like he was seriously considering what he might do, and like she wouldn't like the answer.

"Listen, if you don't behave, I will uproot you like the obnoxious little carrot that you are and drop-kick your ass back to Four Corners."

It was just such an unexpectedly clever thing to say, mean though it was.

She hadn't had a real clear sense of him, because he was guarded with the things that he said, and he took quite a long time to say them. But when it came to insults, he did seem to have a…flair.

And she couldn't help herself. She *laughed*.

She had no idea why she laughed, but once she started, she couldn't stop. All this sniping the whole day, and she was *tired*. Of work, of him, of everything, and then he'd said that.

"Is there something funny?" he asked.

She kept on laughing, and hiccuped, just a little. "It was just a very good sentence. Because my hair is red, so carrot was a really great example. And the image of you…*uprooting* me and drop-kicking me just amused me."

"The hell?"

"I don't know." She wiped the tears that were streaming down her cheeks and hiccuped again. "I thought it was funny. An unexpectedly rich use of language."

"Little bit of a backhanded compliment," he said.

"I didn't mean it to be."

The breeze kicked up between them, and it was cold on her cheeks because they were wet. Her hair tangled into her face and she shook it free, and he was…

Looking at her. He had been, the whole time, but there was something different about this now. His gaze dropped to her mouth. Just for a second. Then he met her eyes again.

"Get your ass on home before you irritate me any more than you already have."

"Aren't you going to drive me back to my car?"

He shook his head. "Lord Almighty, girl, you are a pain in my ass." She thought for a moment he might seriously leave her there. "Get in the truck."

She climbed into the passenger seat, and she couldn't help but notice that now he smelled distinctly of sweat. She also couldn't help but notice that, for some reason, on him it wasn't a terribly unpleasant smell. It was earthy. It seemed to have taken on the sun and the soil, the pine trees and the fresh-cut grass. It was like all the work he had done had bled into his body, like it had become part of him. It was captivating. In a way that she hadn't imagined it could be.

He was still mad at her. But he'd made her laugh, even if he hadn't meant to. And that shifted something.

"So, you had soybeans on the whole property for…"

"Why the hell does that matter?" he said, spitting the words like nails.

She worked at being moderate in tone again, because apparently laughing at him wasn't any more appreciated than sniping. "Because. I'm curious about the ranching operation, how long exactly it's been going and what all it entailed."

"Why?"

"If you haven't noticed, I'm interested. I said that I wanted to help, and I do. Your sister has concerns about the organization of the paperwork, and I kind of want to get an idea of what sort of help you might need."

But apparently the moment for sharing was over. Because he didn't answer. And she could see she'd hit a full-on brick wall with him.

They got back to the house, and blonde, sunny Camilla was standing outside the front door watering a potted plant. She shaded her face as they drove up. "Hey," she said. "Did you have a good workday?"

"Just the best," said Quinn, smiling widely.

"Great. I have to ask you something," said Camilla. "I hope you won't take offense, but I've never been this close to a Four Corners person, you know, apart from the big barn meeting, and then we had to leave because Levi thought you all might shoot him."

"We...wouldn't have shot him."

"That is reassuring. Are you guys a cult?"

For the second time that day, Quinn found herself laughing unexpectedly.

"No," said Quinn. "We are not a cult. Is that a prevailing rumor?"

"Well," said Camilla. "You do kind of all hang out in a commune sort of environment. You and your sisters wear flower dresses. It looks a little Amish."

Quinn couldn't help herself. She was bemused, but she had to laugh. *"Amish.* Believe me when I tell you, we are not Amish. Do you have any idea the kinds of things that have gone on at that ranch in the last couple of years?"

After so many years of the families being separate... they'd started hooking up. Elsie Garrett with Hunter McCloud, Alaina with Gus McCloud. Then there was Sawyer and his mail-order bride. Plus all the babies.

"No," said Camilla.

"Well...it's a lot of sex," said Quinn.

"That doesn't mean it isn't a cult," said Camilla. "It's my understanding that the best cults are sex cults."

"Please. Stop," said Levi, pushing past both of them and heading toward the house. "Talk about sex cults on your own time, please. I can't bear it. I am going to go take a shower. See you at dinner," he said, directing that at Camilla. Then he stormed inside and slammed the door shut, and Quinn spent a full thirty seconds standing there trying not to imagine him in the shower. With water sluicing over all that bronze skin and...

What was *wrong* with her?

He was mean. He didn't like her. He was in no way being kind to her in any way, shape or form, and she was ready to melt into a puddle at his feet.

She was imagining him in the shower. Imagining *joining* him in the shower.

His hands were so big and he worked the land all the time, so they were probably rough, and oh, good Lord, what was wrong with her? *Seriously.*

She'd never even been kissed.

But this was well-worn territory—that was the problem. More understandable, though, when he was merely a fantasy object. Much less so when he was calling her a carrot.

She tamped it down.

"So, not a cult. Sex or otherwise?" Camilla asked.

"No. Not."

"Too bad. I'd be tempted to throw my hat in to be a sister wife. Because some of the men over there are hot."

Quinn laughed, in spite of her discomfort. There was a reason she'd never dated any of the men there. Well, they'd also never dated her because she annoyed them. But even still. "Well. Yes, that is true. Though, I think of them as...well, not brothers. We're not exactly all super close, but kind of like distant cousins. I can't say that I'm really all that interested in any of them. Or in the whole cowboy shtick." She said that just to get back at her imagination, which had momentarily betrayed her.

"Me, either," said Camilla. "I'm going to meet some guy from the city and have him take me away from here."

"If you're going to dream about going away, take yourself away, Camilla. Don't count on a man."

Camilla smiled. "You sound like Levi."

She frowned. "Do I?"

"Yes. He has never been super keen on my romantic daydreams. But someday…someday I'll move somewhere different."

"Except you don't even want to go back to school," said Quinn. She felt old standing next to this bright, sunny twenty-year-old. She wasn't old—she knew that. It was just she had already gone through college, had already made decisions about where she was going to settle. She didn't entertain those kinds of fantasies. Those flights of fancy.

"I… You're going to help him, right?" Camilla asked. "I really do worry about him. He is such a stubborn asshole. I love him. He's my brother. But he can be a ridiculous pill, and he is… He really doesn't have it all together. I know he thinks that he can control it all, and he can just will everything to go his way, but he can't."

Her heart contracted. For Camilla, and *not* for Levi.

It had probably been hard growing up with him. She'd said he didn't like her romantic daydreams and that wasn't fair.

Someone should be interested in a girl's romantic daydreams. No, her parents hadn't been, but she'd had her sisters.

Quinn knew so well what it was like to feel alone. She might not have romantic daydreams, but she'd had dreams. And not really anyone to listen to them.

Who had Camilla had? And now she was all worried about him, and he wasn't being reasonable. Reasonable would be actually taking Quinn's help instead of opposing her.

Reasonable would not be calling her a *carrot*.

Reasonable would have been standing here with her and Camilla for a moment instead of going off to shower.

Naked and wet and...

"It isn't your job to keep everything together," Quinn said quickly.

And that at least jolted her mind away from Levi and the shower. She might as well have been talking to her younger self, or maybe even her current self, she knew.

Because she had always kept it together, and she had always tried to keep the people around her together. And sometimes it was enough, but sometimes it just damn well wasn't.

"Thanks. That's really... It's nice of you. What exactly...? Why are you helping Levi? Did he hire you?"

She sighed. She wasn't going to lie to Camilla. "Not exactly."

"You two were...not on the same team at the meeting."

"No. What do you think? Do you think we're hurting the town with the road changes?"

Camilla shrugged. "I don't think anyone really knows what will happen until it happens. I can see not wanting the road to bypass the town, but...it's your land."

"I'm hoping Levi will let me use the road through here. The customers won't bypass town then, but it's still better than eight miles on our dirt road. I'm trying to show him I can…help. With the ranch. In exchange for that."

"That seems reasonable," Camilla said, sounding slightly surprised.

"I know, right? I mean, I thought it was reasonable, but he's still… I don't know. But I'll convince him."

"Well, good luck. He is a hardheaded fool sometimes. But he had to be. That's the thing. He *had* to be hard. And he had to make decisions. He had to be the adult when he wasn't yet. I was just two when our parents died. Our mom died right after I was born. She had cancer. When she was pregnant with me." That part came out hushed. "I don't even remember them. I remember Levi. He's basically… He's basically my father. And I would do anything for him."

"I think the thing that you can do best for him is going on living a life that pleases you. But maybe don't join a sex cult?"

Camilla laughed. "Yeah. Maybe not. I appreciate it. Thanks."

And then Quinn turned and left the younger woman standing there. She got into her car and headed back toward Sullivan's Point. When she got to the farmhouse, she was delighted to find that all of her sisters were there, including Alaina and baby Cameron.

She smiled and stretched her hands out, taking hold of her nephew and holding him close, smelling his little baby head.

And just for a minute, she ached.

No.

That wasn't what she wanted. She was so glad that Alaina was happy that way. So glad that she had found Gus. That Gus loved her, and loved the baby, and was raising him as his own. Gus was one of those good men. Rare in Quinn's estimation and in her observation. It must be nice, to be taken care of like that. But Quinn had accepted that she didn't want to take that risk. Not ever.

"Any more progress?" Fia asked.

Quinn kissed Cameron on the head. "No. Well. I agreed to work with him for the rest of the week. So we'll see."

"And after you work with him he'll reconsider?"

Yeah. He'd said that. That was the agreement, she was pretty sure. Though, it was difficult to remember what he'd actually said.

Except when he'd called her a *carrot*.

"Yeah. I think he's just… I talked to his sister a bit today. He just had a lot of responsibility put on his shoulders and I think he takes everything really seriously. He had those soybeans in the fields for ten years, and it occupied all of his ranch land, and the more I think about it, the more I think he probably feels reluctant to commit to anything because he's done it before."

"You're psychoanalyzing him now?" Fia asked.

She didn't know why that made her feel defensive. "I mean, you kind of have to, right? It's a tactical move."

"If you say so."

"We have to make preserves on Friday," said Rory, cutting another slice of bread off the thick boule at the center of the table.

"I'm going to be busy," said Quinn. "Doing ranch work."

"Well, Alaina?" Rory turned to look at their youngest sister. "You able to get on that and be of some help?"

"Yes," Alaina said, sounding long-suffering. "I can help."

"Thank you," Quinn said. "It's for the greater good. I'm going to make sure that I prove to Levi Granger that he needs me."

Except when she thought of the strong, angry man that she'd dealt with for most of the day today, she couldn't imagine him ever admitting he needed anybody. But she wasn't going to admit defeat. Not now. Not ever.

She was going to be back tomorrow bright and early, and she was going to gain access to his house so that she could begin to look over his paperwork.

Because she had a feeling that as much as it might help for him to see that she could manage labor, what he really needed was for her to get in there and handle something he didn't want to. She was certain that what he really didn't want to handle involved sitting still.

And while Quinn herself didn't love sitting still, she did love to solve the problem.

Levi, for all that he was a massive pain, was becoming the most interesting problem she'd had in a good long while.

CHAPTER TEN

SHE WAS THERE. Bright and early. Standing on his porch holding a cup.

"Ready." She grinned at him.

Today she was wearing a pair of jeans that looked so tight he had no idea how she was going to bend over and do any work in them. She had on her work boots, and a black tank top that scooped low over the curves of her pale breasts.

They were freckled. Like her face.

He was trying to recall if he'd ever made love to a woman who had freckles on her tits.

He did not think he had.

"Hi."

He looked up, meeting her gaze, suddenly very aware that he had been obviously looking at her rack. "Morning," he said.

She wrinkled her nose, and her cheeks went vaguely flushed. "What's on the agenda for the day?"

"Work," he said.

"When you say work…"

"I mean work."

"So as far as the year goes, do you divide certain work up into quarters?" she asked.

"No. I don't work in an office. I've never seen the point of playacting like I did."

"It's for… It is to help organize the business."

He shrugged. "Sounds boring."

He took long strides toward the truck, leaving her behind, and she took four steps to his every one, doing her best to keep up.

It was like he was being followed by a particularly persistent squirrel.

"*Boring* or not, it is reality. And if it's boring to you, then what you need is for somebody…"

"Listen," he said, finally losing his patience. He stopped and turned to face her, standing there in front of his truck, staring her down. "I got fucked over on that deal with your dad. I was too stupid to understand what mattered. I don't take on things I can't handle myself. Do you understand?"

She'd been badgering him about this yesterday. She'd been badgering him since she appeared. So sure and certain she knew it all. If she really wanted to know it all, then he'd tell her.

"I…"

"I was an idiot—is that what you wanted to hear? Because I didn't have anybody advising me, because there was nobody with a fancy degree hanging around. Because…" He shook his head. "The details aren't important. But the thing is, I don't need you to lecture me. You went to college, little girl, congratulations. But that's not the real world. In the real world, people die, and you have to pick up the pieces and move on. There are kids to raise. There's shit to take care of."

He could see that he'd hurt her. And he didn't really care. Because who was she to come in here and start lecturing him on all these things like she knew better than him?

Like he didn't know anything. About the life he'd

been baptized into by hell fuckin' fire when he was eighteen years old.

"I talked to Camilla a little while yesterday," she said, her voice surprisingly soft. "She told me that she was two when your dad died. And that you're basically her father and… I'm sorry. I think I didn't fully give enough weight to that."

The apology was shocking enough that it stopped him cold. Because one thing Quinn had proved about herself was that she was determined, and a little bit *mean*. He liked that about her, if he were forced to pick a thing to like.

That she was sharp and a bit pointy, that she wasn't afraid to burrow down into an issue and refuse to come out. But she had backed way down this time. And it made him wonder what the hell emotion he had actually shown beneath his anger.

He needed to get a grip.

She was a *Sullivan*.

"You don't just want an easement. You want to use my land. You want strangers to drive onto my land."

"Just the road…"

"You never asked me what the road went past. What it might impact."

"I'm sorry," she said. "What…?"

"Let's get to work."

He felt like an ass, because he had let her talk her way into this, had let her talk herself in circles.

And she had seemingly not noticed that he had never agreed to readdress his answer, just because she was working for him. He had thought it was funny that this woman who thought she was so damn smart only listened to the words coming out of her own mouth, and not the words coming out of his. That she was so certain of her logic, and her understanding, that she genuinely hadn't heard him say *no*.

But she looked young and fragile just then, and he did have to confront the fact that she was his sister's age, and if a man treated Jessie like this he would've run the guy over.

But it wasn't like that. He wasn't a man in the moment, just as she wasn't a woman. He was a rancher, and she was a pain in his ass.

It wasn't the same.

Right. And you looking at her breasts earlier wasn't about you being a man and her being a woman.

No. It wasn't.

Well, it was. But only in the most basic of ways.

She was... She was a little can of rage and determination under pressure. And the wrong thing was going to make that girl explode. He had no patience for anything like that. He didn't do entanglements. And he didn't do intense. He had a feeling that Quinn Sullivan only knew how to be intense.

So whatever he felt, whatever interest he experienced looking at her body... It didn't go any further than that. It was physical. And it was hypothetical.

It would never be anything more.

This disagreement between the two of them had nothing to do with him being a man and her being a woman.

He could not care the hell less about her gender. Not when she was standing there feeling like an emblem of the mistakes he'd made in the past.

"Let's just go," she said, moving toward the truck.

"Sure."

They got in, and he felt tangled up in his own fury. Even though some of it was at himself.

He had let her think that he wasn't all that smart, and this explosion wasn't exactly going to stand as a testament to his intelligence.

He had thought it was funny, and now he was irritated by it.

But he was also too damn stubborn to simply drop the facade.

The truth was, he did like to move slow. The truth was, he did like to carefully consider every angle before making a decision. And so if the little windup toy thought that made him slow, that was just fine.

Another testament to her inexperience.

They drove out toward the back field again, and he tried to imagine that field being full of Christmas trees. It wasn't a terrible idea. He had done a little bit of research on it. He'd watched a couple of videos on the subject, which was one of his preferred ways of getting new info on very specific topics. The internet was a marvel.

One that he had learned to use to his advantage. There were a lot of good things about the Christmas tree idea, it couldn't be denied, though at this point he did feel like if he took her advice he would owe her something.

Though she was the one who wanted that to be the case. He hadn't agreed to anything.

They worked for a while, and then when it started to get warm, he told her to go back to the truck. "I've gotta go pick up feed today. You want to come?"

Now, that was guilt talking.

"Yes," she said. "I thought you did grass fed."

"I do. For the cattle. But there are vitamins and nutrients to go into that, and then also, there's the non-fancy cows, of which I have a few, and there's the horses."

"You sell regular beef, too?"

He nodded. "Yes. I keep the animals separate, and it is not the biggest part of my operation, but when I was trying to recover from the soybeans, I had to start somewhere, and I started with regular cows and built from there. I'm working on phasing them out, but it'll be a couple of years yet. I have some local accounts that use the meat, and I don't want to lose them."

"Oh."

"Additionally, sometimes families buy cows direct from me before the slaughter. And that way we can bypass some different laws that make it more expensive. There are heavy markups when you sell and store, but a lot of that has to do with the cost of getting the animals to the USDA station, and going through that approval process. So once we circumvent…"

"Right. I know all about it," she said. "We read about it in school."

"Right. Of course you *read* about it."

He could feel her get instantly testy in response to his terse statement. "I did more than read about it. I grew up at Four Corners. The Kings and the Garretts deal with this sort of thing all the time. I've witnessed it. Discussed it as part of business meetings."

He said nothing to that. He didn't owe her a response. He hadn't asked her to be here, after all. It wasn't his job to make her feel better when she said something he didn't like.

"It was smart," she said. "Approaching it that way. You made some good decisions."

He looked at her. "Well, thank you kindly. I don't

know that I could have ever anticipated such a compliment."

"Are you *trying* to be mean?"

"If you have to ask, I'm not doing a very good job."

"I'm sorry. I really am not talking down to you. I promise. I didn't mean to make it seem like I thought I was smarter than you. I just think that I might have a different portfolio of knowledge."

"I know that you think that. But I have a hard time believing that anything you learn in the classroom is going to replace what you actually do out here."

They got into the truck and began to drive toward the main road.

This was the road that she wanted the easement for. And when they drove by the big oak tree with the grave markers for his parents beneath it, he didn't say anything, but he might've slowed down just a little bit.

If she noticed, she didn't say anything.

"Well, I have a hard time believing that you can have a full understanding of the business aspects of running a ranch on a wing and a prayer. I grew up on a ranch. I can't stress that enough. I still learned a hell of a lot going to school."

"And why did you go to school exactly?" he asked.

"Isn't it obvious? I've already talked about how much work it's been for us to keep Sullivan's Point going, to keep us being big contributors to Four Corners. Our parents are gone. They didn't die. They just decided to walk away. My dad abandoned us, and then my mom couldn't stand being there anymore. When he left, she fell apart. It was like there was nothing left of her. And she didn't know anything about running a ranch. So that left us. Her daughters. And I looked at that and I decided then and there I was never letting a man determine how successful I was going to be. My father walked away with all that knowledge. So I went and got my *own*. I'm never going to let a man affect my life that way. I'm never going to let one change me like that."

After the verbal skinning he'd given her earlier, he hadn't expected her to share like that. But maybe it came from anger for her, too.

Maybe she was tired of him making assumptions, like he was with her.

Why did it matter, though? When he'd gone off on her, part of it had been because…

He'd wanted her to know.

Why?

And why would she want him to know?

He couldn't sort it out, so instead, he was terse. "Admirable," he said. "But you know, just because you got a degree doesn't mean you don't have something to learn from a man who's been running a ranch all these years."

"Fine," she huffed. "Drop some knowledge on me."

"Don't sign a contract with a shady factory-farming company. Or your dad?"

She forced out a laugh, and he looked at her out of the corner of his eye, saw her gripping the shoulder strap of her seat belt and looking out the window.

"What?" he asked.

"Sometimes you're so… You seem *almost* funny."

"Maybe I am funny, Quinn. Did you ever think of that?"

She looked at him then, those green eyes clashing with his, and he looked away for a second.

He had to keep his eyes on the road, even if they were still on the property.

"You didn't exactly *brand* yourself that way when we met."

"I was unaware that I was branding myself."

"You…lied to me, in a way. On purpose," she said. "You don't want me to know anything about you."

"That's not true. You know about my parents dying. You know that I leased out the fields and that I regret it. Those things are true."

"But I don't know *you*."

There was something about the way she said that that burrowed its way under his skin. And for some reason right then, he thought about her little white shoes.

"You don't need to know me. I didn't invite your ass to my ranch in the first place. I didn't invite you to know me, nor do I have a particular yen to be known by you."

The words made something in his chest pull tight, because hadn't he just been thinking that part of him did want her to understand?

"Does anybody know you?"

"That's a good question," he said. "And the answer is… probably no. I had to try and be the parental figure to my siblings, and having them know me just would have made that harder. I can't have them seeing my flaws, after all. Not when I need their respect. And as for lovers…well, no. Not even a little."

"Oh, *wow*," she said, sounding irritated again, the words low and vaguely venomous. "You sleep with women you don't know?"

"Now, that," he said, "I am confident had absolutely nothing to do with the potential easement deal."

He looked at her and noticed her ears were pink.

"You're the one who brought up lovers."

"That's true," he said, after a fashion. "I did."

"And my question stands. Does anyone actually know you?"

"No," he said, firm and hard. "I never needed anybody to, and I never asked anyone to."

That wasn't strictly true. He'd always had Damien, but then... They didn't talk about stuff, not deep stuff. Damien had been there for him when his parents had died. And when Damien had lost his mom a couple of years ago, Levi had known just how he felt.

But they worked alongside each other. They didn't bare their souls to each other.

Lord Almighty.

He decided to turn the radio on, because he didn't know how he had gotten walked into a personal conversation with the little hellcat, nor did he particularly want to be in one. So he turned the music up, and enjoyed her obvious discomfort as Luke Bryan demanded that a country girl shake it for him.

They drove down to a feed store about twenty minutes outside of Pyrite Falls, not really situated in Mapleton, but not really anywhere.

It was big, with a chain-link fence around the perimeter, and an industrial-looking building. It was the cheapest place to get the kinds of things they needed for the ranch, and it sat where it did because many people used it, from various outlying areas.

And it was the strangest thing. When they got in there, she was...excited.

Interested in all the products they carried, and it made him wonder how long it had been since she'd left the damned house.

"Are you unfamiliar with feed?" he asked.

"Not at all. But we don't do a lot with animals, so I

haven't had the opportunity to really spend a lot of time in stores like this one. I just think everything's really interesting. Everything about ranching. It is an undervalued profession. Listen, I know that you think that I'm snobby, but I'm not. I am proud of the kind of work that we all do. People with office jobs think they're better than the people out there working the land. In reality, we are all part of an ecosystem. We need people to work in offices, but they need us to work in the fields. I think that what we do is the closest thing to magic out there. You take seeds, and from those tiny seeds something amazing grows."

This little rabbit of a woman spoke more words in a few minutes than most people he knew spoke in a day, and yet this monologue fascinated him, even when it shouldn't.

She went on. "You raise animals, and there are so many things that can be done with them. Flour, salt, yeast, eggs, butter and water, and you have bread, but only when you put it together right. There is wisdom in all those things. I get it. You don't think that I have the wisdom. But I have the passion. And I also took the time to figure out the best ways that I could support what we had. And that's all. I'm just trying to help with that."

He could see that she was sincere. She really believed that. She really loved all this.

With all of herself. And it was rare to meet another person who did.

It was especially strange to discover that they actually did have something in common. He'd heard her speak, he'd known she was Brian's daughter, and he'd decided he knew who she was.

But he hadn't.

But they were more the same than they were different. That was the weirdest realization.

Because they were both standing in a feed store like they'd rather be there than anywhere else on the planet, and she was practically in tears over the miracles of the land.

And that was the kind of thing that he'd felt in his soul from the time he was a kid. Though, he'd lost that over the years. Because the ranch had become something he'd had to do, and not the promise of a future.

That was the toughest thing.

When his mom had gotten sick, right at the beginning of her pregnancy with Camilla, he'd been sixteen.

Before then he'd had his dreams. Rodeo dreams.

He was going to get out; he was going to chase glory. In a place where all that mattered was what he could do on the back of a horse, not whether he got good grades.

What would it be like when he was grown and he didn't have to take that hour bus ride into Mapleton to go to school anymore? To sit there all day in a classroom, when he hated it more than anything else, and felt dumber than a bag of rocks by the end of every day. Listening to teachers go on and on at him about how he just didn't try or didn't apply himself.

Like it was his fault the words were backward and he couldn't put numbers in order. Like it was his fault that he could sit there and stare at a page for an hour and not get any of the information. Like he chose for it to all be so hard he couldn't get a grip on it at all.

They all acted like he chose that. And it had never made any sense to him at all. Why it seemed easier to think that a kid was stupid than that maybe you needed to change the way you were teaching them. But that was what happened to him.

And he had been champing at the bit for the day when all he would have to do was get up in the morning and ride.

Leaving school had come sooner than he'd expected, but it hadn't been a dream.

He'd lost his parents, and along with the grief had come the reality of being responsible for everything. Everything and everyone.

And the death of his dreams, too.

He was thirty-six now. You didn't join the rodeo at thirty-six.

It was fine. His life was here now and it didn't matter.

In the scheme of things, it didn't feel like the worst thing.

The people he'd lost, the years he'd lost with them, that would always matter more.

He could remember distinctly when he'd gotten cut on some barbed wire after his mother had died. He'd gone into the bathroom to get the first aid kit, and as he'd fixed the wound, he'd realized he didn't have a mother anymore.

He had to dress his own wounds.

Her soft hands wouldn't be the ones soothing him, not anymore.

He'd sat in that realization for a long time. His mother had been wonderful. She'd cared for him like no one else.

No one would ever love him or care for him like that again.

He'd cried that night, over that cut on his arm. Over the realization he'd lost something he would never get back.

He hadn't known that he'd be without his dad a year later.

That he'd watched the strongest man he'd ever known go down in a field, felled by that same strong grief that had immobilized Levi that night when he'd cut himself.

Grief was a monster.

He'd tangled with it too many times.

No. Losing his rodeo dreams wasn't the tragedy.

Even though ranching hadn't been his immediate dream, he'd imagined he'd settle into it someday. He'd always known this place would go to him. Just not when it had.

He'd imagined life away from the tyranny of school would be carefree.

Wonderful.

He'd never had a carefree moment from the time his mother had first gotten sick.

Really, the closest he'd come to that was in the last few years. After the kids had grown and gone, and he had finally started finding his feet with what he wanted to do with the land. Finally found a way to make it profitable for him. Now he had a little bit more of that.

But he'd had it from the time he was a kid. Those big, blue-sky dreams that had stretched out before him like the promise of a new day.

It was just that they'd been taken away.

Because that was what life did.

But it seemed to him that Quinn might even understand that.

Based on what she'd said about her father, based on what she'd said about the decisions that she'd made in order to protect herself, to keep herself safe. To make sure that no one could ever take anything from her.

He hadn't anticipated standing there in a feed store feeling like maybe Quinn Sullivan was more his kind of person than he might've been able to imagine.

"I'll show you the vitamins we need."

He took her over to the corner, and she was messing with all the different syringes.

"Those are for calves."

"All right. Do you do your own castration?"

"Yeah," he said. "Though, you might want to be careful with that. You go asking men that out of context and it sounds a little bit rough."

Her cheeks went slightly pink again, like they had that morning when he had been looking at her breasts.

Lord Almighty.

"Right." She cleared her throat. "But you knew what I meant."

"I did. I'm just being difficult."

"You seem to specialize in that," she said.

"Yep."

They purchased all their goods, and he pushed the big flat cart out to the pickup truck while she tagged along to the side, fluttering with nervous energy over the fact that she had nothing to do. He picked up a very small bag from the top of the flat. "Here." He handed it to her and she looked up at him like he was nuts.

He didn't explain himself.

"You hungry?" he asked, as he finished loading the last of the bags into the truck.

"You don't have to keep feeding me." She threw her little bag on the top.

"Oh, don't go getting excited. It isn't going to be anything fancy like Becky's. I just figured we'd stop at the Minute Market up the road at the gas station."

They trailed into the little store and he grabbed a deli sandwich out of the case. Quinn had disappeared into an aisle—not tall enough for her head to be seen over the top of it—and emerged with a bag of candy a minute later.

She then went to a milkshake mixing machine and got herself vanilla.

A stark contrast to yesterday's Caesar salad order.

He felt it was tantamount to having driven her to drink.

He took the items from her while she glared at him, and he paid for them all.

"I want to see your paperwork," she said, taking a big sip of the milkshake.

"Nope," he said.

"You don't owe me anything. I mean, if I look at it, and I give you some advice, you don't owe me anything. Flat out. But I want to see. When I said I want to help, I'm serious. None of the way that it's charity or anything like that. It's only that I really do like solving problems."

"I said no."

He put the last bite of his deli sandwich into his mouth and oriented the truck toward home, driving down the highway just a little bit too quickly.

"Just let me see."

He looked at her. She was all glittering, sparkling, annoying. Beautiful.

His gut went tight and his body burned. And what the hell?

What the actual hell?

It was like he was drawn to bullshit. That's what it was. Because she was the most annoying, high-handed female he'd ever had the misfortune of meeting and his body reacting to her was egregious.

"Quinn," he growled. "You need to learn when to step off."

And he thought she'd argue. But suddenly something like knowing moved through her green eyes, and instead, she leaned back in her seat.

She didn't say anything more for the rest of the trip.

AT DINNER THAT NIGHT, he and Camilla had pizza, and a FaceTime call with Dylan.

"How are things?" Camilla asked.

"Hot as hell," said Dylan.

"Well, it's Jordan," said Levi. "I'm not exactly certain what you expected."

"See the world, they said," Dylan said. "Join the military, they said. Not exactly the vacation that I was hoping for."

And all he could do was worry about his brother, which just irritated him. And when they got off the phone, Camilla looked at him, a little bit too sharply for his taste.

"You're going to accept that girl's help, right?"

"I don't know," he said, because at least that was honest.

"I don't know why you're so hesitant to do it."

Of course she didn't know. Because she couldn't possibly understand. The ways in which he felt like he had let them all down. How compelled he felt to keep control now.

"Because I am," he said. "Can't that be enough?"

"No."

"You are a stubborn little hellcat, Camilla. Has anybody ever told you that?"

"I don't know why I'm so stubborn," she said, looking at him, her expression bland. "It's weird. Almost like it runs in the family."

"Yeah." He couldn't help but smile. "Almost like."

"She seems smart."

He frowned. "Who?"

"Quinn."

He had known full well what his sister meant but he felt that showing he did was too…validating to Quinn, and even without her here, he wouldn't do it. "She's Brian Sullivan's daughter."

"I know."

"Why do you think she seems smart? Because she went to college? And because she's encouraging you to stay at college?"

"You're encouraging me to stay at college," Camilla pointed out. "Why are you being mean about Quinn doing it?"

He *was* being unnecessarily rude. Quinn did seem smart, that was the thing. She was sharp, and more than that, she had a real love for the land. He was just being irritated. And he was letting himself be irritated. Because all this nonsense was digging under his skin. Because he had life sorted out for himself. And having somebody meddle in it right now just felt annoying. And like something he didn't especially want to deal with.

They finished their pizza, and he went upstairs, pausing by the door to the office.

It had been his father's office before his. The place where he had sat with his papers, and his pipe, and gone over the financials of the ranch.

His father had been a simple man. And all of his records had been physical, not digital.

Personally, Levi found digital easier to manage. And easier to read. Particularly in certain fonts.

Another thing that he'd learned.

He had work-arounds, but it didn't mean that it made any of this easier, or that he felt more inclined to jump in and do things.

It was just…possible now.

He was holding on by the skin of his teeth when it came to filing taxes and all of that.

Keeping up with business licenses and email communications.

He did pretty well.

But that didn't mean that he didn't let it get to where it was all piled up. It didn't mean that he didn't procrastinate something terrible.

Maybe it wouldn't be the worst thing in the world to let Quinn have a look at it all.

Maybe it would be a reasonable thing to do.

Maybe it was something he should consider.

Giving her access to the road…

And that was how he found himself going back down the stairs. He did not go into his office. Instead, he went out the front door. Instead, he got in his truck and began to drive down the road.

Toward his parents' graves.

He parked his truck in the middle of the gravel road, because he could do that. The sky was pink, the sun going down. It was late, but these endlessly long days in the summer meant that the sun was still hanging on.

He took his hat off and looked down at the graves.

"Hey," he said. "I know it's been a while." He bent

down and brushed some leaves clinging to the headstone away. He hadn't stopped by in at least a month.
Sometimes grief was hard like that. Sometimes he didn't
want to stop and feel it. Other times he did. "I should
come by more. It isn't like you don't live close. I know
that I really made a mess of things with the soybeans.
You would've called that a sissy crop anyway, Dad. You
would've hated it. You'd like the cows, though. But I got
this woman, and she wants to help out with things, and
you would've been suspicious of her, too, because she's
full of book learning from a college in California. And
what the hell is a California school supposed to teach
anybody about ranching, is what I want to know. And
I think it's what you would ask, too."

He cleared his throat. "So yeah. I don't really know.
But this is our spot. And I don't think I really want
people here. And they'd have to drive by to get to the
barn. Have to cut in some new gravel. I don't know."

He wasn't expecting an answer—he just wanted to
be here. Because the office made him wish that he had
never inherited the ranch. And this... Being able to
stand on the plot of land where his parents were at rest,
being able to connect with them while he looked at the
mountains, while he looked at the sky, that was why
he liked this. It was why he liked being here. Why he
valued it. And he needed the reminder today. Because
the truth was, if he let Quinn Sullivan into his office,
he might end up changing his mind about everything.
Because she might just give him what he needed, and
he didn't really know what to do with that.

If he let her into his office, he might have to bleed out
some of his issues, and he really didn't want to do that.

He never talked to his siblings about it. It wasn't that he was ashamed.

He was self-diagnosed through the internet, which was the thing that kind of irritated him, because he would love to be that crusty old guy who said this generation was soft and always looking for excuses. But for him, it wasn't an excuse. It wasn't an excuse. It was something that made the whole of his life make all kinds of sense.

Dyslexia, sequencing disorders, dyscalculia. All those things. They had shown him that his brain just wasn't put together the way that a lot of other people's were, but that didn't mean that he was dumb.

Knowing that, though, didn't solve the issues. It didn't erase the shame that he felt.

He wondered…

Like the cut on his arm he'd had to dress on his own, he'd often wondered. If his mother hadn't gotten sick, if his father's sole focus hadn't been that sickness, then the loss. If either of his parents had lived…

Would they have discovered his issues sooner?

Would someone have helped him?

It didn't matter. He'd had to become an adult and take care of the people around him.

He'd had to bandage his own wounds, and his siblings', so they wouldn't feel the loss in the same way he did.

Anyway, he'd figured out what was wrong with him eventually.

It didn't take away the mistakes that he'd made in the past.

But it had helped him come up with some workarounds, so there was that.

But he didn't want to talk to Quinn about the fact that

he struggled to read even basic sentences. That he used voice and audio to get most everything done.

Because it was bad.

Because hell, when he was out on the range, he didn't really think he was stupid, but when he had to deal with this kind of stuff, it felt like he was.

Quinn was a shining emblem of those issues, of his failures.

And it made him a bit feral.

Or maybe it was life that made him that way. Some kind of unavoidable combination of things, and he was just kind of a difficult monster.

Usually at his parents' graves, he felt some kind of connection. To them, to the land. Right now he felt weirdly alone, and that wasn't the kind of thing he liked to indulge in.

So instead, he put his hat back in place and wandered back to the truck.

He would be seeing Quinn tomorrow whether he wanted to or not. And then he would have to make a decision about what he was going to do. With her. With the ranch.

He hadn't felt uncertain in a long time.

He resented that she had the power to do that. Right now, the impulse to hold on to that resentment was pretty strong. Because it seemed easier than a whole hell of a lot else.

So maybe he would just do that.

CHAPTER ELEVEN

THE NEXT DAY she wore overalls. She was an absurd little varmint. And none of the behavior should be cute in any way.

Yet he found it was.

He wanted her to leave and not come back. He wanted her to show up every day when she said she would. He wanted her to keep her damned mouth shut. And he wanted her to chatter like the ridiculous little squirrel that she was. He wanted to pull the girl's pigtails. That was the problem. He couldn't recall the last time he had felt an impulse like that. Not even in school. She made him feel that way. She made him feel some kind of riled up that he didn't quite understand. And that was another thing. He didn't like not understanding. He had put himself in a position in life where he never felt stupid. Except for the rare moments when he had to disappear into paperwork in his office, he didn't do things that made him struggle.

He'd overcome. In a very specific way. He had made it so that he never had to feel that way again.

She made him feel that way. On so many levels. In so many ways. Not the least of which was that he didn't understand this pull.

He didn't do complicated attraction. He never had.

Because complicated would necessitate a relationship of some kind, and he didn't do those, either.

Shit. You'd think with that kind of thinking he'd be a total manwhore, but he wasn't. It wasn't about that. It was...

Love hurt so damned much. And his desire, his ability to feel any more, had been killed hard the day his father had gone back to the earth.

Knowing what he did, seeing what he'd seen, he'd have to be dumb to want to indulge attraction like this.

Quinn Sullivan made him feel dumb.

Overalls.

Pigtails.

Dammit.

"Ready?" she said, grinning up at him.

"Sure."

The freckles on her face had intensified since they had begun working together. And her nose was a bit pink from the prolonged exposure to the sun in the afternoon heat.

"I thought you put sunblock on."

She frowned. "I did."

"Are you reapplying every two to four hours? Because you're supposed to."

Her mouth opened. "I... Yes. Maybe."

"You look a little sun-kissed there, honey."

Her eyebrows shot up, and she blinked rapidly. She pursed her lips and frowned. *"Honey?"*

"What's weird about that?"

"It's weird."

"I called you a carrot the other day," he pointed out.

"That was less weird."

"Come on," he said, beckoning her into the house.

She followed, and, with the full intent of being a condescending asshole, he got out the bottle of sunscreen
that he used every day and put a measure on his palm.
Then he swiped at it with his fingertips and put some
on her nose, rubbing it across to her cheek, and then
again to the other cheek.

She only looked at him, her eyes filled with a mix-
ture of anger and...

Shit. He'd made a mistake.

Her skin was soft, and being this close to her was
dangerous.

She smelled like flower petals and sleep. Like coffee.
Like the kind of morning he never had with women.

Well. And coconuts. But that was the sunscreen. And
because he was a stubborn asshole, he put his other
hand on her face and rubbed from both sides, getting
the cream worked into her skin, because he wasn't backing down now, even though he knew that he was doing
an idiotic thing.

It was too late to turn back, so he might as well be
in with both feet. Both thumbs.

Whatever.

Lord Almighty.

Her lips parted, and they were pink and soft looking, and far too lovely for his own good.

That was the problem with Quinn Sullivan; she had
been too lovely for his own good from the moment she
showed up on his doorstep.

He didn't have time for this. He didn't need it.

He didn't like what she did to him. What she did to
his life.

And he had no room for anyone else in his world.

He was done. Done helping people. Taking care of them. He'd done it. He was living for himself now.

And Camilla was hovering around and Quinn was here, and none of it was fair. He still had to worry about fucking Dylan, who was out in the middle of the desert, and… At least Jessie was with Damien.

As weird as he had found that whole thing, at least his middle sister was with a man that he trusted, so he knew that she was all right day to day.

He could not say the same for his other siblings, and he didn't like it. Because he wanted all of this to be over. He had been under the strain of needing to take care of everybody else from the time he was eighteen years old. Hell, really from the time he was sixteen.

He hadn't asked to be a parent.

He had just wanted to be a kid.

And he didn't harbor any fantasies about having a second adolescence or anything like that, but he definitely wanted a little bit more freedom.

And that did not include being tangled up in Quinn Sullivan in any regard. None whatsoever.

"Levi…" she whispered.

That was when he knew. She felt it, too.

That was the most dangerous realization he could have had.

And he took a step back, and he pretended that he hadn't noticed anything. Pretended like nothing had just passed between them. Like there was no electrical current, like he hadn't been looking at her the same way she had been looking at him. Like her skin wasn't a revelation, like flower petals in springtime. Like she wasn't making him think poetry.

Yeah. Like that.

Because poetry had no home between himself and Quinn Sullivan.

Poetry had no room within him.

For more reasons than he could name.

"Let's get to work."

"Fine," she said.

"You need some coffee?" he asked.

"Oh, I had my cup before I left, and I couldn't find my thermos and…"

"I have time to get you a cup of coffee."

"You said you didn't share."

"I don't," he said.

But he poured her a cup all the same, and stuck it in the service and put it in her hands.

They were pretty hands. Petite.

And he was a man, so in that moment, he wasn't picturing her hand wrapped around the thermos. He was picturing it wrapped around *him*.

He gritted his teeth and took a step away from her. "Let's go."

He knew that in a few minutes she would be annoying. Just like clockwork. It was one of the things he liked about Quinn. That when things did begin to get too companionable between them, he could count on her to say something irritating and undo it.

To take any of the attraction that was burning beneath the surface and douse it with some cold water.

She…had been doing that on purpose. After that moment that had passed between them, he was sure of that.

"I was doing some research on Christmas trees," she said.

"Were you?"

"Yes. I was."

"Great."

"We can talk about it later," she said. "I want to know what our assignment is for the day."

"Our assignment. Well. Charity McCloud is going to come by a little later to do some vaccinations. We need to get the calves all rounded up so that they're ready for her. And after that, we need to get one of the herds moved from the upper pasture down to the lower pasture. So we'll be doing a bit of riding again today."

"Not my favorite," she said.

"I don't understand how it cannot be your favorite."

"Because it just isn't. Because horses are big and kind of unpredictable." She waved her hand over her whole body. "And I'm very small."

He chuckled. "That you are. I love horses."

He hadn't meant to say that last part. Not that he was such a caveman he couldn't admit to loving something, but still. He didn't much see the point in telling her that.

Or anything about him.

But what had been the point to the sunscreen?

It was a weird day and it wasn't even seven.

"You do?" she asked.

He nodded slowly. And he really had no reason to go on about this, but it just seemed a natural thing. Anyway, he was looking. Searching for the thing. Because Quinn would say something. And as long as he kept talking, it would make her keep talking, and then she would bring that verbal bucket of water his way. He wanted that. Needed it.

"When I was younger I figured I would be in the rodeo. Riding horses was about the only thing that I ever cared about. As soon as I got off the school bus, I would head out to the field every day. More often than not, I would cut, pretend to go to the bus and then not go, get on the horse and ride him around."

"You skipped school?"

And there she was. Sounding so offended. Like he had just confessed to cussing in church.

"Oh, yeah. I was always way more interested in physical pursuits."

He looked at her, and he smiled.

And he had not meant to introduce a double entendre, but he saw something spark in her green eyes. And then he felt an answering heat low in his gut.

Physical pursuits.

"I see," she said, her voice sounding scratchy now.

"People have different priorities," he said, his words hard now, whether he intended them to be or not.

"Yes," she said. "Of course they do. Different philosophies."

She said nothing for a moment. "You never got to be in the rodeo, did you?"

Her voice sounded soft all of a sudden, and he couldn't say he cared for that.

"No," he said. "I was kind of busy."

"Right. Levi, that must've been really difficult. I mean, that is such a limp thing to say. In the face of everything. I can't imagine what you went through. And I'm sorry that you had to give up your dreams. That is the one thing about having my parents leave like they did… I didn't have to give anything up. They didn't care about the ranch anymore. And yes, I think to an extent I felt like I needed to support Fia. After all, she is our older sister, and she did take care of us and everything, but she wouldn't have been alone if we had left. And I did get to leave, for school. I was always planning on coming back, sure, but still."

She did this, too. It was part of the dance of the last few days. Anger, warmth, prickliness, sharing. A tango he hadn't asked to do, but here they were. And like he had several other times, he resisted this.

"I don't need your pity," he said.

"Why not? A little bit of pity isn't the worst thing, is it?"

"Yeah, it can be. Because when people pity you, you begin to buy into the idea that you're worthy of pity. And when you feel like that, then you expect the whole world to treat you like maybe you're a victim. Like maybe you deserve to get something nice, something extra. But let me tell you, all that you get with that kind of mindset is wolves. Wolves smell blood. They know when you're weak. And I don't want to be weak. I never have been, not since any of that happened. I had to be the wolf. I had to be the strong one. Defending my pack. So I never could afford to sit down and indulge myself. Pity can be damaging. If you buy into it too much. There's always a danger in believing your own bullshit—you have to remember that."

"My dad was a wolf."

"Quinn… I think that's something you and I should leave alone." It wasn't about protecting her. It was him. Because when you got down into the fine details of it, it exposed his own weaknesses, and that was something he couldn't stand.

"Why? It's between us. We don't have to talk about it for it to be between us."

"So why talk about it at all?"

"Because would it be so bad to have someone know? To have someone care?"

"It depends. Like I said, it can lure you into a situation where you begin to think of yourself that way. Then get taken advantage of. Listen, I signed those contracts. I can't put all the blame on your father. But I was eighteen years old and doing my best. It just wasn't good enough. But you tell me—was he opportunistic or not?"

"He was. I don't have to know…everything to know that."

"And I seemed easy to take advantage of. Because I was. That's what I mean. You don't want to give them that kind of opportunity."

"You can't count on anybody, right?"

"No, you can't," he said.

That wasn't exactly the conversation he'd been trying to walk her into, but it was a life lesson that she needed. She might rub him the wrong way, but he didn't want her to get hurt, and the truth was, that kind of bravado she carried around with her was liable to get her ass handed to her one of these days.

They drove out to the field, and he was feeling a little overheated from sitting in her presence for all this time.

He needed a new system. A new system for getting laid. If he went out, he could get it done. Women liked him. Well, women didn't like him. They liked his *body*. Women didn't know him well enough to like him or dislike him, and it didn't matter to him at all what they thought of him as a human being. It just mattered whether they wanted to take a ride or not. Mostly they did.

But he had never really gotten in the pattern of going out, and he would have to go out by himself, which, again, was fine, most especially when he was in the mood to get laid. He had old-man patterns and old-man habits. That was the truth of it. He just didn't especially know the social scene, not that the town really had one anyway, but couple that with the fact that he was an empty nester and thirty-six... Well. It was what it was. But that was why Quinn was getting to him.

Because she was just a skinny little redhead—with some decent curves, sure, but lots of women had curves. She wasn't anything special. And in fact, she was infuriating. So there was really no reason in all the damned world for the woman to be under his skin quite like this. The relative dry spell was to blame, he was sure. He wasn't entirely certain when the last time he'd had sex was. But it had been a little bit.

He didn't think of it that way, normally. Hazard of going without for long periods of time while single parenting.

If not for Hannah, that girl from class who'd paid him a visit that night, he'd have ended up the world's oldest living virgin. God bless her. She'd given him just the right way to experience sex for the first time. A pattern he'd kept forever on after.

He didn't want connections. He didn't want to know anyone. He didn't want them to know him.

Maybe that was why Quinn's sharing moments irked him so much. She made him almost wish...

It didn't matter.

They worked until it was time to gather the calves, which Quinn did with almost amusing determination. She was amped up, and she may not love riding horses, but she was pretty damn good at it. She helped him corral the little calves, and got them ready for Charity's arrival.

The sweet-natured veterinarian had always been

well-known in the community. Her father had been the veterinarian before her.

She had always been tied in with the McCloud family, best friends with Lachlan, and even though Levi couldn't say he really knew the McClouds at all, he had always known Charity to be exceptionally good people. He had been pretty damn surprised when she had married Lachlan.

One thing he did know about Lachlan McCloud was that, prior to his marriage, the man had a reputation for being a huge player about town. Hooking up with a different woman pretty much every night. And then there was Charity...

Well, Charity seemed happy, so all must be well.

Quinn seemed delighted to see her, and it was clear to him that the two of them knew each other.

"I'm excited to get to watch you work," said Quinn, planting her hands on her knees and bending over in the ridiculous overalls. He did not know why she was the way that she was.

"Yeah, you normally aren't around for the animal stuff," said Charity, getting the vaccines out and lining them up.

"No. Though, I've been getting to do quite a bit of it with Levi this last week. It's great."

He studied her face, trying to see if she was lying. She seemed like she was telling the truth.

Which was weird. He wasn't sure what she would've thought of their time together, but enjoyment was not really what he'd been expecting.

"What are you working on here?"

"Remains to be seen," said Levi.

Charity looked at him speculatively.

Well. He had probably deserved that. Because yeah. He could see that an answer like that left things open to interpretation. And he decided he wasn't going to overcorrect or disabuse her of the notion.

Quinn, for her part, seemed oblivious to what Charity had been musing on.

Fine with him.

It was hot, sweaty work, but done fairly quickly, because Charity was a professional, and that was one reason he had her out to do it.

He probably could've bought a supply and done it himself, but it didn't appeal. He knew that there was some truth in that to be examined. Because he had learned to hire out when need be. He had learned to hire out for work that he didn't enjoy doing, or that took longer for him to do than something else might.

He had learned to play to his own strengths, so it wasn't that he had grown entirely insular.

It was the control stuff...

Well, hell. Whatever.

He didn't like all the navel-gazing that Quinn was forcing him to do. Not in the least. It was boring.

By the time they were finished, they were both sweaty, and hungry, but it wasn't time to stop for lunch yet, not when they needed to get the cows moved from the upper pasture.

"It's hot," Quinn groused as they rode the horses up the side of the hill that led to the upper pasture.

"I know," he said.

"Yeah, but I'm really hot."

"I didn't make you come today."

"I know," she said fiercely.

"We gotta get the cows from here down to the lower

pasture, because the water dries up this way this time of year. It's better for them to be down there where there's a year-round pond. I move the grazing about seasonally."

"Smart," she said.

"Smart? I thought that was a word that wasn't reserved for me."

"Oh, don't," said Quinn. "You make so many assumptions about what I think, and it's not fair. I never said that you weren't smart."

"You just think it."

He could feel her fuming.

The herd was small, and it was easy for the two of them to get them corralled where they needed them to go, and when it was time to get them to move quick, he urged his horse into a trot, then a gallop, and Quinn followed suit.

The cows thundered down right where he wanted them to go.

And for a moment, he shut everything out but this. Because this was where things had always made sense. This was where he had always been able to find some kind of bliss.

This was where no man stood taller than him, and no one had more power.

This was his land. *His*.

No one and nothing could take that from him, and it was everything.

It was just damn well everything. By the time they got the cows down to the lower pasture, near the pond, he was drenched in sweat.

"Let's stop for a second," he said.

He stripped his shirt off and made his way over to

the pond, dipping it down into the water, because that would feel better than wearing a shirt soaked in his own sweat.

He turned to look at Quinn, who was furiously looking down at her phone, and not looking at him, with what seemed to be great determination.

So.

She had to make an effort to not look when he took his clothes off.

Nice to know. But it shouldn't be.

"The Christmas trees," she said suddenly, very loudly.

"The Christmas trees?"

"Yes," she said. "The Christmas trees. I was doing some research on different outfits who will lease…"

"I'm not interested in leasing anything," he said.

"No, just listen to me."

He straightened and looked at her, and noticed that she still wasn't looking at him. "Quinn," he said.

"No, you're not listening." She took a step toward him and held her phone out, but she still wasn't looking at him.

"Just read this," she said.

She shoved the phone in his face at a weird-ass angle, and even if it had been straight on, there was no way in hell he was going to be able to stand there and read articles with tiny lettering on demand like that. He could barely sit down and read when the font was altered to something friendlier and he didn't have any pressure put on him.

"Stop," he said.

"You're just being stubborn," she said. "If you'll just look at it."

She shoved her phone into his hand and looked at him expectantly.

He looked down at the screen, and it infuriated him to see the letters scramble. It was nonsense. Might've been in some alien language. Might have been in Russian. Didn't fucking matter.

And right then he just about hated her. For being so damned full of her own mission that she couldn't even stop to…

She just didn't think. That was the thing. She thought everybody was her. She thought everybody was her with her exact same brain and her exact same array of choices. And she had no concept of the fact that things were different for different people.

She thought it made you less. But it made you dumb.

And he felt his anger rising.

"If you'll just read the article."

"I told you, I have no interest."

"It's just…"

"Look at me," he said.

And he saw that it took a great and mighty force of will to get her to turn her eyes upon him. "Why can't you look at me, Quinn?"

"I don't have any problem…"

"Seems like you do."

"I don't," she said.

"Got a problem with me taking my shirt off?"

"No. I don't. I mean, I think it's a little bit gratuitous, but I'm used to men and their muscles, and their frequent need to strip half the way naked just because the sun came out from behind the clouds, but you don't see me climbing out of these overalls running around in my panties, do you?"

Damn. That put an image in his head that he didn't need.

He wondered if her thighs were freckled, too.

Damn her.

"No, I don't. But I do think that you should cool off, Quinn."

"I don't need to cool off."

"You don't? You seem a little bit heated."

"Heated? No. I'm just irritated that you are being a stubborn, ridiculous, hardheaded..."

And that just did it. He wasn't listening anymore. And he still had her phone. So everything that was about to get wet would dry just fine.

He picked her up off the ground with one arm and draped her over his shoulder. His bare shoulder. And he had a feeling she was getting a good look at his bare back while she dangled there.

Then he walked her over to the edge of the pond and flipped her down into it.

The unholy shriek that she made before she hit the water, and then submerged, almost made him laugh. Almost.

"You bastard!" she screamed as she sputtered up to the surface of the water.

"You can swim, right?"

"Lucky for you."

"It would be a real waste if you had all that fancy college learning and didn't know how to swim. That's pretty basic."

"But you didn't know," she said.

"I could fish you out easily enough."

"You…you…"

"You'll dry just fine, little carrot. We'll put you in a bag of rice."

"I don't need to be put in a bag of rice!"

"Then what are you complaining about? You probably just need a little bit more sunshine."

She sloshed over to the shore. "I am in overalls."

"You could strip down to your panties," he said, making direct eye contact with her. "I wouldn't mind. Would be fair, after all, all things considered." He gestured to his bare chest.

"Bastard," she spit as she got out of the water. And then she was racing toward him. And she planted both hands on his bare chest and shoved him backward. "I got into a fistfight with Trevor Morton in the ninth grade, and I will fist-fight you, too."

"Calm down. You don't want to be fist-fighting me."

"Yes, I do," she said, shoving him again. "Because you're infuriating."

"Your fists are the size of tiny little pebbles, sweetie. They aren't going to do anything."

He'd be lying if he didn't say he found her fury *interesting*.

It was so potent. He could taste it. It was heavier than anything he'd ever experienced.

It was strange to think that his experience of women was so *limited*. He didn't often think of it that way.

He had hookups in bars. Women who were done up to the nines, because they'd gone out for the same reason that he had. Everybody on their best behavior, in their best clothes, with their best underwear. It was a fine, civilized way to get sex.

But that meant he didn't see things like this. Meant

he didn't often see a woman looking bedraggled and somehow still sexy. Meant he didn't get in fights with women. *Fights* that produced the kind of palpable sexual tension that could grab a man by the throat and strangle him.

It meant he hadn't ever looked at a woman all waterlogged and wrecked and thought that he probably wanted her more than he had when she was wearing little white socks and shoes.

Well. Maybe not more. But it was definitely still want. A particular kind.

What made him angriest was that, right about now, she seemed like she could show him a particular kind of thing that he'd never known he'd wanted.

He gripped her wrists and held her back, away from him, until she stopped huffing and trying to hit him. She hadn't hurt him. He was more concerned she'd hurt herself. Though she'd deserve it.

She took a deep breath. Then another. And another.

Her face contorted, her eyes going wide with horror.

"I hit you."

"You did," he said, standing there holding on to her still.

"I'm so sorry. I am so sorry. I don't do that kind of thing anymore. I don't. I…"

"Chill out, Quinn."

She frowned. "You just told me to chill out."

"I did. Calm the hell down. I'm fine. You didn't hurt me. I threw you in the water but I didn't hurt you. It's all fine."

"You were really mad at me," she said.

"I was."

"You aren't now, though."

"I'm more amused than I am mad right at this moment, yes."

She sniffed loudly and he released his hold on her. She took a step back, and somehow managed to look both down and up at his chest right at the same time. Then she looked away. Resolutely.

"It's okay that you like the look of me without my shirt, Quinn."

"You…!" She was mad again.

"What? I take it as a compliment. But you don't need to worry about me."

She didn't. For every reason he'd already listed, but frankly, her age, too. Now he'd gotten to thinking about his own sexual history and…no.

When he went out, he found women who wanted the same thing and who were close to his age. Older, younger, didn't matter, but in the same ballpark.

Quinn was young. Eleven years younger. And that was a big no in his book.

Her personality was the bigger barrier, but still.

He ignored the kick in his gut that called him a liar, because there was nothing at all that made him feel deterred from looking at how pretty she was.

"I don't… I… No, I'm not worried because I wasn't looking at you. Be shirtless. I don't care. You're just a basic…bro…muscle…hunk cowboy."

"A muscle hunk?" he repeated.

"You heard me! Basic. Nothing special. Seen it all before." She waved a hand.

"Oh, have you?"

"Um. Yes, I went to college in California, remember? Surfers, cowboys…whatever."

And then he quite literally hauled her up by the back

of her overalls to position her to where she could get on the back of her horse. She looked like an angry kitten that had been collared by the scruff, but she scrabbled back into the saddle.

"You got something to say?" he asked.

"You going to put your shirt on?" she asked.

"Not planning on it."

She took several deep breaths, and he could see that she was trying. Trying to not be outraged. Trying to not be angry.

And she was all of those things, but he could see that she was trying.

She felt guilty about hitting him. She shouldn't.

He'd been an asshole. That was the truth of it. And maybe, maybe, she had deserved it. But what he had gotten afterward had been well deserved, as well.

It was the truth. "Listen," he said. "I started a fight with you, so you don't need to feel guilty about fighting back."

"I don't feel guilty. I feel as if I let myself down. That's it. I have a personal ethic, and this was not it."

"Okay," he responded.

"You know, you could try to not be condescending to me."

"Only when you try to not be condescending to me."

She shook her head, and water droplets flew off the ends of her pigtails. "Our issue is that we are too different," she said. "We don't see the world the same. At all. You are an absolute hardheaded, stubborn pig of a human being, and you don't care if you get in an altercation. I absolutely…do care if I get in a confrontation."

He couldn't help it. He laughed at that. The same way she had laughed when he'd called her a carrot.

"Yeah. I mean, that is true. Way too different."

"You don't value the things that I value."

"No," he said. "I don't. And I'm not worried about that, carrot. Truly, I'm not. You're the one who came here. You could leave."

"I can't, though," she said. "Because I…I have to make it work."

"Why?"

"Because I do," she said. "Because I do. Okay?"

"Fine. But this is the thing. You made your little pond bed, so you have to deal with it."

"I said that I would finish out the week. I'm going to. I'm going to."

And he could've told her right then that she was wasting her time. But he didn't. Maybe it was the pile of paperwork sitting in his office, or maybe it was something else. He didn't know.

But they rode, wet and half-dressed, back to the ranch, and when they got to the barn, he got off his horse and reached his hands up, offering to help her down, too. She looked furious, but reached down, almost reflexively, and he gripped her by the waist and lifted her off.

And she just looked at him, those ferocious green eyes burning into his and making his heart speed up.

The woman got his blood pumping harder, faster.

He'd been furious, frankly still was, but he wasn't dead to the attraction that burned between them.

He didn't want to call it that. Didn't want to acknowledge it. But there was no way around it. She was gripping his forearms with her hands, and when her eyes met his this time, they were worried.

She was afraid of this.

Maybe that was why she hissed and spit quite so loud.

But he could show her. He could show her there was nothing to be afraid of. That it would feel good.

What the hell is wrong with you?

He took a step back, letting go of her.

"I think that's it for the day. You need to go home and get dried off."

"Yes," she said. "I do."

"Get."

And there was a warning in that word, and she, for the first time in his acquaintance with her, heeded it.

She didn't get in his truck; instead, she turned and took off back toward the house on her own two feet.

And he decided that he would get the horses finished, and when he came back, she'd better be gone.

She was, thank God.

He growled into the house, and Camilla was sitting there at the kitchen bar, eating a bowl of ice cream. "Well. What happened to you?" she asked.

"Nothing," he said.

"You just always roam around shirtless like you're some kind of hot cowboy calendar just waiting to break out into a photo shoot?"

He glared at his sister. "I got warm."

"You weren't by chance cavorting with the pretty redhead that's supposed to be helping you with your paperwork?"

"I was not," he said. "It isn't like that."

"But you're kind of mad about it."

"You don't know what you're talking about, Camilla, and you know what? If you would like me to have some time to cavort with women, *maybe get your ass back to school.*"

She rolled her eyes. "Levi, I don't need you to pretend that you're a monk for my benefit. I know that you're not."

"Maybe let's not talk about this. Ever."

"I don't really want to talk about the details of it, but you have to stop." She pushed her bowl of ice cream back dramatically. "You have to stop sacrificing everything just because I exist. You have to stop putting your life on pause every time I show up, because it makes me feel like you don't want me here."

"It isn't that," he said. "I love you—you know that. Camilla… You…you could literally be my daughter, and I raised you as such. There is not a person in this world…" His chest went all tight. "Nobody else is quite like you. Okay? But I don't want you to be stuck here. I don't want you to choose this life, just because you're worried about me. That I couldn't take."

"You're going to accept her help, right?"

"Yeah," he said, making his way toward the fridge.

"Why don't I believe you?"

"It isn't up to you to believe me or not. You're not the parent."

"You aren't, either," she said softly. "Not really. You're my brother. I love you. I don't even remember what it's like to have parents, Levi. So yeah, you are kind of it for me. But it isn't really fair, is it? Because you *are* my brother. And you were sixteen when I was born. You're not really old enough to be my dad. You weren't really old enough to take all this on. I don't want to be a burden."

"*I* don't want to be a burden," he said. "Don't you get that? That's the thing that I can't stand, Camilla. You can't treat me like I'm a burden just because I don't do things the way that you would."

"I'm just worried that you need help."

He looked at his sister, and he just felt...defeated. Like he might have to give in to Quinn. And he couldn't even quite remember why that was such a bad thing now.

The graves. The road.

Admitting that he needed help. Maybe it was all those things.

"I'm going to handle this the way that I see fit. Like I did the whole time I raised you. You don't get to tell me what to do. Not now. If I'm like a parent to you, then do what I tell you to do. Go back to school."

"Levi..."

"We're done with this conversation. You can sit there and have your ice cream. Let me have a beer."

She nodded slowly, and he could see that he had kind of hurt her feelings. He didn't like that. But he didn't need her being a mother hen to him. That actually felt like it undermined everything he'd sacrificed, and he didn't want to get into that. Because he didn't want to go on about his sacrifice. Because that was a shitty thing to do, and he didn't want to make her feel bad. He just...

He didn't know why he was beset by so many difficult women.

But rather than continuing to talk, he and his sister sat there, her with her ice cream and him with his beer, and after a fashion, he had to admit to himself that he wasn't all that sorry that she was there.

But he did need her to leave. Because he needed her to get on with things.

And as for him? Things would just keep clicking along like they always had.

That was all he expected. It was all he needed.

And there was nothing wrong with that.

CHAPTER TWELVE

BY THE TIME Quinn got back to the farmhouse, she was shivering. Soaking wet in her overalls, and not at all cold.

She was just…

Shaken.

The whole thing with him had been…a lot. Too much, really. He had stripped his shirt off, and she hadn't had any idea where to look, so she had looked down at her phone and decided to dig into the whole thing with the Christmas trees.

But the sight of him was emblazoned upon her soul.

Broad shoulders, perfectly sculpted pectoral muscles and a washboard-flat stomach. The dark hair on his chest had done something strange to her.

She had never considered herself a fan of a hairy chest—she had never really put that much thought into it, in all honesty—but she was a fan of his chest.

Why? Why this man that infuriated her so much? Why did he dig down in the things that she had never wanted to examine before? Why did he uproot all of this stuff inside her? Maybe it was because he irritated her that he managed to get down to the attraction.

Because he was peeling back all kinds of things that she normally kept covered up. From her temper, to her desire, so it sort of stood to reason that all of it could easily be refocused onto him.

She didn't want to be out of control. It was a horrible thing. For her, that had always been anger. Her temper would spark and off she'd go, the red haze driving her forward, making her say things, do things, she hadn't even had time to think about.

And he made her feel this horrible, layered emotion that seemed to have her in a headlock she couldn't break out of. When he'd taken his shirt off, everything in her had been thrown into a tizzy, and her go-to for that sort of thing was…being mad. But it was all awful and out of control. It was all letting someone else derail her. Steal her focus. Make her so disoriented she couldn't find her way to her goals.

Wanting to please her dad had been all-consuming. The pain when she'd failed to please him, and he'd left, just as much.

When she'd had her punch-out in ninth grade, the teacher had threatened to kick her out of the school. She'd nearly compromised something she cared about so much because she couldn't control herself.

You thought being angry made you different. But you really are kind of like your mom. Burning it all down over a man.

She rejected that, wholly.

"What the hell happened to you?"

She looked up from the driver side of her car window and saw Rory standing there, looking shocked.

"Nothing," she said, getting out of the car, which just revealed that she was soaking wet.

Of course, Fia chose that moment to come out onto the porch.

"I'm fine," she said.

Fia frowned. "You're soaking wet."

"Yes, thanks, Fia. I did notice that," she said dryly.

"What happened?" Rory asked again.

"I fell into the pond at Levi Granger's." And she tried to smile, and she tried to look like she wasn't holding back some of the truth. "It was silly. And not a big deal. I am no worse for wear, just a little bit damp."

"You *fell* into a *pond*," said Fia, her eyes narrowed. "That is suspicious."

"It isn't suspicious. I was hot, so I leaned down to try and get some water, and I fell in. It was not a big deal, and that's why I'm home early, because I am soaking wet."

She was *furious* was what she was, and addled and perturbed, and any number of other things that she didn't want to be, and *yet*.

But she didn't want to talk to her sisters about it, not even a little bit, not even at all.

Rory would begin to romanticize it. Because Rory was like that.

Fia would get angry, and overly suspicious, and would likely go over there with a switchblade and no small amount of outrage, and she didn't want that, either.

And she didn't want to expose herself. All of these burning, confusing feelings were her burden, and her burden alone.

"What really happened?" Rory asked.

"Nothing," said Quinn.

"I think you're lying, Quinn. And I don't often think you're lying."

"Fine. He dumped me in the water because I made him mad. I deserved it. I punched him. After he threw me in the water."

Rory and Fia just stared at her. "He...*threw* you in the water," Fia said.

At the same time, Rory said, "You *punched him*?"

"Yes. It's fine. I'm going back over there tomorrow, as planned. Everything is patched up."

"This sounds...like not at all what we sent you over there for," said Fia.

"I'm going to fix it," said Quinn. "I'm going to end it. Tomorrow I'm going to actually go in and tackle his office." She had decided it. Just then. Just right then. Because it seemed like the thing to do. Because it was time to stop messing around. Time to get an actual commitment out of him.

And she would prove to him that she belonged there. She would prove to him that she could help.

"I don't know. I kind of want to go punch him in the face," said Fia.

"I already hit him," said Quinn. "Levi Granger is my problem, and I am going to solve him. I'm not worried about it. So don't take on any worry for me."

"Fine," said Fia. "But if he manhandles you again, I am going to intervene. Okay?"

"Fine," said Quinn. "You're welcome to intervene then. But it's not going to be a problem."

She was going to get back to herself. To catching flies with honey, rather than vinegar. She was going to make this work.

And tomorrow she was going to show up, ready to do what she actually did well. And then he would be absolutely powerless against her. And one thing she was not going to do was think about how he looked without a shirt.

CHAPTER THIRTEEN

WHEN QUINN PUT on her white shoes the next morning, and her short floral dress, it was every bit a tactical maneuver.

She had pushed her way into working for him for the rest of the week, and she knew that it was risky to dress to work indoors.

Especially because he hadn't agreed to any of it. But she was going to prove herself, by God, and she knew she was better in the office than she was out in the field.

Though, she did feel a little bit of regret over the idea of not spending the day with him, and she didn't know what that was.

He was a compelling man.

It had to be said. Handsome, too.

She spent way too much time thinking about that. And the whole shirtless thing really had messed her brain up.

Except she just thought of his sister, and the way that she talked about him, and then the way that he smelled. Even after a long hard day's work.

Or maybe *especially* after a long hard day's work.

She frowned.

She was not going to let this get into *crush* territory. Crushes were feelings. She didn't want feelings.

It was good to acknowledge this. Good to try to take

it all and sort through it, untangle it, because yesterday had been unacceptable on all fronts. His bare chest didn't make her angry. She thought it was nice-looking. Maybe if she could admit it, put it all where it belonged and stop it all from becoming this big, rolling ball of overlarge feelings that were threatening to bowl her over, she could actually focus on the task at hand.

She was acting like she had no control over this. And okay, she wasn't choosing to find him hot. But she could choose what she did about it. She could choose how she reacted to it.

He was good-looking, yes, point established many years ago, but there were a few things to consider. He was eleven years older than her. Which was outrageous. He was more in line to be a mentor, if anything, when it came to ranch work, and definitely not anything else.

Plus, and most of all, she didn't even like the man.

Well, that wasn't true. It wasn't like she had sworn off *physical* relationships forever. It was just that she had no desire to be entangled in something serious.

She hadn't seen romance work well in her family. And yes, she was rooting for Gus and Alaina, she really was. But Alaina's situation was very specific to her. She'd been pregnant, and she had been headed a specific direction because of the decisions she made regarding that pregnancy anyway.

Quinn wanted to be established in herself before she introduced anything new into her life.

And a sexual relationship would be something new.

How did you go from thinking that he was handsome to thinking about sex?

She wasn't exactly sure how she had managed that, and she didn't especially like it. It was unnecessary.

Deeply unnecessary.

But she was committed to her task. And she didn't need to be regretful about not spending the day with him.

Not at all.

She got into the car and began the short drive over to his place.

It was funny. This reminded her more of being in school than it did anything else. Because, of course, to work at Sullivan's she didn't have to commute.

She'd lived in dorms at school, but even that had felt like more of a commute than the ranch. Especially because there were many days where they simply got up and baked in the kitchen, started working on preserves. Put things in the root cellar, wandered around the gardens.

They worked the closest to their house of any of the other families. And they had really made the place a home. Getting up in the morning and driving to a job was strange.

Not that it was a job. It was more of a forced bartering situation. Assuming he agreed to the barter. Otherwise, she was basically just offering to do the man's paperwork for nothing.

Joy.

She arrived, coffee cup firmly in hand, and walked to the door, feeling very determined and hoping the look on her face was appropriately determined, as well.

He opened the door and regarded her with suspicion. "Morning."

"Good morning."

He looked down. "I thought I put a moratorium on those shoes."

"You did. For outdoor work. But I would like to take a look at the paperwork."

"Quinn…"

"Let me see it. It's not going to kill you."

Except he had a look on his face like it might.

"You know I can't make you do anything. You really could uproot me like a carrot and drop-kick me, and we both know it." She said it very gravely, which she thought he'd like. "But you let me come around. And I know you haven't agreed to anything. I know that it's been me talking over you and running over you, and I know that you think I'm a pain in the ass. Well, I am a pain in the ass. I have always been a pain in the ass. Just ask my dad. Or maybe you could ask my dad if he didn't leave because I'm such a pain in the ass."

She had been meaning to be funny, but her own words hit her with a strange sort of sharpness, and it made her heart ache. "Whatever. The point is, I get it. I am difficult. I have always been difficult. And I know that I kind of weaseled my way into this. But I really will help you, regardless of whether or not you help me."

"Why?"

"To show you that we are committed to the community. To show you that I do just care."

"You still think you're going to get your way."

And she stopped, sloshing coffee over the top of her little white shoe. And she howled. "Yes. I want my way. Dammit, Levi. Because my way is not unreasonable."

"Quinn…" He slammed the door behind them. "Get in the truck."

"What?"

"Just get in the truck, Quinn."

And she was so stunned that she found herself turning and obeying him. Because he wasn't angry now. He sounded…something else altogether.

Deeply, gruffly resigned to something she couldn't quite figure out.

It wasn't light out yet, and it was a little bit earlier than they had taken off on any of the other days, but he did have his work boots on already. He did not, however, have his coffee, and that made her feel like her life might be in danger.

"Levi…"

"Do what I said."

So she did, climbing up into the passenger seat of the truck and closing the door behind her, buckling up.

It was weird to think that she hadn't known this man just a few short days ago. Not at all. And now she felt like she knew him, and was currently caught up in one of his moods, and yet it felt somehow like…like it wasn't wholly unfamiliar, and she wasn't sure how that worked out.

She couldn't do this math equation. It was frustrating.

He started up the engine and began to drive down the dirt road, the easement road, the one that she wanted access to.

"You need to see it. You need to see what my problem is. First of all," he said, pointing out at the fields, where the cows were grazing, "these were all soybeans. For ten fucking years, Quinn. Tied up because…because of *me*. Because I made the decision that I made. Because I…I acted in haste. So keep that in mind as we go." They kept on driving for a minute, and then he stopped, right in front of an oak tree. "Get out."

She got out of the truck and walked over to the oak

tree, where he was gesturing, but she did so slowly. And then she looked down. And saw them. The gravestones.

Belinda Granger, beloved mother. Miles Granger, beloved father.

His parents were buried here.

On the road that she wanted to use.

"Levi… I…"

"Do you see what you're asking me? You're not just asking me to give you access to my land again, which feels like giving blood, it really does. You're asking me to let strangers drive up here. This is my home. And my family. And those are my parents. And this is sacred ground. And you think that I'm just being an asshole, and I'm not." The words were heavy. It was all heavy. "And you… You're a Sullivan. And it was your dad who talked me into giving up my fields, and when I say he took advantage of me…so much money, Quinn. He took so much money from us by drawing up an unfair deal and making sure I didn't…that I didn't know."

"I'm sorry," she said, horror mounting inside. "Maybe there's a way… I'm sorry. I should just go. I…I should just go."

Her dad had *taken* money from him. It wasn't just a deal gone sour. It was theft.

From them.

And she had the nerve to ask him to help her, to help them, like he owed them.

He didn't.

They owed *him*.

She got back in the truck, her heart pounding hard, so hard it was all she could hear. Staring at her own self-ishness, her own inability to really understand that this man wasn't simply being hardheaded for the sake of it, but that there was an emotional reason behind it and she hadn't even asked, or bothered to dig deep enough, or really considered him as a human, and not just an obstacle, long enough to think that that might be the case.

No, there was something else. Something that made her feel like crying, and she couldn't quite put her finger on it. He got into the car and didn't say anything, and they drove back toward his house.

"I'm going to go home," she said.

"You don't have to leave…"

But she got out of the truck, and she went straight for her car. And he stood there leaning against the truck, watching her get in and pull out.

And then… For a reason she couldn't quite understand, she did start to cry.

She just felt…bad.

She was so persistent. So insistent. So certain that she was smart, smarter than him. He was right—that was the thing. She had been so sure that she could come in and wow him with her knowledge. And she had never once considered him as a whole person.

She had started to. Talking to his sister, seeing the way that he viewed the land, those things made her feel like he was a whole person, but she still hadn't…

She just felt terrible.

She felt like her old self. That girl who had gone around fighting people whenever they made her angry. That girl who hadn't thought of anybody but herself. Who had never considered other people when she was acting out.

And she had nearly gotten herself pulverized, punched in the face by a boy, because she had picked a fight with the wrong guy, and, you know, she had deserved it. She really felt like she did.

But it wasn't the punch to the face that had started her realizing she had to change.

It was nearly losing what she wanted to her temper.

It had changed her.

Except had it? Because she was still running around looking for an outlet for her emotions. Because she was still acting like she was right and everybody else was wrong.

Was that what had driven her dad?

She'd never considered that she could be like her dad. Because she was here and he was gone.

Because he hadn't even liked her.

But how was she different?

She'd worried only recently she might be like her mom but…

What an awful thing. To realize she was both of their daughter.

Because she had still been certain that she had the upper hand with Levi and all she'd had to do was say the right combination of words, or just keep talking at him. She really had felt like he didn't understand what she had to do was make him understand.

She'd been trying to manipulate him.

And it was like he had taken the whole script and flipped it. Just taken the world and turned it entirely upside down and shown her that she was actually the one who didn't understand.

She was the one who hadn't been listening. She was the one who needed to learn.

When he said that his land was part of him, he meant it. When he said that giving a piece of it would be costly, he was talking about something she hadn't even understood.

She had been the one who had something to learn. She was just embarrassed.

She pulled back up to the ranch house, and went inside to find Fia and Rory sitting there with their morning coffee.

"What are you doing back?" Fia asked.

"I'm an asshole."

"Well, that's quite a declaration before seven a.m.," she said.

"I just have to rethink all of this. I'm sorry. I might need to go back to the drawing board with the county or something. But I can't keep pushing him. I just can't."

"What happened?"

"I don't want to talk about it."

Quinn could still hear herself being stubborn, and suddenly she just hated the sound of her own voice.

She was just so obnoxious. How did anybody deal with her ever? She wanted to curl up in a ball, and on some level she was aware that this reaction was strong and weird, and may be related to the thing that she had said about her dad, which she had meant as a total joke, but she felt like maybe wasn't.

She had meant to say something to put him off his guard and had ended up stabbing her own self.

She was just a fool. In every way Levi Granger had outmaneuvered her. She was defeated.

Really, Quinn? You experience a little bit of emotional turmoil and you're defeated?

Maybe it was just *surrender*. Maybe that was a better word. Maybe that was fairer. She was ready to surrender.

Maybe she was running scared.

Because this made her back into childhood Quinn. The one who felt it all. She just didn't like it. It hurt.

Maybe he was just too much for her.

She put her sweats on and got back into bed. She would come up with something else. She just needed to start the day over again.

Because there was just something about this, the impact it had on her, combined with the way she felt about him, and it…

It was for the best. She needed to be done with Levi Granger. She needed to be done with that endeavor.

She could figure this out. She was smart.

But she didn't want to try to outmaneuver him. Not anymore.

CHAPTER FOURTEEN

HE SHOULD BE *grateful* that she had run off. He thought that multiple times over the course of the day, but right around lunchtime, it started to get harder to ignore the fact that he wasn't grateful at all.

He hadn't meant to hurt her.

He'd wanted her to understand, sure.

He'd felt like she wasn't listening, like she didn't understand, and hell, he had a stake in that. He hadn't explained. So he'd decided to explain.

He hadn't thought she'd run away.

In truth, he hadn't thought that she had it in her to run away. She had proved that she was such a stubborn little cuss, he had imagined that she would offer to build a wall or something to keep the grave area private.

He certainly hadn't imagined that she would look like she wanted to burst into tears. But that was exactly how she'd looked. And so he found himself doing something he'd never done before. He went down the main highway, and when he saw the sign over the big wide dirt road that read Four Corners, he turned right onto that road.

There was a sign right up front that said King's Crest. And then there was Garrett's Watch. McCloud's Landing. And a few minutes later, he saw a sign with directions to Sullivan's Point.

He turned, heading toward what he knew was Quinn's domain.

The site of the white ranch house surprised him. It was pretty and pristine, a big green yard out front, with glorious weeping willows all around. There was a large fenced-in garden with barricades tall enough to keep deer out.

It was a beautiful place. It really was its own world, though, and he could see how people got lost in it. How it became the only thing. Hell, if he lived in a place like this, he might feel that way, too.

It was like a house from another era. And when the door opened, and a pretty redhead in a long floral dress came out, he really felt like it could be another era.

"Levi Granger."

The woman tilted her head and gave him a skeptical look.

"You must be Fia Sullivan."

She smiled. "I am."

"The older sister."

"Yes."

"I came to see if Quinn is here."

Fia arched a brow. "Why exactly are you looking for my sister, Mr. Granger?"

"Because she left my place very upset this morning, and I wanted to make sure she was all right."

Fia nodded. "Yes. She came back here very upset. So you can see that I'm not altogether amenable to the idea of giving you her location. I want to know what you did to make her upset."

"I showed her my parents' graves. Which as it happens is right off the road that you want to use. So it was part of the discussion. She was unhappy when I showed it to her, and she ran away."

Fia frowned. "Oh. I'm...I'm sorry to hear about that. Maybe you and I should talk about..."

"I just want to talk to Quinn."

Fia nodded. "She's out back."

She gestured around the side of the house, and he walked to the backyard.

Where he saw her. She was sitting on a swing that hung from a long oak branch. She had on a white dress that billowed around her, her red hair loose. Her feet were bare; it felt notable in the same way her white shoes and socks did.

She was holding a book, clutching it tightly in her grip. He wondered if she was reading or just staring at the pages.

"Hey there."

She looked up from the book she was reading. He didn't know what kind of book it was. She liked to read. Just for fun.

He couldn't imagine that.

"What are you doing here?"

"I came to check on you. I didn't mean to make you that upset."

Her eyes were round, her cheeks pale. She blinked for a moment, looking at him like he might be an apparition.

"It wasn't your fault. It was my fault. I was an idiot, Levi. And I'm sorry. I was pushing you and acting like you were dumb. That's how I was acting. It was. You had reasons, and I refused to see it, and I feel badly about that. And personally responsible for what my father did. I couldn't handle it."

"So you ran away?"

"Yes. I did."

"You only know how to win or retreat?"

"I don't understand."

"If you can't hammer me to death, you don't know what else to do."

She lowered her head. "Yeah. Okay. I don't know what else to do. I don't know the right thing here. And I don't actually want to try and talk you into something you really don't want to do. I just thought you were being stubborn and... Yeah, that I was willing to push up against."

"It's a whole thing where I'm a human being that has feelings that baffles you?"

She leaned against the rope. "Yes. Because I didn't consider them."

"Am I understanding you right, that actually what makes you mad is that you don't feel like you have the moral high ground anymore?"

She wrinkled her nose. "Well. That's part of it."

"So what really bothers you is that you aren't right."

"Don't make it sound like that. That still makes it sound like I'm not very nice."

"Are you very nice?"

He shouldn't badger her. Or maybe he should. He didn't owe this little creature anything. She was the one who had come into his life and put things in relative turmoil. She was the one who had caused all of this. He had just been ranching and minding his own business. He hadn't asked.

"I want to be nice," she said. "But I just...care a lot. About everything. When I get into that space I do things sometimes that don't seem nice because all I can see is the goal." She looked up at him with glassy eyes. "I never feel mean because I know how much I care. Well, I didn't used to feel mean. I have recently."

She felt bad, and he could see it. And worst of all... he related to her. He wondered if they suffered from the same problem. Her life had been singularly devoted to proving herself. And while his had been more practical— he had to do a good job by his siblings—it had hacked limbs off his personal development.

He wondered if her own narrow focus had done the same to her. She'd gone away to college, yes, and she clung to that now like it validated her. So whatever she said about that, and surfers, he wondered if she'd actually been social there at all. Or if her singular mission statement had taken over all of it.

He was pretty sure he could guess.

"I care about the ranch," she said softly. "I... It has felt easier than caring about other things for a long time, and I feel like my degree is what makes me...important."

"I don't care about your degree, carrot."

"I know you don't. It's why you make me so mad. If my degree doesn't matter to you, then..."

"Here's the deal," he said, wondering why the hell he felt compassion for her. "If a degree is all that mattered to me, I'd have to discount my own experiences, right?"

"I suppose."

"And I'm not doing that. The degree isn't what makes me think you're smart. It's what I've seen you do. It's the amount of care I've seen from you as far as the land goes. That's what matters to me. Come back to the ranch. Take a look at the paperwork."

"But you said..."

"I have real reservations, Quinn. I was going to tell

you unequivocally *no*. Because of the graves, yes. Because of your father, yes. But also because I'm a control freak. I just got all my control back."

She nodded, slowly. "I'm not asking for any control. I do promise you that. Everything is still going to be up to you, and if there's too much traffic, we'll work something else out."

"Come back and look at the paperwork."

"Okay."

She stood up, and he couldn't help but notice the way the diaphanous fabric molded to her figure. She was just the prettiest thing.

She paused and slipped some sandals on.

He found he missed the socks.

That thought didn't belong in this moment. That thought didn't belong in his head. But it was there all the same.

He resented her for that, too.

Because he hadn't asked her to come to his ranch.

He hadn't asked her to come into his life.

He'd said his piece at the meeting in Four Corners and that should have been it. But it wasn't.

And here he was, inviting her right back after she had run away. He wasn't really certain what the logic was behind that. He was a little afraid there was no logic behind it.

Except he did have that pile of paperwork. And the idea of doing it really did bother him.

And he really did need Camilla to go back to school.

She walked back to the truck with him.

"I'll give you a ride over there," he said.

"Are you sure?"

"Yes, I'm sure. Come on."

As they were getting into the truck, Fia came back out on the front porch.

"I'm fine," Quinn called.

"Good," said Fia. "And you're going back to the ranch?"

"Yes," they both confirmed.

"Okay." Fia narrowed her eyes, and he could see the question there. Could see that Fia was wondering about ulterior motives.

He didn't have any.

He ignored the tightening of his gut when he looked at Quinn. He didn't.

Quinn basically melted into the seat when they got back on the road.

And he could only stare at her. She was a funny little thing. All wound up and passionate all the time. And that moment of not feeling certainty had really done something to her.

She was fascinating. And he couldn't recall ever being fascinated by another person before.

"Thanks for giving me the chance to do this," she said. "After everything. After I was a dick to you."

He laughed. "Yeah. You were."

"You were playing a game with me, though."

"I admit it."

"Yeah. I know you did. I'm just saying."

"You're just justifying," he said.

"Maybe."

"Quinn Sullivan, you are kind of a brat."

She huffed a laugh. "Not the first time I've heard that, oddly."

And then he remembered what she'd said about her

dad, and he knew a moment's guilt, which was sort of a novelty.

"If your dad left because you are the way you are, he's a dick. Just so we're clear."

"I am totally aware that my dad is a dick," said Quinn.

"I mean, we all are. I just wanted to make sure I said it. My dad loved us, loved my mom, loved this land until it put him into the ground. Do you understand that? He loved my mother so much that when she died, his heart was never the same again. He literally died of a broken heart. And we were a ragtag group of imperfect people. He loved us like that anyway. He's still here, even though he's gone, you know? Because that's how much he loved us. That's how much he loved this place. So yeah, if your dad could leave because you are a stubborn cuss, he's no kind of man, in my opinion. And definitely no kind of father."

He looked over at her and saw that she was staring at him. She had the oddest look on her face. Her expression sharpened and incredulous.

"What? Has anyone ever said that to you before?"

"No. Maybe because I never said to anybody what I said to you."

"Why did you say it?"

"I don't know."

He was happy enough to leave it there. Because he could well understand saying and doing things you couldn't explain. He felt like all the last few days were that for him. Why the hell he had indulged her for even five seconds was kind of beyond him. Not something he could wholly grasp. And then they pulled up to the house, and he was saved from his own thoughts.

They opened the doors at the same time and got out, and she followed him up to the house.

"Do I need to take my shoes off?" she asked, looking down at the pile of shoes by the door.

"No. You know, I think Jessie still has shoes there. And Dylan, for that matter. He hasn't been home since Christmas."

His younger brother was a whole thing. Loud and brash and filled with bravado. Which he supposed wasn't actually bravado, since he went out and risked his life every day in service of the country.

Dylan had definitely changed in the years since he joined the military. He had been idealistic at first. And had behaved like he thought he was bulletproof. And every year, there'd been a little less of both those things. Every year, it had become more and more obvious that he had seen things. That he questioned things.

But Levi still respected the hell out of what his brother was doing. Even while it terrified him.

"That's just…a dumping ground, then?"

"Yeah. You know, the house was new and we thought maybe we'd keep it all nice, but we did have too much living to do in here."

"Right. Has Camilla gone back to school yet?"

"Not yet. She has until the end of the week. But she needs to get gone. And frankly, having you up here in the office will go a long way in getting her there."

"I really will just help."

"Why?"

"We've gotten to know each other, and now I just kind of want to. What you did for your siblings is a big deal. I want your sister to go finish college. I don't want her to just stay here."

"Like me, you mean?"

He waited a beat, and saw as shame flooded her cheeks. "That isn't what I meant. It's not."

"It's okay. You can say it. You think an education is necessary for someone to be qualified."

"No, that's not it. I am afraid to have…nothing to fall back on. No credentials. My dad left and my mom fell apart. I wanted to make sure that I was more than that. More than a marriage or a vague connection to something. That I had something I could take with me wherever I went. And I didn't know how else to make sure of it. I wanted to make sure that I was more than what I became when my dad left. Specifically."

"And what was that?" Maybe he shouldn't be curious about that, but he was.

Curious about what Brian had done to her.

"*Angry.* So angry that I thought I was going to implode from it. So angry that I thought I'd explode. And I nearly did, quite a few times. I was just running around venting all of it on other people, and it wasn't fair. I was so mean. Just so toxic, all because of him. And I needed there to be more to me than that. I needed something that made me…that proved to me that I was qualified, I guess. Because why? When you lose the foundation of that, you do question everything."

He nodded slowly. "You know, I lost my parents, too, but in a way that made me feel more certain that this was where I needed to be. They died working this land. And I know that I want to do the same."

"Maybe the difference is the way they left it. Like you said, your dad died of a broken heart. That was how much he didn't want to lose what he had. My dad ran from his life. He chose to leave it. To leave us. All

I could see were broken dreams, and I never wanted to be in that space. Where everything that I worked for didn't matter anymore because of the decisions of somebody else. I wanted to know why I did what I did. Why I lived the life I lived. I wanted to know why I chose the life I chose.

"It was really important to me. To know that. And I do now. I went and I learned all about ranching, and I made my choice, not my birthright. And that changed things for me. It did. I'm not sure if it makes any sense to you. But I promise you it isn't about looking down on you still being here. It's about understanding why sometimes you need to make sure that you know why you ended up where you did. So that a life doesn't choose you, but you choose it."

They were such strange words to him, because he'd never had that opportunity. He'd never even really thought about it. His life was his birthright. And that was it.

And really, in many ways it was a good thing, because what the hell would he have had if not for this land? If not for this land, Quinn would probably be working in a high-rise office building somewhere. She would probably be a city girl. Or not. But she had an array of options in front of her. Because she had gone to school, and she had gotten a degree. She had done well for herself. He was just a guy who could barely read. He would probably be doing work that was twice as hard for half the pay if he didn't have this land.

Things had to be rough for him. That was just the honest truth.

He didn't feel burdened by this land. It was a gift to him.

But he wondered, if the land wasn't there for Quinn, how different her life would be.

"Come on upstairs." They started up the stairs, and he led her down the hardwood-floor hallway, to the office door. And he felt a little ashamed, actually. The idea of showing her this place where he worked, which was an absolute disaster and was probably much worse off than she could ever imagine, made him hesitate.

It reminded him of school, quite frankly. He didn't like it.

But he opened up the door anyway.

"Come on in."

There were papers everywhere, and he quickly moved to the computer, leaned over and turned off the accessibility feature that he always used. He didn't want to start talking to her.

There was admitting that he was messing with her, and kind of exposing the way that he felt about her degree snobbery, and then there was letting her in on the extent of his own issues, and he didn't let anybody in on that.

"Okay, Quinn. Here it is."

CHAPTER FIFTEEN

QUINN WAS STILL feeling rattled by everything that had happened in the last few hours, and now she was looking at his desk, which was…a mess.

"What's the most pressing issue?"

"Just look at the budget files and the taxes on the computer. Nothing else."

"I'm sure that I can figure it out. You can leave me to it. You can go back to your work."

"Okay, then." He turned, and she had a feeling that leaving her here was costing him, but she also had a feeling that he wanted to be here even less.

"It'll be fine," she said.

She started going through everything, and there weren't a lot of handwritten records. There were a lot of things that were typed and printed. None of the typing had any punctuation, and he didn't use capital letters. There were a couple of correspondences that had pretty atrocious grammar, considering that the computer would take care of most of that for you. Levi spoke fluidly, but that wasn't how he wrote, that was for sure. She frowned as she looked at a communication with the shipping company where he had made a few homonym errors.

He was behind. On everything to do with paperwork, much more so than he had let on. There were a lot of invoices that weren't completed. And it wasn't even him being behind on making payments; it was *him* needing to collect payments, for meat that had already been shipped and sold.

It was not comprehensively put together, and it was definitely hurting him and his bottom line.

She wondered if he even knew at this point how far behind he was, and what all he had missed.

She started working her way through accounts, and then stopped to take a break, to do a little bit of research on Christmas tree farms and what large companies might be looking to contract out for the next few years. And if not contract out, then would take inventory on from a ranch. Because that would be the best, she figured. Somebody who would agree to buy the trees, in the way that he sold the cows. She could see there might be a little bit of convenience in doing the contracting, because then he wouldn't have to invoice and manage sales individually, but she also knew that he was particular about maintaining rights to the land, and she could understand that.

She looked over at a file cabinet. He'd said to stick to the computer but…well, there was more to do. And wouldn't it be helpful to keep on organizing?

She opened up the cabinet and laughed, because the files were just shoved inside in a stack. She moved one and frowned at a Post-it note on the front of it. Not what it said, but the writing. There was a phone number, she was pretty sure that's what it was, and the fives were backward. And then there was a name, with a backward *J* and *D*. Her stomach squeezed tightly. He had obvious hallmarks of someone with dyslexia. She remembered when she had brought the binder, and he hadn't actually read it. She thought he was being mean, but…

She felt uncomfortable, worse even than she had earlier, and that was saying something. Because she had been just so snotty to him, and she had made so many assumptions.

This was clearly a struggle for him, more than just not wanting to do it, which was what he pretended.

She sighed and pinched the bridge of her nose, and started putting different types of papers into categories.

She hadn't even realized that four hours had gone by until he opened the door. "Hey. You hungry?"

"Yes," she said.

"My sister is bringing a pizza from Mapleton. We do pizza a lot, even though it's a big drive to get one."

"Oh, I'd love that. It's been forever since I've had takeout. Well, I had it more with you than I have for ages. That was my favorite thing about being in school, actually, the ease with which we could order food. So different than here."

"I bet," he said. He looked around the room. "You survived it."

"Yeah. It's… We should come up with the system," she said.

If he wanted to tell her he was dyslexic, he would. And he hadn't. So he clearly didn't want to talk about it. So it probably wasn't the right thing to do to bring it up. Anyway, maybe she was wrong.

Maybe he was just careless, but nothing about him seemed careless.

She walked out of the office slowly, and brushed past him closer than she meant to. She looked up at him, and she was startled yet again by the clarity of those blue eyes.

He was unknowable. She felt in so many ways like

she had gotten to know him in the last few days—that was why the whole thing with his parents had affected her so deeply. She felt like she was wrapped around him somehow. Maybe because their fates were tied together, because his ranch was now connected with the success of hers—even if it wasn't entirely fair of her to think of it that way because he hadn't agreed to anything and none of this was his fault—or what, she couldn't say. But she also felt like she hadn't even begun to scratch the surface of who he was, and more than that, she had never really felt the desire to know another person.

She had grown up with her sisters, and they had always been her best friends. Growing up on Four Corners, there was a rotating cycle of people who came and went, and there was really no point bothering to get to know them all that well. And then there were the original four families. The ones that were always there. And they were their own thing. She had never particularly clicked with any of them.

That was just the truth of it.

At school, she hadn't really bothered to get to know anyone well because she had been so busy with school. That was what she told herself.

Was that really true? Was she busy with school or did she avoid getting to know people?

Did it all seem pointless because it always felt like they would leave? Except for her sisters, who were the only ones that she could trust?

That was such a weird realization to have standing in his house, about to have pizza with him and his sister. She didn't know what it was about him that made her reflect on these kinds of things. Except maybe it was that he was different. A new person. And one that in-

trigued her in a way that no one else really had before.
Part of her wanted to run away from that, and part of her
wanted to lean in to it because it was just so interesting.

She liked to learn, after all. And this was an aca-
demically rigorous exercise. At least, it was a new experience.

Maybe that was all it was.

Except it felt different from that. She felt different
from that.

"I mean, if you can. I would be thrilled with it."

"I would have to know what works for you."

He nodded. "I'll have to get back to you on that."

"Levi, if you need some kind of particular sort of
system…"

"What exactly…?"

"I'm back."

Just then, Camilla came into the house, holding a
pizza.

Quinn felt startled by the intrusion, like somebody
had come in and popped a bubble that they were standing in. She had no clue why it felt so jarring. Why she
felt vaguely embarrassed.

"It's nice to see you again, Quinn," said Camilla.

"You, too," she said, still feeling slightly edgy and
electrified.

"I hope you were helping him with his admin."

"I was," she said.

She wondered if Camilla knew how bad it actually
was.

"Thank you. It makes me feel a lot better to know
that he has some oversight."

"I'm right here," he said.

"I know," said Camilla, smiling at him all bright and

sunny, and it amused Quinn because Levi was so very not bright and sunny. She was glad that he had his sister in his life. She wanted to meet his other siblings. She pushed back hard against that impulse. Because it was just so out of the blue. And had absolutely nothing to do with any of this.

Why they were here, why she was helping.

Except she wasn't really helping him just to get something in return anymore, was she?

Whatever. She was getting pizza for dinner. If that was all the payment she got, it was all the payment she got, and maybe it would do something to make up for what an asshole she'd been the past few days.

"This is from Mapleton," Camilla said, plunking the pizza down in the middle of the table. "It's a newer place. It's really good."

"It's pizza," said Levi. "It is the safest food on the planet. Even bad pizza is edible."

Camilla wrinkled her nose. "I don't know about that. I remember when you tried to make pizza one time when you were maybe... I don't know. I was probably like six? That was bad. I don't know how you did it, but I think you burned the olives."

"You ungrateful little weasel."

"So calling people animal names is just something that you do?" Quinn asked.

Camilla cackled. "Have you been on the receiving end of his insults?"

"I have. He called me a carrot."

"Levi used to try to not swear when we were little, so he got really creative with the stuff he would say. Funny. Until he uses it on you."

That was like peeling back another layer on him.

She sort of wished it wasn't happening. Because she found all the top layers attractive—the way he looked, the way he moved. Seeing him as a whole person made it all so much harder.

But there was no point in getting mired in questioning it. She was here for dinner, so she might as well just…be here for dinner.

"I have noticed he's very good at that."

"Yeah. Well. Hopefully he's not insulting you too much, since you're helping him and all."

"I'm not being altruistic, so don't go thinking that I'm just doing him a favor."

"Yeah. I know. Is he being reasonable?"

"I'm right here," he said. "And I kind of resent being talked about like I'm not."

"Welcome to my world," said Camilla. "I'm only the youngest in this family. That's basically my entire life. You people talking about what I want or should want while I'm right there."

"Yeah. Well. Shouldn't have been born last."

"I had to be born last. Our mother died so quickly after me, there was no chance to get another one in."

Quinn was a little taken off guard by the gallows humor, but Levi laughed. "Fair enough, Cam. Fair enough."

He took a stack of paper plates out of the cabinet and set them on the counter, and she felt like she was getting a small window into how he had done things when his siblings were at home. Paper plates, pizza. And he had tried to learn to cook pizza, but was apparently very bad at it. And suddenly she was curious.

"Can you cook?"

"Yes," he said. "I would never have survived if I couldn't."

"He learned eventually," said Camilla.

"Yeah. The casserole brigade was around most nights before I did."

Suddenly, he got a strange expression on his face, his jaw going tight. He looked away. She couldn't read that moment, and Camilla hadn't noticed it.

It was weird, to feel this companionable with him. Especially after the fight this morning. And after being dumped in the pond yesterday.

But she wanted to talk to him about the extent of the issues in the office. And the ways in which she could maybe help him organize if she understood exactly what his issues were.

But she didn't want to bring it up in front of his sister, either.

They were sweet together. And it was strange, to see him be sweet. Maybe *sweet* was the wrong word, because there was a roughness to him no matter what.

But he had learned to cook for her.

For all of his siblings.

She was resisting this, him becoming more of a three-dimensional human. Especially one with deep, hard struggles.

Because it just made her feel even worse. This morning, she had felt overwhelmed by the unveiling of his parents' graves. And then this evening, she kept thinking of all the times she had shoved text in his face, and the way that she had acted about college degrees.

Of course he felt like she was belittling him. This was a deep wound. Something that had undoubtedly colored his whole life. Made things difficult for him.

Made him feel like less.

When he had said that he skipped school, she could see why now.

It wasn't about different values; it was about different strengths.

And she had been awful to assume the things that she had.

"Well," said Camilla, "I think I'm going to go pack, since I'll be leaving tomorrow afternoon. I have to drive all the way back to Santa Clara. I appreciate you being here, Quinn. Even if Levi won't say it, I will."

"It's not a problem. I mean, it isn't a burden. It hasn't been."

Levi didn't say anything.

Camilla waved and then walked out of the room, leaving the two of them alone in the kitchen.

But suddenly, the room felt too small, and she looked out the back window. "You have a firepit out there, don't you?"

She had noticed it when it was still light outside.

"Yeah," he said.

"Can I see?"

"Sure," he said.

If he thought it was strange, he didn't say.

She was…searching for the right words. Because she knew that he was going to be angry that she had deviated from her exact task. Because it was what had exposed the dyslexia. He knew that he had it. He must.

But what if he didn't?

She swallowed hard when they got outside. "This is pretty," she said, looking around the area, all done with pavers and with seating everywhere. "I bet when everybody's home it's really fun."

"Yeah," he said.

She wondered if anybody really understood. She hadn't, until today, somehow.

The weight that he carried. The way that he clearly wanted to be left alone to do his own thing, but how he was so enmeshed in the lives of all these other people, and solitary and not quite whole without them.

It must be awful.

She imagined it was what being a parent was like. Well, if you were a functional parent, and not like hers.

And she wanted to help him. Even though she knew she'd make him mad. She wanted to…to do something. To take care of him, maybe. It was the strangest, biggest burning shock of emotion she'd ever experienced. It was a callback to old Quinn.

To the one who had wanted to do well so badly, she'd insisted on herself. Followed her dad around day in, day out, chattering, badgering him.

Quinn, not today. The constant chattering is too damned annoying.

And the next day he'd left.

She knew there was a cost to this, and she still couldn't help herself.

But you don't love Levi. You just want to help. So you can handle it.

"I just… I needed to say something," she said.

He looked at her, his expression sharp.

"What?"

"I went through some of your files, and I know that wasn't really on the table. But I noticed some things."

"Quinn, I didn't tell you to look through it. It's because I didn't want to talk about it."

"I want to help you."

And maybe she was blowing up the whole thing.

The whole easement and everything. But it wasn't just about that, not now.

"I wanted to talk to you about the... You're dyslexic, right?"

"Quinn, I said I didn't want to talk about it."

"There are systems. For people with dyslexia. And there are ways that..."

"Are you going to stand there and tell me about my own brain? You must think I am really stupid, Quinn Sullivan, if you think that I need you to sort out what I have known about myself for most of my life. How do you think I've gotten this far?"

"Levi, I am not insulting you. It's just that there are some things in the office that could be fine-tuned."

"Yeah. Well, great. Well identified. I'm dyslexic. I can't read. Not very well. How does that make you feel? That make you feel smart? Does it make you feel like you have something to teach me? Is this like some movie where you come in and transform the lives of people who are dumber than yourself?"

"You are not dumb, and I don't think that you are. I never said that you were. I already told you it's...it's my own insecurity that makes me cling to the degree. It's...it's not about you."

"But you value that degree, don't you? I don't know a whole hell of a lot of anything about book learning, do I? I know you can see that I don't. I never will. I'm never going to read a book for fun, Quinn. I'm never going to read a book. It's too fucking hard. I can't do it. You shoving that shit in my face the other day on your phone... I couldn't read it. I couldn't read it. Not that I don't want to. I can't."

He was angry.

She'd known he would be, but she'd lied to herself so well. She'd told herself she could handle it.

Now she felt bad. Like when he'd shown her his parents' graves. She was digging into things that she knew he had put a fence around. But she was being understanding, and she really couldn't understand why it was setting him off like this. Surely the dyslexia wasn't anything to be ashamed of. It explained things. It made her understand.

She didn't understand why he should be so mad that she knew.

Because he's proud. And you're stepping all over it. This is why he didn't want help to begin with. This is why...

"This hurts you, doesn't it? Knowing this about me. Because I'll never be anything you value, and you still want me."

That shook her. Jolted her out of her thoughts. "Excuse me?"

"You want me, even knowing that I am an illiterate idiot. You were looking at me that day down by the pond. You couldn't stop yourself—that was why you had to so determinedly stare at anything else. Because even knowing that I am basically a caveman, you burn for me. Not those asshole college boys that you went to school with. Me. Because you know that I might not know how to read, but I could show you a damned good time. I don't have to be smart to know how to find exactly where you want me to touch you."

She started to shake, that familiar adrenaline from sparring with him rising up inside her, but more. It was always more. With him, always.

That shameful desire that she felt burning for him

in her gut, but she wasn't ashamed for the reason that he thought.

You're not ashamed. You're afraid.

Yeah. She was terrified. Terrified of this man, all six-foot-two muscled cowboy, furious and filled with the kind of sexual promise that she had never wanted to desire quite this badly. But she did. Hell, she really did.

And they could never be anything. Because she didn't want anything, and neither did he. Not because she was smart and he was dumb, or whatever narrative he thought lived inside her.

But it was just impossible. They didn't like each other, let alone…

But he was calling it out. Identifying it. Saying exactly what it was, and she wished to hell that he wouldn't.

She really wished that he wouldn't.

Because it made her feel… It made her feel…

"Levi, that is not what I think, and it is not… It's not what I think."

"I think on some level it is. Because it excites you, doesn't it? The idea of slumming it with me. And, you know, maybe you're not totally wrong. I'll be way better than any of those guys ever were. Because I don't need to think. I have instincts. We have chemistry."

"No," she said. "It doesn't make sense."

"Yeah, I know, because I should be a big turnoff for you, shouldn't I?"

"Stop it," she said. "Stop trying to make it seem like I'm a snob, or like I disdain you. I don't. You know I don't. I'm not my father and you know that, but you want me to keep my distance right now and I'm not sure why. But don't make it about me when it's actually about you. When I saw all that up there, I realized how hard you work to do as well as you do and…"

"You are a condescending, mousy little carrot," he said. "And why the hell I want to kiss you, I don't know. I'm sick of it. I'm sick of you, and I'm sick of this. Walk away right now."

"No," she said, standing there, knowing that she was tempting him. Knowing that she was pushing it, and not caring. "I'm not walking away."

Fourteen-year-old Quinn, whose crush had been abandoned so long ago in an act of self-protection, cheered.

"Then on your head be it, little carrot."

CHAPTER SIXTEEN

HE COULDN'T SEE STRAIGHT, couldn't think straight. He knew that he was acting like a wounded animal backed into a corner, and he knew he wasn't being fair. He had wanted to make her feel threatened the same way that he did, but she wasn't backing down. Instead, she was standing there, staring at him with clear green eyes, breathing hard and heavy and making him feel like there was no other option.

He couldn't think. He couldn't do anything but feel. And what he felt was rage. Rage and a deep, calling need that he had never felt before.

Because there had never been a specific woman. Not for him.

There had been generic desire and sex, the satisfaction of a few hours well spent in a stranger's arms.

But he had never wanted any one person specifically, and he had sworn to himself that he would leave her alone for a variety of reasons, all of which were valid, all of which were good.

But she had pulled the pin in the grenade that was just barely holding the two of them back.

It was an explosion now, and he didn't know what the hell he was supposed to do about it. Didn't know if he wanted to do anything about it. Hell, he knew that he didn't. What he wanted right now was her.

What he wanted was to prove that he was better at something.

He hated that. Hated that all the shame still lived inside him, that he hadn't really worked it all out.

Hated that he still felt broken and wrong, and frankly, dumb sometimes.

Especially when compared with her.

Especially when he tried to do things that were beyond him.

But this wasn't beyond him.

And so he closed the distance between them and wrapped his arm around her waist, and finally, it wasn't just to hold her in a pond or lift her up onto a horse. Finally, it was so he could do this.

He lowered his head and pressed his lips to hers, and she was frozen, immobile for a second, before she wrapped her arms around his neck and started to kiss him back.

Her movements were tentative at first, hesitant, but they were sweet. So damned sweet.

And this was the question in her eyes answered, this was the provocation down by the pond fulfilled.

It had been nothing but this. This heightened, angry awareness that was trying to keep them away from this. Trying, and failing. Because he had told himself that he wasn't going to do this. He had told himself that he wasn't going to run roughshod over all of her sweet, young beauty.

He had told himself he didn't even like her, and honest to God, he didn't. But that wasn't what made him angry. Her hair was loose, and he took advantage of that, letting his fingers sink into the silky strands as he cradled her face and kissed her harder. Deeper.

She did not pull away. In fact, she gripped his T-shirt, arching her body against his and whimpering as the kiss went on and on. As he parted her lips and let his tongue slide against hers. The little sound she made was more like a whimper, and for some reason, he thought of her socks.

Those little white socks.

He was so hard he thought he was going to die from it, and he couldn't recall feeling that way before.

He could remember the first time he'd gone out on his own to find a lover, the kids all packed away at sleepovers, and the sense of freedom giving him a little bit of a high.

But this wasn't about the act of sex, which he was familiar enough with. It was about Quinn.

It was just about Quinn.

He backed her up against the side of the house, pressing his body hard up against hers and moving his palms over her curves. He brought his hand up to cup her breasts, and she gasped, arching hard into him, filling his hand with her.

Then he slid his thumb over her nipple, and she wiggled against him, and he knew that she must be able to feel the obvious evidence of his desire for her pressed right up against her.

She pulled away from him, breathing hard, and he couldn't figure out if she was trying to angle her body closer to him, or if she was trying to escape, so he released his hold on her.

"I…" She was panting hard. "You don't like me."

"No, carrot, I can't say that I really do."

"Why did you kiss me?"

"The same reason you kissed me. You might not like me, but you want me. You can't help yourself."

She didn't look away. Instead, she met his gaze. Full-on and clear. "I don't think that you're stupid. I'm not ashamed of being attracted to you—I just don't understand it. I don't understand how I can want somebody that I can't say two words to without making them *furious*."

"Maybe that's what it is. Maybe it's the spark."

It was as true as anything, probably. At least as he figured. "I am sorry," she said. "About invading your privacy. I didn't mean to do that. Well, I did. But I didn't mean to upset you."

He breathed out hard. "You sure you don't just want to keep kissing?"

She laughed, a kind of frantic, helpless-sounding laugh. "Sure. The kissing is nice. But I can't keep kissing you as long as you think I'm trying to hurt you. Or that I look down on you. It was never about you. It's about me. I had to make myself feel important because otherwise I just feel…" Her chest hitched, a cross between a sigh and a sob. "I must not matter that much. That's what I feel. My dad might have sucked, but he was also the one person I wanted to please most in the world. I didn't have friends because I wanted to make him proud on the ranch and I worked the land instead of playing with other kids. And he…he chose a new life over me. A lover over me. He…he made me feel like I didn't matter and I had to make myself matter, Levi. I had to prove I was good with ranching, and I'm never going to be the strongest, am I? So I had to find a way to convince myself I was the smartest. It was never looking down on you. I look down on me."

"Don't hurt yourself," he said, feeling heavy with

tension, and with some of his own shame. Because he had been hard on her. He had assumed the worst to try to push her away. And he didn't even think he believed any of it. Because absolutely nothing that she had said to him today had been condescending. Absolutely nothing that she had said had been in that vein. She had not acted like he was less because of the dyslexia. He had simply felt it.

And he had felt it because he didn't know how to talk about it. He didn't know how to be vulnerable about it.

He hated being vulnerable more than anything, so even if he did know how to be vulnerable about it, he didn't want to be. Not with her, not with anybody.

Because what he'd said to her the other day was true.

Vulnerability led straight to victimhood.

Because it let people get in. It let them get under your skin. He would be damned if he ever did that again.

And then there was the sole carrot.

Up in his grill, up in his life, who drove him absolutely crazy… And maybe that was the key.

Because he didn't feel especially vulnerable to her. She wasn't somebody who was tangled up in his life. So why not share with her? Why not? He wanted to kiss her. He wanted to dump her in a pond. He wanted to drag her upstairs and take her to bed, even though Camilla was here.

He wanted her.

And that could never be anything more than desire, because he just didn't do anything deeper than that, and he never would.

The truth was, he didn't have it in him. He didn't want to have it in him.

He wanted his freedom.

And maybe that was part of the problem. He had only ever experienced personal affairs when he was young. When he didn't understand that sex didn't have to be meaningful or connected. That it didn't have to matter.

He had only ever signed a contract for the use of his land back when he'd been naive.

He wasn't naive anymore, and he wasn't inexperienced.

And he had first realized that he had a problem with letters and numbers in school, back when he'd been a kid, and all the teachers had given him a very specific vocabulary to deal with that. *Lazy. Lazy* was the big one. *No drive. Doesn't apply himself.*

So that was what he believed.

And in the years since, he had clawed his way to a new understanding of all of those things.

None of these things with Quinn needed to be personal. And none of them needed to make him feel bad about himself.

Not at all.

"I'm dyslexic. I learned that a few years ago. I know it's stupid, but I didn't know... For a while, I didn't know there were names for all the things wrong with me. I just thought I wasn't smart."

"Levi, I am so sorry."

"Don't *pity* me."

"No, I didn't mean that I was sorry for you—I'm sorry for me. I'm really sorry that I didn't listen to you. And that I judged you. And that I thought somehow going to school for four years meant that I was smarter than you. When you have been running this place since you were eighteen years old, and I don't know very many people who would've had the inbuilt instinct and ability to do that. You are clearly incredibly smart. Incredibly strong."

"Well, don't go crazy with the compliments. I signed a contract that I couldn't read, because I listened to the guy who was talking to me. Not only did I not do a lot of digging, I let my skimming and my own reading comprehension be the guide to signing a ten-year lease for my field. It was stupid. I knew my own limitations, but because I wasn't willing to ask for anyone's help, because I wasn't willing to expose myself, I got myself into a heap of trouble. I worked hard after that. To never be dependent again, while at the same time understanding what my own limits were. That's why I don't find deals anymore, Quinn. I just… I made a big mess out of it. And I never wanted to go through something like that again."

"Of course you didn't," she said.

She did look sorry then.

And he didn't want her to look sorry. He wanted her eyes to be full of desire again. He wanted her to want him.

He really wanted her.

"I think I might also have sequencing disorder. And also maybe some dyscalculia. Basically, the grab bag of learning disabilities. And you have no idea how pissed off that makes me. I thought my whole life that I just didn't want to work hard at school. All these things that other kids could just do easily, and I knew I couldn't do them. I knew it was harder for me. My parents were consumed with my mom's illness. In hindsight, I think my dad had some of my same issues, so he didn't really care about school. The teachers would tell him I didn't apply myself, but my dad saw a hard worker, so he thought they were liars. At school I got told I wasn't trying. I knew that I wasn't lazy when it came to doing real work. Work on the ranch. I wanted to get away and go to the rodeo, where all that would matter was how good I was on the back of a horse. Where nobody would give a shit whether or not I could read a crusty old novel about a man on a fishing boat."

"*The Old Man and the Sea*?"

"*Moby Dick*."

She wrinkled her nose. "Men really do like to write about travails on the water, don't they?"

He laughed. "I guess so. And when you showed up, it seemed like a game at first to go ahead and play down to what I knew you thought. But eventually…"

"Eventually it got old."

He nodded slowly. "Eventually. Apparently I don't possess the ability to toy with you indefinitely."

"Don't take this the wrong way," she said. "But especially as I've gotten to know you, I really wouldn't have assumed you struggled with that. Because of the way you talk."

"Audiobooks," he said. "Nothing has ever made me feel more smug than the ease of access that you have to all kinds of information on audio nowadays. And video, too. Videos online were how I found out about the different learning disabilities I probably had, how I figured out how to set up my computers so that I can do most of it through voice. And have it read things to me. It isn't that I *can't* read. I can. But it takes a hell of a long time, and a lot of times I don't retain some of the things. It's just easier to have a little bit of help, and to not turn everything into a mission."

"I definitely understand that."

She was silent for a long moment. "Why didn't you want me to know?"

He didn't have a ready answer for that. Not really. Except...

"Remember what I said to you about vulnerability?"

"You don't want anyone to use it against you."

He shook his head. "No. And... Quinn, I learned a long time ago I had to take care of myself, and the people around me. I can't be vulnerable. I have to be in charge. In control. For Dylan, Jessie and Camilla. At least if people think I'm dumb, I'm in control of that. Because I know I'm not dumb. So I can do things like I did with you. I played with you. It was easy enough to do. When someone's underestimating you, it's pretty easy."

"Yeah," she said. "I get that. And also...I bet me being a Sullivan..."

"At first," he said. "But it doesn't now. So now you know."

"I meant what I said. If you still don't want to do the easement, I am more than willing to look at the paperwork anyway."

And he looked at Quinn, and he realized that he was just... He wanted to give her an award. For being the stubborn little cuss that she was. For sticking it out through all of the different tantrums he had at her, and for going right at him and having several tantrums right back.

She was the only person that he had ever told about the dyslexia. She was the only woman that he had ever kissed in this house. She was something, whether he wanted her to be or not.

"The easement is yours," he said. "Because I do trust

you, Quinn. Even if I don't particularly like you all the time."

He was lying. He did like her.

He liked her a whole lot.

She nodded slowly. "Right. Well. I appreciate it."

"You have to finish working for me this week."

"I will. And I'll work on the papers, too… I…" And then she leaned forward, and curved her hand around the back of his neck, and kissed him. It was deep and lingering, and he returned it, desperate for more of her.

He wasn't familiar with this feeling. With it feeling so necessary to have a particular woman.

To have her.

But he wanted her. Quinn Sullivan. Lord Almighty.

It was a different kind of want. Something that had more to do with the fire in his blood than the purely physical.

Something indescribable, incalculable.

And not just because he had difficulties with math.

But because it was part of a great universal mystery.

Chemistry.

He'd never taken chemistry.

Maybe that was it.

Maybe she had.

Maybe she understood it better than he did. But when they parted, he could see by the confusion in her eyes that she didn't.

"I'll be back tomorrow."

"Yeah. All right."

And tomorrow Camilla wouldn't be here. Tomorrow, he would be back to the kind of freedom that he had always wanted.

Tomorrow, he would be alone with Quinn Sullivan.

And he already knew what was going to happen.

He didn't say anything, though, and neither did she.

She gave him a slight smile, then moved away from him. "See you tomorrow."

"See you tomorrow. I'll share my coffee with you, Quinn."

She nodded.

And then she went back inside, closing the door behind her.

He leaned back against the house and let out a long, slow breath. He tried to walk himself slowly through all of this, every step of the way from the moment she had first appeared at his house to now, and he gave up. Because everything was just an explosion.

And he was going to keep on standing in the rubble.

Regardless of the consequences.

CHAPTER SEVENTEEN

IT WAS GETTING DARK, more and more stars peppering the sky as it turned from blush pink to purple to midnight blue.

And Quinn just sat there in her car, in the middle of the dirt road that was supposed to take her back home to Sullivan's Point.

Because she didn't know how she was going to face Fia and Rory. Because she was sure that she looked changed. She felt changed.

It was a kiss. Just a kiss, but she had gotten the easement. And whether or not it was because of the kiss, she couldn't rightly say.

She had been kissed.

Her first kiss.

By Levi Granger, the object of her fantasies since she was fourteen. The man she would've said that she didn't like, except after tonight she felt like maybe she did.

And that was confusing and upsetting, and made her want to scream and shout.

Because she didn't want to care about him.

She didn't want to be entangled with him in any regard.

He was far too…too *him*.

He was…

He scares you.

Lord, how he did. Because he was unearthing old Quinn. Not angry Quinn, though he'd done that, too. But Quinn who felt it all. Who wanted it all.

She didn't want to be involved with anybody.

But she was getting to know him, and she had whispered one of the more vulnerable things that she had never told anybody to him, just this morning. Had it been just this morning?

That he had taken her to his parents' graves, that he had come to get her at her house.

That they'd had pizza and conversation, and another fight, and a kiss that had scorched her soul.

She let out a slow breath, jagged and shaky.

She was going back tomorrow.

Camilla would be gone.

Did he want...?

Did she?

She drove on toward the house, finally ready, because she at least got to tell them that she had secured the easement.

Now she just had to not screw it up. She didn't worry, not even for a moment, that he was holding sex hostage for the easement. That just wasn't him. He was hardheaded, and he was stubborn, proud.

But he would never manipulate her.

He was way too straightforward for that. It was why he had thrown her in a pond, and yelled at her when he had thought she interpreted his dyslexia as stupidity.

He was a man of deep feelings, and they were real.

He was not the kind of man who would hold something over a woman in exchange for sex.

And anyway, it wasn't like she was so sexually appealing that a guy would do that just to get with her.

Here she was, thinking about sex again, after something that might well not actually connect up to sex.

It stood to reason. She was, after all, a twenty-five-year-old virgin, which was pretty old, but it was intentional on her part. Not out of morals or anything like that, just because she had been focused.

And afraid.

If she were very honest.

Because how could you ever forget the feeling of gravel cutting into your feet, the hot tears streaming down your face and the unending ache in your chest, as you chased your dad's car down the drive, begging him not to leave.

You didn't.

She'd never wanted to chase a man again.

She got out of the car and turned the engine off. The headlights had obviously alerted Fia to her appearance, and the porch light flicked on, and the door opened.

And there her sister was, looking hard out into the darkness.

She got out of the car.

"Good news," she said. "The easement is ours."

"Is it?"

"Yes. I went and helped him with his paperwork, and after he saw how good of a job I did, he agreed. He will be happy to work with us."

"Is that it?"

"Yeah," she said. "That's it."

"Are you okay?"

How was she going to encapsulate everything that was Levi Granger and what had happened with him today? It was a full emotional roller coaster. She felt like she had lived three lives in the last four days, and she didn't know how to communicate that to Fia. Most especially not without exposing him, and suddenly she felt as if she would protect those things that were harmful to him with her life.

Because he had told her. He had told her about himself, and the way that teachers had made him feel, the way that he had felt about himself, and the way that he been taken advantage of. He had told her about it, and she couldn't violate that. She wouldn't.

"I'm going back over there tomorrow to do a little bit more admin. The easement is contingent on that."

She walked up the front porch and into the house. "And then we really will be on our way to getting the store open."

That was why she was doing this. And somehow, it all kind of felt lost. Lost in the happenings of the last few days. Lost in everything. But, of course, this was about Sullivan's Point. It was about the farm store. It was about proving...

Proving herself.

Proving herself to...just herself.

Because she wasn't a kid anymore.

And she knew better than to blame herself for her dad leaving. She did.

But still, her stomach felt like acid when she thought about it.

"Are you okay, Quinn?"

"I'm fine," she said.

"You look upset."

Upset really wasn't the right word. She was stirred up. She was something new. Something different. Something she had never fully experienced before.

But she wasn't hurt or angry.

He had kissed her. And it had been amazing.

She was attracted to him.

Her chest felt a little bit cracked.

She felt sensitive and fragile, and like she didn't know whether she wanted to go to her room and cry, or get in the shower and relieve the sexual tension that had built up in her body.

Her older sister looked at her in the glow cast by the porch light, her eyes filled with concern. "Something happened with him, didn't it?"

"Why do you say that?"

"Well, first of all, because you didn't deny it with your first breath."

"Something's happened with him every day," said Quinn. "Something that turns into a fight or ends up with me being thrown into a pond…"

"You care about him, don't you?"

"No," she said too quickly. "No. It's not like that. Isn't… It's not. Okay? I don't have any desire whatsoever to get involved with a man. There is too much to do here on the ranch, and there is too much to do in my life, and there is…"

"You're lying to me."

"Fia, why do you think you get to know about my personal life? You won't even tell anybody what happened between you and Landry King, while the two of you hiss and spit at each other like cats every time you're in the same room. You have never once confided in me about that."

Fia's face went cold. "And I won't. It isn't what you think, I'll tell you that."

"Why won't you tell me…?"

"No. What's between Landry and me is between us. Okay?"

"And what's between Levi and me is between us."

"I don't want you to get hurt," said Fia. "I don't. I don't trust random men. I just… He's not one of us. And even though… Our dad was one of us, Quinn, and he still hurt us. And… You just cannot always trust people."

"I don't trust him," she said. Except it was a lie. She did trust him. She trusted him not to hurt her on purpose. She trusted him not to take advantage of her.

She trusted that he was a man of his word.

She trusted a whole lot of things about him that she would've said that she didn't just a little bit before, but she did now. She did.

"Just trust me. I've got the easement. The rest of it… It's my business."

She walked into the house, past her sister, letting the screen door slam behind her.

And there was Rory, standing at the base of the stairs, her red hair already piled in a bun on her head, her white nightgown more suited to that of a Victorian orphan than a grown woman.

"What was that about?"

"Our sister being overly protective."

"Do you need protecting?" Rory asked.

"No, Rory. I don't. I do not need to be protected. Not from him, not from myself. I don't need to be protected from anyone. Least of all Levi Granger. Or my own self. Because that's what it comes down to. Fia doesn't trust me. And she doesn't have the balls to say that, so she's acting like she's worried about him."

She stomped up the stairs, past Rory, who followed her up. "Did you kiss him?"

She turned to look at her sister, who was overly romantic always.

"No," she lied. "I didn't."

She didn't know why she wasn't telling either of them.

You know why. You don't want them to tell you to rethink it.

You don't want them to tell you to stop.

True. Because she wanted to go over there tomorrow. She wanted to go over there tomorrow, and with all the freedom that she possessed, she wanted to make whatever decision she did about him. Without them hovering in the background, worried about her. Without them acting like they knew best.

So there.

So she went up to her room and closed the door behind her, and she didn't even take her clothes off. Instead, she just fell into bed.

She didn't sleep for a long time, and she just replayed the kiss. Over and over again.

THE NEXT MORNING she left the house early enough that she didn't encounter anyone, and she was grateful.

She wore a dress and her white shoes and socks, and she didn't bring coffee, just like he'd said.

And when she arrived at the house, he wasn't holding a thermos, but a mug.

"Come on in."

It was weird. It felt like the dawning of a new day in so many ways.

He was greeting her differently. Treating her entirely differently.

"Good morning."

"Come on. Sit down with me."

"Is Camilla…?"

"She's gonna leave in a couple of hours. She is not up yet."

They went and sat down at the kitchen table. She held her mug between her hands and let it warm her palms. She looked up and met his gaze. There was a fire in his blue eyes that resonated inside her.

"So I'll be working in the office today. I'm going to do a little bit of research on some systems I might be able to put in place for you, but you know, I think you just might want to hire somebody to do a lot of this. To make it kind of automated. I think it would be best, and I'm going to go through your financials and tell you where I think you can spare some expense. Okay?"

He nodded. "Okay. I don't take being told what to do all that well."

She laughed. Because she couldn't help it. Because obviously.

"I hadn't guessed that."

"Yeah," he said gruffly. "Well."

"Don't think of it as being told what to do. You already know that sometimes it's good to take… Not help. Sometimes it's good to get someone else involved in doing the parts of the job that don't come as easily to you. It makes sense."

"That's why I'm having you do it," he said.

"And I can help for a while. But once we get the store up and running, then… We're going to be busy with that."

He looked at her hard for a moment, and she realized that she had just turned on a ticking clock.

It was good. It was for the best.

Because she was tangled up in him already just after a few days, and that wasn't going to work.

It wasn't sustainable.

"So, Camilla is going back to school, and then you're back to the empty-nest life."

He nodded. "Yep. And in two years, I'll be done paying for school, and… Well. Really, the freedom is almost unimaginable."

He took a sip of his coffee and she watched him. The way his hands gripped the cup handle, the way his throat worked as he swallowed.

And then he looked at her, and she felt…caught. And pinned to the spot.

It was weird to sit here and have a conversation with him. One that wasn't so tinged with hostility. But it was like when their lips had touched he had taken away her anger, and she had taken away some of his.

It was like they were transforming each other, even if just a bit.

And now she was sitting there staring at his Adam's apple. And his chin, his lips, back up to his eyes.

"Stop looking at me like that," he said.

"Why? How?"

Both valid questions, though she hadn't really meant to ask the last one.

"Because it's dangerous."

"You already threw me in a pond. What else can you do to me?"

"Not the best question. I have work to do." He drained the last of his coffee. "But this time when you go up in my office, you are welcome to look at whatever you want. I eagerly await your report."

"I get the feeling that it's not exactly all that eager."

He shrugged a shoulder. "Maybe I oversold it a little bit."

"Right. Well. I'll see you when you get back."

She stayed firmly rooted in the office, even when she heard Camilla walking around in the hall, getting ready to leave. She just didn't have it in her to face the other woman after she had... After she had kissed Levi.

And especially not when the sound of Camilla's departure amped up the excitement, the desire that was burning through her.

Yeah, especially because of that.

She shifted and continued to pore through all of his records. In truth, there was a meticulousness to the way he did things. She could see where he got behind, and then got overwhelmed, but when he was keeping up, everything was perfect. Probably because he did have to work so hard to make sure that it was right. It was apparent, the amount of work he put into that.

The biggest thing was looking at his budget, and at what he had coming in.

He was making a ton of money, which of course he must know. He was paying tuition every quarter, and seemed to be doing it without any real hardship. But he had more than enough money to make sure that he never had to do any of the invoicing. But she knew the key would be to find somebody that he felt comfortable with. That he trusted.

The same would be true if they started doing the Christmas trees. She would not be looking for a leasing situation. And not just because she didn't want to get thrown in the pond again.

Because now she understood. What drove him. What made him such a stubborn cuss.

And she couldn't help but respect it.

She settled into daydreaming just a bit while she thought of the way he looked at her this morning over coffee.

When he came back, would he kiss her? Would she let him? There would be no reason to stop.

And maybe this was the real life lesson for her. That she couldn't plan everything.

That she couldn't control everything.

Levi made her lose her temper in a way she hadn't since she was a kid.

And he made her lose her head in a way she never had.

She wanted him.

She wanted to explore desire with him.

That was normal. And it didn't have to be a huge deal. They had a working relationship, and they had already gone through being bitter and toxic at each other. So she wasn't even really afraid of that.

They hadn't even liked each other yesterday morning.

So what was there to fear in terms of what would become of them? Nothing, as far as she was concerned.

It was sort of a no-risk thing.

And there was already a deadline.

When the front door opened and closed, she froze. She heard footsteps on the stairs, and her breath caught in her throat. She expected him to open the office door, but he didn't. Instead, the footsteps went past her down the hall, and she heard a door open and close.

She waited.

Waited, and heard the sound of water running through pipes.

He was taking a shower. She was almost certain of it.

She swallowed hard, and asked herself if she was half as determined that she had always imagined she was.

She was.

She had spent all day thinking about him. Thinking about this.

It was a change. A shift. She hadn't known it was what she wanted.

But she did now. Quinn had always been book-smart.

But maybe it was time she got a little bit street-smart.

She walked slowly down the hall, and listened for the sound of the water. She could hear it faintly through one of the doors. She opened it, and saw that it was the master bedroom. His room.

And with only a small amount of guilt, she paused at his nightstand and opened a drawer. And breathed out a sigh of relief when she saw a box of condoms there.

She grabbed a packet and took another step. Then she stopped and stared at it.

She'd seen condoms a lot of times. She'd gone to college. They were literally in giant bowls at the health center. They handed out massive bags of them if you went in for a sniffle.

Everybody wanted the college kids to be practicing safe sex. Quinn had been practicing the safest sex of all.

Abstinence.

But she had never *announced* it. So she had amassed quite the collection of condoms, which she had gladly given to her roommates whenever they had a need.

And when she had lived in a small studio apartment

by herself, she had simply donated them back to the condom bowl in the common areas of the school.

She had never once held one and looked at it with the intent of using it.

She had never once thought of them as anything other than an abstract object.

Her breath started coming in short bursts, her heart beating more and more rapidly.

She was doing it.

After all, she was a student of many things, and one of the biggest mistakes she had made when meeting Levi was assuming that he didn't have anything to teach her. She blinked and headed toward the bathroom.

She pushed the door open, and she could just barely make out the shape of him through the steamed-up glass. Her heart was now beating in triplicate, the pulse at the apex of her thighs fluttering, the nervous energy going through her body enough to make her expire then and there.

They had kissed once. She was making a big leap. A big assumption.

And she wasn't going to give herself time to think.

She walked toward the shower and pulled the door open. His head jerked up, and steam poured out, slowly revealing his body. Broad shoulders, muscular chest, those washboard abs, and…

Oh, boy.

"What are you doing here?" he asked.

"Was this not an open invitation?"

"It wasn't."

"Is it now?" She sounded too hopeful, and for a moment, she knew a moment of real fear that she'd be rejected.

That she wasn't enough after all.

That fear was mitigated almost immediately.

"Hell yeah."

He reached out, wrapped his arm around her waist and pulled her into the shower fully clothed.

She squeaked as she found herself being trapped between the slippery shower wall and his wet, hard body.

Her dress was saturated quickly, and she was thankful she had at least taken her shoes off, but she still had her socks on, which was a bit distressing.

He pulled back and looked her up and down. "Lord Almighty."

"Yeah," she said, because it was the only thing she could say.

Her dress had buttons on it, and he popped the first one open.

"I do not have any other clothes with me," she said.

"I'm sure my sisters have some things around that you could wear."

And that was how she found the whole rest of her dress popped open completely. Exposing her white bra and panties.

And he made quick work of the dress, flinging it over the top of the shower door and consigning it to the ground outside.

"The *socks*," he growled. "Why are they so fucking hot?"

Right now, her socks were soggy, and she could imagine nothing less sexy, really, except everything felt sexy right now, so it was some kind of sock paradox, and she didn't know what to do with that.

"I don't... I don't know..."

He gripped her hips and held her still as he pressed the hard evidence of his arousal against her body.

She looked down, and she could see him. Hard and so much bigger than she had anticipated. His skin was flushed with desire, and it made her feel powerful.

She had spent years at college ignoring this kind of thing. Ignoring men.

Or maybe she had been ignoring boys, and that was why it had been so easy.

Young and reedy and not this.

He was intense.

And it matched her own intensity.

She'd said, flat out, that he was a hardheaded pig. And that she was, too. And maybe that was how it worked. Hardheadedness saw hardheadedness, and it couldn't help but want to test itself against it.

In every way that she possibly could.

All she knew was that this was compelling, he was compelling, in a way that she couldn't turn away from. In a way she didn't want to turn away from.

He made her feel things, made her want things, that she couldn't deny. She had never considered herself a person with a lot of self-control. In fact, she had always known that she was impulsive, hotheaded and led by her baser instincts.

That considered, it was somewhat surprising that she had never had sex before.

Except it made sense. Now.

Because this was the first time her blood had ever been heated like this.

This was the first time she had ever wanted, ever needed. And she was jumping in headfirst, because what else was there to do?

She knew the giddy power in surrendering to lost temper.

In letting anger flow through you, control you, dominate you.

But she had never experienced *this*.

And one thing she knew about giving in to temper was that there was shame waiting on the other side. And maybe there would be shame on the other side of this, too, but for all the times that she had made that bargain with anger and accepted the consequences, she would do the same here, because at least this felt glorious.

And she felt new.

She had been defined, utterly, these last few years by her drive. By her ability to shut out exhaustion when she needed sleep, but there was work to be done. Anger when she wanted to yell, but she had to let cooler heads prevail so that she could negotiate something. To just give in to what she wanted... It was a glorious, headlong trip into the kind of excitement she'd never experienced before, and she wanted it.

She wanted it badly.

To open this door to another part of herself that she had closed down for so long.

And of course it would be him.

Because he was the only person she'd ever met who was as stubborn as she was. The only person she'd ever met who felt about ranching the way that she did.

A man who was holding everything together for the greater good, and she really understood that.

Down to her soul.

He unhooked her bra and sent it sailing the same direction as her dress. And then he kissed her neck, down her collarbone, and excitement built low between her legs, an ache building and building that made her wiggle her hips restlessly, made her cry out in agony. She felt him smile against her skin as he made his way down to her breast and sucked her nipple into his mouth.

All she could do was stare. Watch as his mouth fastened itself over that intimate part of her; it was the most erotic thing she'd ever seen. And more erotic than anything she'd ever imagined, that was for sure.

She didn't know herself in this moment. She just wanted to surrender. And that really, really wasn't her, and there was something wondrous about it.

To be lost to this. To be sexual. To be overwhelmed.

She was mesmerized by the feeling of his tongue circling her tightened bud, and by the sight of it, too.

By the way his large hands skimmed over her rib cage, down her waist, to her hips, and she watched as his dark head continued down her body, a trail of hot kisses left in his wake.

She moaned when he kissed just beneath her belly button, when he reached the waistband of her panties.

And then he moved his hands down to her thighs, and back up again, his thumbs going underneath the sodden white fabric as he pulled them down slowly, leaving him eye level with the most intimate part of her.

Her head fell back against the shower wall, and she was breathing hard and fast, embarrassment warring with curiosity to see what he would do next.

She hoped that she knew what he was going to do next.

She was aching for it. Desperate.

And when he leaned in and stroked his tongue over that place that was most needy for him, she grabbed the back of his head with one hand and braced herself against the wall with the other, trying to keep herself from melting into a full-on puddle.

"Levi," she said, his name coming out a breath she sighed.

He moved his head back and forth, burying his face there between her legs as he began to lick and suck and create a tormenting rhythm that he played like a song through her body. Through her soul.

She was lost in it. She could no longer analyze the moment. She could only feel. It was this. This glorious tipping point that took her over into the land where she was all feeling.

No thinking at all.

Where she was everything she had worked all these last years to not be.

Book-smart. And that was Quinn Sullivan.

She had put away those feverish feelings that often roiled over into overbright tempers, but apparently contained all her passion, as well.

And now… Now it was like she had found it again. Like she had found herself.

In the stroke of his tongue, the tease of his fingers, and then, when he pushed one inside her body and began to move it rhythmically along with his tongue, it was like stars burst behind her eyes.

The climax hit her so hard, so unexpected, that she let out a short, sharp scream, moving her hips helplessly in time with the demands of her body.

"Levi," she said again.

And then he kissed down her inner thigh, down her leg, and stopped, looking at her socks.

"They just are the cutest thing."

And he took one sodden sock off, and then another,

and looked up at her, the expression on his face dumb-founded. Like he had no idea what he was doing here, either. Or why. Like he didn't understand this connection between them any more than she did. Or maybe she even understood it more.

Hardheaded seeing hardheaded.

Water seeking its own level.

Because they were the same. They weren't different. And she had been foolish when she'd said to him that they saw things differently. They didn't.

They didn't.

He wrung her socks out, laughing before he threw them over the top of the shower door. She hadn't known that sex could be funny, but that was pretty funny.

Then he got back to his feet and kissed her. Kissed her deep and hard.

"I brought a condom," she whimpered against his mouth.

"You really are smart, Quinn," he said.

He opened up the door and reached out to the counter, where he found the packet.

And then she found herself being kissed again, long and deep, pressed against the wall as he maneuvered around, tearing open the packet and rolling the condom over his length.

He grabbed her thigh and lifted it up over his hip, and she had the dim thought that she should maybe tell him she hadn't done this before, and that it might hurt, or that she maybe didn't have the skill level to be taken against the shower wall, but then he was right at the entrance to her body, and she couldn't think, because she wanted him so badly. Because she needed this so badly. Needed him.

So what was experience?

She knew about sex.

Her sister Rory left her romance novels lying around all the time, and Quinn had read them before.

She had also been around the internet, so she had seen some things. She knew what sex was.

She wouldn't say she had made a study of it or anything, but she had a fair idea.

She didn't need to announce her inexperience.

She relaxed, or at least she tried to, taking a deep breath as his eyes met hers. And then she forgot. Everything. Because he was looking at her. Those blue eyes staring straight into hers, but he wasn't angry, or upset with her. They weren't sparring outside. He was about to be inside her.

Levi Granger.

This man that she had thought she hated... Was it twenty-four hours ago that she thought she hated him?

This man she'd wanted since she was fourteen and hadn't fully known what it meant. This man she'd told herself she just liked the look of, not the heart of.

How could she have gotten that so wrong? And right then, just before he thrust inside her, she realized she didn't know anything. And that felt like a free fall.

And that was when he gripped her hips and thrust deep.

She cried out, the sharp, tearing pain of the invasion a shock she hadn't seen coming.

She didn't know anything. She didn't know a damn thing. She wasn't ready for this. She wasn't ready for him.

She thought that grabbing a condom and ambushing him in the shower put her in charge? She wasn't in charge.

He was huge, and he was inside her, and he was so much bigger than she was, and she had made a mistake.

She froze, because she didn't know what else to do. Because she had no idea...

And then he was kissing her, slow and tender, and she felt the panic begin to recede.

So her desire began to come back. That ache in her body suddenly recognizing that this was what it had wanted all along. To be filled by him. This was the answer.

She just hadn't known it.

And maybe it was okay that she didn't know. Because he did. She looked at him, asking all the questions that she didn't have a voice for with one look.

But in his eyes, she saw questions, too, and she knew that he was going to ask them when this was over. And it would be over whenever she said—she recognized that, too. She could tell him to stop now. That it hurt too much. That she was too afraid.

And right in that moment, she would never know if she was driven by pride or desire. Because later it would be lost in all that need.

But for now...

"Please," she whispered. "Show me."

He let out a long, slow breath that broke right at the end, the only thing that really betrayed how on edge he was.

He drew back, then thrust deep, and she dug her fingernails into his shoulder when he did. Then he pulled out again, thrusting in again. She couldn't say that it felt great, but it felt right.

But each subsequent thrust changed. Built. Showed her something.

And her body began to move to welcome his. More than just accommodate.

She got wetter when he met up against that sensitized bundle of nerves there, and as she got yet slicker, it felt better and better.

He thrust into her until she was trembling, until they both were.

Until she was on edge.

And then he reached his hand between them and pinched her there, just gently before stroking her. And that sent her right over the edge.

She cried out his name as she clung to him, wave after wave of pleasure rolling through her.

It was different. Different from having an orgasm alone. Different even from the one he'd given her earlier.

She felt exhausted with it. Spent.

But it kept on going. Deeper and deeper into her, and that was when he went over the edge, too. On a growl, he thrust hard inside her twice more and froze, his arousal pulsing inside her. And she turned to look at him, at the vein standing out on his neck, at the tension in his jaw.

She had done that to him.

She had made him come apart the same as he had made her come apart, and that felt right.

Except then... Her eyes filled with tears.

And Quinn Sullivan didn't cry. Not in front of anybody. Not ever.

But her heart was beating hard, and her body felt boneless, and she was trembling. And she didn't have any idea how the hell to stop it. Because she didn't know how to do this, and it had been fine when he was leading the charge, when he was showing her how good it could be.

And now it was just... Now it was just done.

And she'd had sex with him, and he was still inside her, and she felt like maybe she was dying.

"Quinn," he said, his voice quiet but scolding.

"I...I..."

"Come on."

The water was still pounding down on them. She'd lost her sense of it at some point, but when he reached down and turned it off, she was unbearably conscious of how quiet it was. How she could hear her heart beating in her own ears, how she could hear their breathing, ragged and far too intimate for her to handle.

"Come on," he said, picking her up so she didn't really have a choice and depositing her outside the shower. He grabbed a very large towel and wrapped it around her shoulders, and then he began to dry the water droplets from her body.

It wasn't wholly dispassionate. There was still some fire in his eyes.

But it was banked. And she could tell that he was exercising control now.

She couldn't help but watch his body. The play of muscles.

The look of him when he was relaxed, having just been satisfied.

Except he wasn't totally relaxed; there was tension in his jaw and his shoulders. She could see it.

She was about to ask, and then she found herself being lifted up off the ground again and carried into his bedroom, where she was deposited, still wrapped in the towel, at the center of the bed.

"That was swinging a bit above your pay grade," he said.

And very suddenly, she decided she couldn't deal with the conversation, and so she did a very mature thing. She crawled out from beneath the towel and slipped beneath the covers on the bed, all the way under, making sure they were over her head.

She hadn't acted this much like a child in more years than she could remember, because she hadn't been able to take that luxury.

Her father had left when she was fifteen. Her mother had been gone since she was nineteen, abandoning the ranch and her daughters to kind of just deal with it. And even before that, her mother had been gone.

So they'd all had to find some kind of new normal. Some kind of levelheaded in all of that.

Quinn had never been that good at it. Until she had fought herself right to the end of what was reasonable.

Until she had exhausted herself with her outrage and realized it wasn't leading anywhere. And that was when she had locked it all away. Apparently so many things. Things she hadn't realized had gone in that big metal box, along with her anger.

All things that Levi had dragged out.

Her desire to hide under the bed when she did something naughty among them.

"Quinn," he said. "I literally just watched you go under the covers, so you're not very well hidden."

"I'm tired," she said.

"We need to talk."

Then suddenly it was bright and cold, and she looked up, seeing Levi had stripped the covers from her.

He was looking down at her, all muscular and sexy, and not angry, but not relaxed, either.

She wasn't quite sure what the expression on his face meant.

"I'm chilly," she said.

He dropped the blankets back down over her, but beneath her chin, so that he could still look at her.

"You hadn't had sex before, had you?"

"No."

He rubbed his hands over his face. "Lord Almighty, girl."

"What? I was ready. I wanted to."

"And you didn't think that I might want to know about all that?"

"I didn't really see how it was relevant to you."

"Because it is, Quinn. Because it mattered. Because I wouldn't have had you up against the wall in the shower, and maybe I wouldn't have had you at all. Maybe we would've had to have a discussion about what sex means to me, and what it can't. Maybe we would've had to have a discussion about—"

"You are really not making me feel all that guilty about it, Levi, because I wanted to have sex with you." She didn't like saying it like this. That sounded harsh, and it sounded very much like something clinical, which it had not been. It had been hot, and it had been filled with emotion. She had enjoyed it. And even if she did feel a little bit turned inside out, a little bit rocked, she didn't see why she needed to be scolded. Why she needed to be told. Yeah, she panicked right at the pivotal moment, but she was over it now. Kind of. She only felt a little bit panicked. A little bit scared, and a little bit...

A tear leaked out the corner of her eye, and she could've cursed herself.

"Quinn," he said, his voice getting soft, and then suddenly she was being lifted from the mattress and pulled into his arms, pulled onto his lap. He reached down and gripped her chin, tilted her face up and looked at her. "I'm not designed to be a woman's first lover, Quinn. I probably wouldn't have turned you away, though. But I might've been a little more gentle. A little slower. Given you time. I wouldn't have been that fast."

"I liked it," she whispered.

"Yeah, but you might've liked it more if you weren't terrified."

"I'm *not* terrified."

Except her heart was pounding far too hard even now.

"You aren't?"

"Well, I've done it now," she said. "There's not really any point lecturing me. Not really any point scolding me. I've done it now."

He brushed his thumb over her cheekbone. "Yes, you have. We have. It wasn't just you. It doesn't matter that it was your first time and not mine." He paused. "I've never been with a woman in this house."

"You haven't?"

"No." He shook his head. "I have kept sex separate from my life at home. For all these years." He closed his eyes. "That's not strictly true. But this house was built long after the only time I ever had an entanglement that felt a little bit personal. So there hasn't been anyone here."

"What personal entanglement did you have?" She felt suddenly outraged, wanted to find whoever the woman was and...

What was wrong with her? That sudden rush of possessiveness was not her. Not at all.

It was messed up, that she would be jealous of another woman, angry at her instead of Levi. She would say that she stood against such things. Her father had had an affair, and even her mother had said it was a poor showing of feminism to hate her. And that all the hate should be reserved for their dad. Quinn had happily and easily obliged.

And yet… She certainly wasn't doing a good job of applying that element of sisterhood to this moment. And whoever the woman was, she hadn't even betrayed Quinn.

"It's not a great story. I'm not sure it's a good time to tell it."

"I want to hear it."

"I'll tell you what. I'm going to find some sweats for you, and then we're going to go downstairs and have some ice cream. And we'll talk about it at the kitchen table. But not in my bed."

"Okay."

CHAPTER EIGHTEEN

LEVI FELT SHAKEN to his bones. He hadn't been able to resist her when she'd come into the shower. It had been the slippery, wonderful surprise of his life, and he had been uninterested in resisting.

She was beautiful, and he wanted her.

So why the hell not? She was there, she wanted him, and he wasn't going to protect the girl from herself.

He'd expected to be in control of it. He hadn't expected her to be a virgin.

He got ice cream out of the freezer and set two bowls on the table.

And waited.

He heard soft footsteps coming down the stairs, and when he looked up, his whole being went tight. His groin, his chest, everything in between. She was wearing a very large red sweatshirt and some plaid pants that were far too big for her. And the pants were seemingly held on by boot socks that she had pulled up over the bottoms of the pants, which were... Why were socks so cute on this woman? He had never given a single damned thought to socks a day in his life, and here he was with Quinn Sullivan, obsessing about socks regularly.

Her red hair was wet and bedraggled, and he wanted to pick her up again and carry her to the table.

But he didn't.

He let there be a little bit of distance, because he felt like he needed it.

Dammit all, he needed it.

She padded to the table and sat down, right in front of one of the bowls.

"Mint chocolate chip or salted caramel?"

"Salted caramel," she said, pushing the bowl toward her preferred ice cream container. He started to scoop it for her.

"Okay. So, you know my dad died when I was eighteen."

"Yes," she said.

"I wasn't an adult. I felt…half-finished at best. I had to figure out how to be the caregiver and I was fighting blind. I still didn't know that I had all those learning disabilities and suddenly all this paperwork was on my lap. Plus, three kids. The first time I had sex it was some girl from school who pitied me. Who came by and had a quickie with me on my couch after the kids went to bed, when she dropped off a casserole her mother had made. I was glad, because it felt like I needed to get it over and done with. I needed to be an adult. An adult ought to know what sex is, right?" He sighed. "I don't know how to do the emotions, though. I'm not… I know how to take care of kids. I raised my siblings. I love them. In a lot of ways I never learned how to really take care of myself. I learned to stitch myself back together. To make sure I wasn't bleeding all over, but I'm not… I'm not the kind of man who should be having sex with virgins."

"I literally jumped you in the shower and brought a condom. And news flash—I knew I was a virgin."

"Yeah, you did, but… Quinn, I can't do the whole true-love thing." His chest felt like it was full of ground-up glass. He wondered if that's how his dad's heart had felt. Before it had given out.

The image of him dropping to the ground played in Levi's mind.

He did his best to block it out.

"I understand that," she said softly. "I don't want it, either, actually. I want… Why do you think I'm a virgin, Levi?"

"You made it sound like you had an array of surfers."

"I lied. I went to college, and I didn't really make any friends. Even when I had roommates, I didn't get to know them. Because I was so busy policing myself, making sure that I was there for the right reasons. Making sure that I was doing the right thing. I was trying to…to prove myself. To someone who wasn't even there anymore."

"Your dad," he said.

She nodded. "Yeah. My dad. I told you I followed him around every day. I cared so much about the ranch and about his approval. He used to like it. He changed. He got short-tempered. My chattering started bothering him. The day before he left…he had a blowup at me. He said I was too much. Annoying. I…I thought he liked being with me. And then the next day him and my mom just…blew up. About his affair. I trusted my dad, Levi. I didn't think he had a secret life. But he did. And he packed up his bags and left us." She heaved a deep breath. "I chased him and I begged him to stay. I cried and cried. I ran after his truck. He didn't stop. And I know he left because of him. I know the changes in him, the year he screwed you over, the year he started to get impatient with me, it was about him." She breathed deeply again, like she was trying to shift a weight in her chest. "But it felt like maybe it was because of me. And I got so…so angry. It felt better than crying."

She continued. "I was angry like that for a couple of years. Fighting with everyone, all the time. Until I got into a fistfight with a kid at school and got knocked flat on my ass. That's why I was so horrified when I punched you. I…had decided to never be that person again. It's when I decided I needed to get myself focused, because I couldn't let what my dad did take my future from me."

He felt understanding begin to shift inside him. "He was setting up income for himself. For when he left the ranch. When he screwed me over. Because he got money from that for nearly a decade."

Quinn nodded. "I think you're right."

"Then it wasn't you, Quinn. He was planning on going all that time. You get that, right? He…he was treating you like a dog you can't stand to have following you around because you're going to give it up." He grimaced. It didn't sound as flattering as he meant it to be.

But she just smiled. "I guess he was." She shook her head. "I don't ever want to rely on a man. Not like that. My dad already just about screwed me up for good. This…this is helping me. I didn't know how to be anything but one thing after he left. I knew how to be angry. Then I knew how to be driven. Now I feel like I'm finding me again, so don't regret the sex. It was time for me. And don't think I'm going to expect more from you than you want to give."

He needed that to be true. Because he needed her. Right now he needed her, but he didn't want to hurt this woman who had already been so badly burned.

"Quinn, I am tired," he said, his voice rough. "I'm

really tired of being responsible for people. I can't do it anymore. I don't want to get married. I don't want to have kids. I'm done."

"Okay," she said.

She looked so young then, pale, the freckles on her skin standing out even more than usual.

"I just need you to understand that," he said.

"I do. When we open the farm store I'm going to be busy. Very busy, and it's what we've been working toward. This next phase of Sullivan's Point. And that's the most important thing to me. I don't want to get married. I'm a Sullivan. I aim to stay one."

"Okay."

They were both silent for a long moment. "Just so you know, I don't think you should hold on to that pain that you carry."

He looked up at her. "What?"

"I know you blame yourself. For what my dad did. But just like with me…he had a plan and he was willing to take advantage of you to see it through. Your vulnerability wasn't wrong. My dad was."

He looked down at his hands, and he felt like he couldn't fully turn over those things she was saying.

"Well, just so we're clear, it's the same with your anger. Did you ever think that you were entitled to it?"

She blinked three times. Four. "No. Because…"

"Quinn, you had every right to be angry that your dad left. It's normal. And maybe you shouldn't have gone punching somebody, but maybe they deserved it. I did. I made you angry. I can take responsibility for that. That's why I wasn't upset when you punched me. I deserved it. People have to take responsibility for their actions, too. Everything your dad said to you at the end, everything he did, was him trying to make his own actions seem justified, and they weren't." For a minute, the only sound was their spoons scraping against the ice cream bowls.

A small smile curved her lips. "You do admit that you deserved to be punched."

"In this case."

He realized he didn't quite know what to do with a woman in his house. Maybe he was half-feral. He had often thought so.

He didn't have the occasion to hone social graces, and he really didn't have experience with this kind of thing. Sharing food with someone he'd just had sex with.

It struck him how much he felt like a virgin right then.

And he didn't like that. And every time, he realized, Quinn did something that butted up against that insecurity of his, he got mad at her. He was really just mad at the world.

He had a feeling Quinn could relate.

He wondered then if he was no better than a little boy who had been pulling pigtails on a playground.

He liked her. And there was part of him that had acknowledged that already. He liked her.

She was spirited, and she was beautiful and cute. All those things.

He'd tried to compete with Four Corners by signing that contract, and he'd let Brian Sullivan guide him because it had seemed like someone from Four Corners would understand the business of making money.

For all the good it had done him.

But Quinn wasn't at fault for that. She hadn't caused any of the problems.

She hadn't created any of the systems.

And he'd been so busy feeling threatened by everything that she was...

You were probably right to be.

Maybe. Because here she was in his kitchen, eating his ice cream, so that said quite a few things about just how much of a threat she was.

He wasn't going to get mad at her. Not now.

Because it wasn't her. It never had been.

And one thing was certain—he wasn't sharing. He didn't want to take advantage of her. In fact, apparently he had something to learn from the situation.

"I don't really know what comes after this," he said.

"Me, either," said Quinn. "I'm blessedly free of expectation."

So was he. Because sex had never been this.

Another area of his life where he'd had to skip important steps.

He laughed. "Oh, come on now. I don't totally believe that. You must have an expectation of some kind."

"I really didn't. The ice cream has actually exceeded any expectation I might have had."

"Right. Well. Quinn... Are you able to get home all right?"

He felt wrong asking that, but they had already left his room, and he didn't fully feel right about having her spend the night, either. So maybe he should. Maybe he should put her dress and socks and underwear in the dryer and take her back up in his bed.

Then he could have her again.

That, he realized right away, was a bad idea. She was new at this. He couldn't go doing it all over again so quickly.

"Yeah," she said, nodding, digging into the ice cream bowl even deeper. "I can make it home. I should get home soon anyway. Because, you know… My sisters."

She couldn't spend the night. That was kind of a relief. She couldn't spend the night because her sisters would worry.

He nodded slowly. "Right. I'll pitch your things in the dryer and have them all ready for you… You're coming back tomorrow?"

She nodded. "Yeah. I said I would do the week. And now I'm committed to doing whatever… I don't want you to give me the easement just because we had sex. Because you know that feels a bit like prostitution."

He laughed, but not a rolling, roaring laugh, just a short chuckle, mostly because he hadn't expected that. "First of all, I told you it was yours after we *kissed*."

She sniffed. "I felt there was an expectation."

"Right. Well. I would never give you the easement just because we had sex. But I do feel more like giving it to you, now that I am sitting back and being honest with myself. It isn't you I don't trust, Quinn. You didn't do anything to me. You just showed up looking a lot like my issues. And I reacted badly to that. And yes, I don't have a great well of love in my soul for Four Corners. I have some issues with that whole collective, and I'm not the only one in the community who does. But it has nothing to do with you and, really, has nothing to do with an easement on and off the property. I trust you."

Her green eyes looked suddenly dewy. "You trust me?"

"Yes. I do. You've proved to me that you are honest, and that if you tell me to make sure it's all okay, you are. I don't believe that you would dig into a situation that feels untenable."

"I wouldn't," she said.

"So it isn't about kissing or sex or anything like that. Okay?"

She nodded. "Okay. I believe you."

"Good."

She stood up, still adorable in the too-big clothes. Her sisters were probably going to question that. But that, he figured, was something she would either be concerned about or not.

"I'll see you tomorrow."

He thought about leaning in and kissing her, but he didn't know about that, either.

And she didn't make a move toward him. She seemed suddenly a little bit skittish. And he didn't think—he just reached out and put his hand on her cheek, stroked down the back of her hair. And she seemed to still.

"Good night, carrot," he said softly.

"Good night."

She turned and walked out of the house, and he felt like he shouldn't let her go.

But what he did do was go to his room and collect her clothes, pick up her bra and drape it over the shower, because he wasn't going to put it in the dryer, because he did know better from a particular disaster that had happened once when Jessie was in high school. But everything else went straight in with a dryer sheet that was going to make her clothes smell like his.

He stood there for a while pondering that.

He wasn't quite sure just what in the hell he'd gotten himself into here. But he was into it.

So, there was nothing else to do but be in it.

CHAPTER NINETEEN

QUINN FELT LIKE CRYING. And like laughing. As she drove back home shaking inside, she was glad that he hadn't asked her to stay. Part of her wanted to. Part of her wanted to climb into bed with him. But part of her needed the distance, and if he had asked her to stay, she wouldn't have been able to tell him no. She needed to process what had just happened, and she was very aware that she was driving home without her shoes, wearing a very large pair of boot socks that were clearly not hers. And that it was late.

She really hoped—she really, really hoped—that her sisters had gone to bed.

She just wasn't ready to talk about it. She wasn't even really ready to deal with it in her own soul, but it was what it was, she supposed.

When she turned onto the road that led to Four Corners, she really looked at it in a different way.

A big, mysterious collective that no one else in town could access unless they worked there.

A gigantic ranch that almost nobody could compete with, that had been there since the dawn of time.

Of course it was a big deal for Levi to agree to work with them. It would probably even make other people feel like he was a sellout, or like he was suspicious.

It was… It was difficult. Of course it was.

But he'd said yes, and now they were just working together.

Not just working together.

She felt something. She felt *something*.

She pulled up to the house and got out of the car, wincing as the gravel bit into her sock-covered feet. She squeaked, and then started humming as she hopped up the front steps.

"There you are."

Her hum turned into a short scream, and she turned and saw her sister Fia sitting there in a rocking chair.

"You're back late," she said, accusing.

"Yes," she said. "I am."

"Why?"

"Work," she said.

"You're in pajamas."

"I'm not in pajamas," she said. "I'm in sweats. I got cold. I was working inside today, and..."

"You were working inside?"

"Yes. I told you, I'm going to be helping more with his paperwork. He needs somebody to organize." That was all she was willing to share. Because Levi didn't want to share about his dyslexia, and neither was she. And she certainly wasn't going to make it sound like he was failing in some way when he wasn't.

"I guess that means we can get moving opening the store."

"Yeah. We can set a grand opening and everything. He and I need to work out some papers. And we're going to have to get lawyers."

She knew that he'd said he trusted her, but she wanted to take that a step further by making sure she demonstrated to him that she was protecting his legal interests.

He'd been through enough. And she wasn't going to be part of putting them through any more.

And she just…

Standing there in the socks, and his clothes, in front of Fia, she felt vaguely ridiculous. And a little like she was falling apart.

She felt happy, in the strangest way. Felt like there was finally something good happening in her life. Something that she wanted.

But it wasn't something she could share.

It was like she had met herself for the first time tonight.

A woman who could be passionate in a positive way. A woman who could feel everything, but it wasn't just anger.

It was amazing, and she wanted to continue to examine it on her own time. She wanted to keep on thinking on it, without allowing anybody else's opinions to change it.

Because one thing had become clear tonight when she'd been talking to Levi. The way that her dad had hurt her had shaped her.

For better and for worse.

There were no decisions to make. She was having her first fling. Which felt like a really bad word for it. Because it didn't feel like a fling. A fling, as far as Quinn was concerned, sounded light. Fluffy, even, and this was not that.

She'd told him things she'd never told another person. She had a feeling it was the same for him.

She understood why he didn't want forever. She didn't want it, either, but that didn't make this shallow.

It was too personal to share with anyone.

After what he'd told her, she didn't want to fight him. But she did want to fight for him.

"Gideon Payne contacted us," Fia said. "He wants to rent one of the houses for a few months."

"Gideon… Rory's friend's brother?"

"Yes. He's coming back to buy his old family homestead. They lost it when his dad died. I want you to look over the agreement I drafted for him."

"The rentals are kind of Rory's purview, aren't they? Plus, she knows him. He used to drive her to school every day. I swear, she was closer to his family than she was to ours."

Fia shrugged. "I really value your input on things, Quinn."

Quinn looked at her sister. "What's sparking this?"

"Well, sometimes I feel like I don't acknowledge enough the work that you put in to get the education that you did. I understand that it took a lot for you to get there. And believe me, we all understand how little support you had. Mom and Dad certainly didn't…"

"Fia, you don't have to be Mom and Dad. It isn't your responsibility. You've done so much." And it was knowing Levi that really underlined that. Really drove the point home. And suddenly, she wondered… She wondered how much Fia held herself back because of them. Was her sister living a relatively celibate life because she felt like she had to set an example or be responsible? And now Quinn was out having hot sex and her sister wasn't because…

Well, she knew that there was a possibility that Fia had been with Landry, but her sister never dated. And she didn't spend nights away.

"You don't have to give your whole life for us," said

Quinn. "We're not kids. We don't need for you to act like you're some kind of a saint for our benefit. Anyway, Alaina already entered into a life of sin."

Fia laughed. "Do you think that I...? You think that..."

"I know that you're not dating anyone, and in my memory you haven't."

"Nothing that I do in that arena is self-sacrificial. Believe me."

"If you're sure. It's just I've been spending a lot of time over at the Grangers', and Levi's sister Camilla was there." She chose her next words carefully, because she didn't want it to sound too intimate, but there were many things that she had found out about him prior to the kiss. Prior to them making love.

"And he raised his siblings, and I can see the places that he sacrificed everything. Absolutely everything for them."

"Don't worry about me," she said. "Believe me, if I wanted to bang a guy, I would bring him back here, hang a tie on the door and do it in the living room. I'm not worried about your delicate sensibilities. What I do and don't do is about me."

They'd never talked about it. They'd never talked about a lot of things. They loved each other and they bonded over the ranch, but in so many ways it was like they'd gone off to lick their wounds in separate corners. Alaina had Elsie. Rory'd had the Payne family. Fia had been their sister and their caregiver.

Now that she'd spent time talking to Levi...she fully realized how lonely that must have been for Fia.

"Do you ever need to talk about it?" she asked.

And suddenly Fia looked desperately sad. And what Quinn could see right then was that the real cost of being the strong one, the parental figure, was that she couldn't share. She felt like she had to be strong and stoic and she was alone in whatever her pain was.

"Maybe someday. It's not something that I know how to talk about. Not with anybody. Anyway, you don't need me to heap my problems on you. You, Rory and Alaina have been through enough."

"We love you, though." And she felt disingenuous because here she was, not sharing her own situation at all. Not telling Fia what she had been up to tonight. Though, she had a feeling Fia could hazard a guess if she really wanted to.

Maybe that was part of how they all got along so well, in truth. Fia just pretended not to see what she didn't want to. And that kept them all out of each other's hair.

"But you know what's really not fair about us?" said Quinn. "It's that our parents are still alive—they're just not around. And that means that half the time we have to manage their emotions along with our own."

Fia nodded. "That's the truth. And it is indeed the most unfair part."

"I'm heading upstairs to have a shower." The word *shower* made her feel fuzzy and fizzy.

"Okay. If you need something, you will ask me, right, Quinn?"

And that was the first time Fia really showed that she might not fully believe Quinn's story.

"Yes. I promise. I do know that you are there for me no matter what."

"I appreciate that."

She went upstairs and walked into her bedroom, looked around for her nightgown and then stopped. She realized that she wanted to sleep in his clothes. And she also realized she didn't even actually want to shower. Because that would wash his touch off. So she sat down on the edge of her bed and looked at the faded yellow wallpaper. She wasn't a virgin anymore. But the virginity thing never really mattered all that much to her. It hadn't been about not doing something. It had been about not especially wanting to yet. And so she had, and she did. She closed her eyes and thought about him.

How intense he had been. How beautiful.

How for all that she had only known this man for a few days, she now knew something about him that was intimate. Deeply so.

He had been with other women—she knew that. But maybe he hadn't also told them about his dyslexia. She was sure that he hadn't.

She knew about his dyslexia. About his parents. About how her dad had taken advantage of him and made him feel stupid. About his first experience with sex. She had worn his socks. She'd been naked in his house.

She had all these pieces of Levi Granger that she didn't think anyone else in the world ever had.

And if asked, she would say she didn't know the man all that well. Especially when compared with all the people she'd known every day of her life on Four Corners.

Except she did know him.

She'd seen him naked, and she'd seen him undone. She was wearing his clothes.

She lay back on her bed, her arm slung over her head.

She would see him again tomorrow.

And she didn't know what was going to happen when she did.

She imagined that some of that was up to her.

She had never been passive. It wasn't the time to go getting passive now, she supposed.

He turned her inside out.

And right now she was still trying to decide if she wanted to flip herself the other way or not.

Or if she wanted to stay like this. New and different.

The heavy truth was, she might not have a choice.

She had taken a plunge into the unknown.

And for all that Quinn liked to be in control, she had the feeling that she had surrendered that. Utterly and completely.

And as long as she was with him, she wasn't going to be getting it back.

CHAPTER TWENTY

SHE WAS THERE the next morning, bright and early with a coffee cup in her hand.

And he really did intend to go out to work, and let her go up to his office. He really did intend to have a conversation with her.

He really did intend to behave himself. But the problem was, he had spent all night dreaming of her. Of her body pressed against his in the shower. Of the cries of pleasure that had echoed in his ears when she'd come.

The way she looked in his oversize clothes and socks. Her sitting at his kitchen table eating ice cream. Her listening to him when he talked about all the mistakes that he'd made, completely without judgment. Her. All night long it had been her. And he had cursed himself for a fool for not asking her to stay the night. He had missed her. All night long, and he had never missed a woman in his life.

Had never slept with a woman all night, so where the urge to hold her came from, he couldn't say. She was different, that was all.

He really did intend to treat her like she was the same.

Until he saw her.

Standing on his doorstep holding a little cup of coffee.

He tried to remember when the sight of her had infuriated him, and he was pretty sure it never really had.

He was pretty sure he was just a liar.

To himself most of all.

He reached out and wrapped his arm around her waist, took the coffee cup from her hand and crushed her against his body, kissing her hard and deep without so much as a good-morning.

And when they parted, she looked dazed.

"Oh," she said.

"I want you," he said.

"Yes," she said. "Yes, please."

That was all the encouragement he needed. He set the coffee cup down on the bench by the door and swept Quinn up into his arms. Like it was some old movie. He held her close, carrying her up the stairs, heading straight for his bedroom. Where he should've kept her all damned night.

Because he wanted her. Because he couldn't deny it. Because he didn't even want to deny it, not anymore.

His heart was beating so hard he thought it was going to burst through the front of his chest.

And when he set her down at the foot of his bed, he cradled her face in his hands and just looked at her. Long and hard.

She was so pretty.

And he didn't know how something so small had re-arranged his life so utterly and completely.

He looked at her for answers. And all he saw was Quinn.

Her pale skin and freckles, her green eyes. That red hair.

She was beautiful. And he wanted her to be his.

In so many ways.

Impossible ways.

But there was one way that was possible. Right now.

He wanted her. He wanted this.

And he wasn't going to stop. Not now.

Today, Quinn had on a long floral dress with buttons, like the one last night.

This time, he didn't pop any buttons. This time, he went slow, undoing them and revealing her skin inch by inch.

It was like a gift he had never allowed himself to have before. This long, slow moment to luxuriate in a woman he wanted.

Not just getting sex to get it done. But *indulging*.

He hadn't told her this last night, but he'd never taken a woman in the shower. He'd never had a woman in his bed.

Not his bed.

He didn't count his experience with Hannah. He hadn't taken ownership of his life yet. Of the bed he was sleeping in. Of the world he inhabited. And since then, it had been a series of one-night stands.

And it didn't allow for him to really want. To really explore. To really get what he needed.

Maybe it had never been there before. Maybe there had never been a woman that he would have wanted like this. Maybe it was only Quinn, and that was why she was here. That was why it was her. That was why, even though he'd had an empty nest for two years, this was the first time he had felt compelled to have a woman here. Now.

Because he could have. He could've extended his time with any number of his lovers in the years since Camilla had left, and he hadn't.

It was just this outrageous little carrot that made him

want to be something he wasn't. That made him want to do things he never had before.

He kissed her stomach, lowering himself onto his knees as he finished unbuttoning her dress. He teased her with his tongue, around the waistband of her panties.

"You...you like doing that," she whispered as he pulled her underwear down.

"What?"

"You like...that."

He lifted a brow and he leaned in, dragging his tongue through her sweet folds. "This?"

She gasped and braced herself on his shoulder. "Yes. That."

"What man wouldn't want a taste of that?"

"I don't know. You know, what with the whole not-having-any-experience thing."

"Right. Believe me when I tell you, it's about the best thing I can think of."

And he proved his point by setting her on the edge of the bed and draping her legs over his shoulders as he went deep, indulging himself utterly and completely.

She arched her hips up off the bed, pressing herself more firmly into his mouth, and he reveled in it.

But she was still partly dressed, and he needed to fix that. He took her to the edge, and then denied her, and enjoyed watching her sweat and pant on his bed, wanting more. Needing more.

He reached behind her and unhooked her bra, removed the dress the rest of the way and took the bra off along with it.

"You are mean," she said.

"Why is that?"

"Because you didn't... You won't let me..."

Something primal and satisfying rolled through him, his body so hard he could barely see straight. Could barely think.

"Because I won't let you come?"

"Levi," she said.

"You're going to get all prudish on me now after I've had you in my mouth?"

"Levi," she said, scolding.

"Tell me what you want."

"You. I want you."

"I think that's something you might have to earn."

He undid the buckle on his jeans, the button, the zipper, and exposed his desire to her.

She looked up at him, her eyes widened, innocent and hungry.

And he felt like he'd been sucker punched with need.

He wrapped his hand around his hardened length and stroked himself with his thumb.

He watched her let out a long, slow breath, a shiver going through her.

She moved to the edge of the bed and wrapped her hand around him, leaning forward, stroking him with her tongue.

He watched her face, watched her expression, wonder, desire, need, reflective of his own all right there as she took him into her mouth.

He pushed his hand into her hair and held her there, as she tormented him with an expert stroke of her tongue, with the force of her need.

It didn't need to be skilled. It just needed to be her.

It was her turn to take him to the edge. He was the one now who wasn't coherent. He was the one who was lost.

"Quinn," he said, ragged, trying to hold back his climax.

He lifted her away from him and set her back on the bed, put his hand between her thighs and began to stroke her with his thumb. She whimpered, moving her hips in tempo with his touch, and he teased the entrance to her body, denying her penetration even as she begged for it with her questing hips.

He brought her to the edge again and again, until he had lost all sense of time. Until he had lost all sense of everything but how soft and slick she was. How rosy her lips were, desire making her cheeks red and spreading that flush all over her body.

Her hands roamed over his body, his chest, his shoulders. And finally, he reached into the bedside drawer for a condom.

For the first time in his life, he was almost sorry to put one on. Almost sorry that he was unable to stop himself from taking things to the next level, because he could've reveled in this, in the touching, the teasing, for an hour or so more.

If he had just a little more willpower. But he didn't. He would finish mourning it later, because for now he just needed to be inside her.

He moved his hand back around under her ass and lifted her off the mattress, positioning himself at the entrance of her body and pushing inside in one smooth stroke.

And that was when she shattered. She cried out her orgasm, digging her fingernails into his forearms, the climax rolling on and on, and he began to move, not even letting her catch her breath, not letting her come down from the heights before he started to chase his own.

Her whimpers, his name on her lips, created a rhythm that he kept until he lost control. Until his climax roared up inside him, desire that he couldn't deny. And when he found his own release, she found hers again, crying out his name and shuddering and shaking beneath him. Then he collapsed beside her, sweat-slicked and spent.

"I really didn't intend to do that," he said.

A delicate hand came to rest on his cheek and he closed his eyes.

"What is it you intended to do?"

"Go to work," he said.

"Sex is a lot more fun than work," she said.

He rolled over onto his back and scooped her up, bringing her over to rest on his chest. "Yeah. It is. But I can't say that I've ever shirked work for sex before."

"Well," she said. "It's fun. You should do it more often."

"Apparently I should."

"I didn't tell anyone," she said softly.

"I don't care if you do."

And then he realized she might be ashamed of him. But he dismissed that. He wasn't going to assume the worst of her. He'd done that too many times. To protect himself.

"Right. Well. I guess that's just a me thing, then," she said.

"What? You're embarrassed?" he asked.

"No. I'm not embarrassed at all. I'd open the window and shout about it right now if you asked me to. I just…"

He understood. Without her having to finish the sentence. It was *theirs*. Whatever it was.

It wasn't for anybody else.

"Yeah. I know," he said.

He'd had secrets. A lot of them. For a long time. It felt heavy. He wondered if she felt the same way.

But this was different.

And maybe they both deserved that. Something nice. Something fun.

He was just completely shocked that it was with her.

"I'm sorry," he said.

"For what?"

"For deciding that you were a certain kind of way based on the fact that you had an education. Based on what your dad did. Every single thing that you said to me I decided was with the worst intent. And all the while I was grumbling about how you make assumptions about me because I hadn't been to school. While I made just as many about you because you had."

"Some of them were true," she said.

"Yeah. Well, some of your assumptions about me were true."

"You aren't dumb."

"I know," he said.

"Do you?"

"I guess, more than knowing that, I've decided it doesn't matter. I know how to run my ranch. I made the place that I could run. That was probably one reason I was so irritated to have to take any help from you."

"You didn't have to take it. But there's nothing wrong with wanting it."

"That hasn't been my experience," he said, his voice gruff. "Wanting and needing help are just paths that people take to get something from other people, and I…"

"I'm not trying to take advantage of you."

"I know that. And I trust you. I swear. Whatever else

is going on in this whole…ridiculous world, I know you're not like your dad."

"Thank you."

She was just so… She was so hurt. And the way that he had lumped her in with Brian wasn't fair. Because she was a good woman.

And that was that.

He might not be a good enough man for her, he might not be able to offer her anything, but he could see now that he'd been very wrong about her. And all his anger had been misdirected. She'd been hurt by her father. Because he was that kind of man, the kind that went around hurting people, just because he could.

But Quinn wasn't like that at all. She was determined, and she was sharp. And sometimes it might come across like she thought she was better than other people, but that wasn't it. She was just passionate. In a very deep, real way.

"I guess we better get to work," she said quietly.

"Well, that sounds like a pretty shitty thing to have to do after all that," he said.

She laughed. "I'm going to finish organizing the office. Levi… Thank you, for the easement."

"In the end, it's the best thing to do. I really do believe that having a road that circumvents the town would've caused harm. I haven't changed my mind about that. I do have concerns…"

"I swear, we will find ways to invest back into the community. Really. I don't know what to do about the fact that we're such a big ranching operation, or the fact that people feel a little bit distrustful of us. I understand now, though, because knowing you like I do… It's forced me to look outside of our whole thing. It's easy for us to get caught up in who we are, and the fact that we know each other. The truth is, we all went through things with our parents. I would say the Sullivans had it the best, and you know my dad, so you know that's saying something."

"Yeah. Well, I remember hearing all about Seamus McCloud."

It was rumored that the McCloud patriarch had been horrendously abusive.

"He was everything that you've heard and more. Maybe worse. That's where... Anyway. It's just that when my sister and Sawyer and Denver and Gus came together to really reinvigorate Four Corners, it wasn't to try and take over anything. It was to try and save us. To save us from all this stuff that our parents were just letting go to waste. Maybe they were the Death Star. The Evil Empire. But we aren't. We actually do care, and we want to succeed without hurting anybody."

"I really do believe you."

He kissed her on the cheek and got out of bed, pushing back against the unfamiliar feeling that was invading his chest.

"I'll see you later."

He got dressed, and Quinn was still working her way out of bed, and he decided that it would be best if he left as quickly as possible.

Because it was one thing to have a conversation with her, it was one thing to have sex with her, but it was quite another to indulge the strange feelings that were expanding inside him. Those, he couldn't quite come to terms with. Those, he couldn't quite understand.

And so he found it best to just go and work. Because that was what he was good at. And that was what he understood.

CHAPTER TWENTY-ONE

QUINN SPENT THE day in the office, and she was happy for the reprieve, even though she missed him at the same time. She didn't care if that made sense. Making sense wasn't really the name of the game at this point.

She just *felt* things.

And she could honestly say it had been a long time since she'd allowed herself to do that.

Even before the anger.

Because the anger had just been a cover for other, more complex feelings.

The anger had been her putting a filter on her feelings so that it was easier to grab hold of them. Easier to understand them. To control them.

And then her solution had been to be…determined. To be the one who always knew what was going on, to be the one in control. But none of those things had made her happy.

When she really thought about it.

She was happy enough with her life, what was in it. She was happy to be at Sullivan's Point. Happy to be Fia, Rory and Alaina's sister.

She was excited about the farm store.

But there were things that were missing. From her life, from her experiences. She knew that for sure.

And she was trying *not* to get all excited about the

idea that Levi was giving her something new. She was, though, and maybe that was the triumph of hope over experience in her life.

When had a man ever done what he'd said? Her father was so disappointing on so many fronts. She hadn't even known everything that he had done to Levi until recently, and it was alarming to believe that one man could be responsible for the emotional scarring of so many people that she cared about.

Her sisters. Her. Her mother. Levi.

Levi.

Her heart had hurt for him the whole time she had worked on the office. All she could think was how hard he must work. She was so proud of all the work-arounds. The way he had accessibility set up on his computer, the way that he had figured out his own brain.

He didn't actually *need* her. But if she could make something easier, she wanted to. Because being able to help and accept help in that way was something she and her sisters had had to figure out a long time ago. To play into their strengths, and let the strength of other people cover their deficits. That was really what was happening here. Levi had so many strengths. When she really looked through his business plan, she could see that he was actually brilliant. On more levels than she had realized.

He was right—competing in beef against the Garretts and the Kings was nearly impossible. The way that he had approached it was brilliant. Specializing was brilliant. And he had done a fantastic job. He had gotten contacts, and he was actually a lot more organized than it appeared on first glance.

Some of her work today was about educating herself. She did some reading on the fact that dyslexic organization tended to be three-dimensional, rather than simply sequential. So what made sense to her wouldn't make sense to him, and what seemed messy to her was actually arranged in a way that worked for his thought process.

She found a bunch of color-coded folders deep in his office and determined he'd meant to get papers organized by color so he would find taxes, invoices and other things at a glance. Once it was all put together, it would be easy.

Well, as easy as this stuff was. Nobody liked doing paperwork.

It was interesting to care about somebody else's success. Their operation. She knew Four Corners, and she knew it well. But watching the way that Levi managed a smaller spread was really interesting.

And it only made her more and more in awe of him.

"I'm back with dinner."

She heard his voice through the door and perked up.

"Dinner?"

"I went down to John's and got some fried chicken. Now, if he knew that I was feeding a Sullivan, he might have rescinded some of the drumsticks."

"I'm starving," she said.

"Well, maybe we should have a picnic."

"Where?"

"The firepit."

He didn't have to ask her twice. She took two beers out of the fridge and went outside, and Levi brought a brown paper bag out and set it down on the small table by the firepit. He took out a smaller bag filled with fried chicken, a tub of coleslaw, a tub of macaroni salad, a tub of potato salad…

"Is everything mayonnaise-based?"

"Everything except the chicken. And the rolls."

"I'm not complaining, actually. It's just interesting how much they are essentially all the same food."

"But they aren't," he said. "First of all, because the potato salad has mustard in it, but also because it has potatoes."

"Good point," she said.

"I make a lot of those."

He grinned at her.

She felt…shimmering and ridiculous, and a little bit like she'd been hit over the head.

Or perhaps thrown into a pond.

"Thank you," she said. "You worked all day and then went and got dinner."

"Well, I like working the ranch. I do not like sitting in my office and going over all the things that you were dealing with. I definitely felt like I owed you dinner."

He started to dish food onto his plate. He heaped food on, in big mounds, and she wondered about him being an eighteen-year-old boy, responsible for those other children.

"How was mealtime? With the kids, I mean, after your parents."

He sat down and dug his fork into a mound of potatoes, and she realized her plate was still empty, so she went and got her own food.

"Well, at first, women in the community brought food. Meal trains are how you take care of people. I was taken care of, Quinn. By some. Your mom even brought some food over a few times. It wasn't all bad. There were people who cared. But that doesn't last. So eventually we had a lot of meals like this, chicken from the store and sides."

"You worked so hard, you must have been hungry all the time."

"I was. And here's the thing… The deal with your dad is complicated. I'm angry about it, because did he take advantage to an extent? Yes. But did I have steady income? Yeah. We weren't rich, but we always ate. I could always go to the Minute Market and grab a bite when I went to buy feed—which I could also afford. So did we get the best deal? No. But did we have enough? Yeah."

"I'm glad you didn't go hungry."

He shook his head. "Nah. It was nothing fancy. I learned to make a few things. I'd put meals in the slow cooker in the morning so we could come back to food in the evening. I adapted. You do adapt."

She was familiar. She'd adapted. The Sullivans kept on adapting. Some of it was good—figuring out ways to use the land that were sustainable for them.

And some weren't. Like using anger as a shield, and then using a sense of superiority and education as another, so you never had to deal with your deeper emotions.

"What were the kids like?"

"Camilla never knew any different. She was barely one when Mom died. Two when Dad did. I think she missed Dad, but she adapted to me easily enough. She needed to be carried around everywhere, though. Jessie was seven, and it was…hard. She was just a little girl whose whole life got upended, and she ended up sticking to me pretty hard all day every day. Dylan was thirteen. He wanted to fight. Everyone and everything. I guess it was the military or prison, so I should be glad he chose the military. But he has taken a few years off my life."

She took a bite of her macaroni salad. "I can relate to him. To the anger. Because the alternative is pain." She met his gaze. "I didn't want to be in pain. I didn't want to grieve. So I just…let my anger power me. Until my goals could. But even those were just distractions from feeling."

"Sometimes keeping moving is all you've got, though. I don't know what else there is."

And neither did she. Except there was this. They had this.

"I like you," she said. "If you didn't know."

"I like you, too, carrot," he said.

"I'm glad to hear that, because just yesterday you said you didn't."

"I'm a stubborn cuss. So even when I change my opinion on something, sometimes it takes me a while to admit it."

"I hadn't noticed," she said.

"Liar."

"I thought you said you liked me."

"I *do*. That doesn't mean you're not a liar."

She was, though. Because there was something else she'd left behind when her father had abandoned them, and that was all those softer feelings she'd had for him. The very idea had felt impossible because she just couldn't want any more things she couldn't have.

But she'd shared all these other things with him, and now she wanted him to have this, too.

To know that…this mattered to her. Because of who they were now, but also because of how she'd felt then.

She smiled. "I have something to tell you."

"What is it you have to tell me?"

"I had a crush on you. When I was fourteen."

"You had a crush on me?"

"Yes. You spent a lot of time at our house back then. From the time I was a kid, admittedly, but I just remembered the first time I noticed you. Really noticed you. My dad left and you didn't come around anymore because, of course, your deal was with him…"

"It's a good thing you didn't actually know what I was talking to your dad about, because usually we were having a fight about the whole thing."

"Yeah, I get that now. But I didn't then. I remember sometimes I'd see you around town in… You know, you're definitely one of the reasons I never had sex in college."

He looked like he'd been slapped with a fish. "I'm one of the reasons you didn't have sex in college?"

"Yes," she said. "Because I was attracted to you, and there was no one, surfer or otherwise, that I met down there who made me feel even half of what you did. And I told myself that I didn't actually have a crush on you, I just thought you were attractive, because it wasn't like I knew you or anything, but you definitely shaped my taste in male aesthetics."

"Thank you, I think."

"Well, I just thought you should know. Because whatever you thought about me, and what I thought about you when we met, you were missing that layer. It's probably why I got riled up so easily, and so quickly. You made me feel things, confusing things. Things I really tried not to feel."

"Your dad made you feel badly about your feelings."

"Yes. I…humiliated myself chasing him. Begging

him to stay. I mean, I had all kinds of dreams. Who doesn't when they're a teenager? I wanted to work the ranch. I wanted to leave. I wanted to go to college. I wanted you to kiss me, and I wanted to travel the world and be tied down by nobody. I wanted to get married and settle down. I wanted everything. All of it. Because that's how it should be when you're young and you haven't been hurt. You should be able to see all the possibilities. It sucks when you lose that."

He nodded slowly. "Yeah. I remember that. Just vaguely. I dreamed about leaving. Riding in the rodeo. All that fame and glory. And the girls. I dreamed about going out to honky-tonks every night and drinking beer, doing whatever the hell I wanted, because, of course, my mother would've taken a dim view to such a thing."

"Right. Of course."

"But that didn't·happen."

"No. Well, I still got to go to college. I knew I didn't want love or marriage anymore, because it was so risky. I knew there wouldn't be any world-traveling. I knew I couldn't let Fia carry everything."

"Is Sullivan's actually in a precarious position?"

"As far as I know, there is a very old stipulation in the agreement that if we're not profitable for too many years in a row, we might have to begin selling our acreage off to the other families. That has never come up. No one has ever acted like they wanted to do that, but it is something that I'm very aware of. We struggled. We struggled because the foundation was never quite as firm as the other ranches anyway, and then we got left to it really abruptly."

"I relate to that, too."

"I know. And a lot of the problems were caused by my dad. So, there's another thing we have in common."

"Your dad's not the cause of all my problems. Definitely one that got me, but not all of them."

"What gave you the strength to do that? To take care of everybody."

"There was no other choice. I love my brother and sisters, and somebody had to take care of them. I could never let them get taken off the ranch. At the end of the day, whatever dream I had out there of the rodeo, of glory, none of that was real. This place is real. My family is real. And they were all I had left. So the decision was easy. And it wasn't even really a decision. It's clarifying, when you lose all that. You cling to what matters."

"Yeah," she said softly. "I know my parents didn't die, but I actually do understand that. We've clung to each other because everyone else is off doing their own thing. So we have to love it. The land. We have to love what we do. We have to take care of it. We have to take care of each other. Because the simple truth is that nobody else will. So we do."

He looked away, distant, and she only stared at him. He was just so handsome. So singular.

He always had been. And back then he had been unobtainable. Much too old. But right now, he was here, and she could reach out and touch him. She felt like that was a lesson. And something. She just didn't know what yet.

"Did your parents know? About your school problems?"

"No," he said. "They just thought I didn't like school. That's all. I'll never know if they'd have figured it out.

There was a lot going on. It couldn't be about me. And then there wasn't time."

"Well, you're allowed to be angry about that. About the fact that...you had to give out care you couldn't have yourself."

He looked over at her, his expression breaking. There was no other description for it. His forehead wrinkled, his mouth turning down. "Well. I guess that I am." He frowned. "I...I wish it was different. Or maybe that I was. I wish I could have... I love my siblings."

"But you never got to be a kid."

"I never got to fully grow up. Which sounds weird, I know. It sounds like I had to grow up overnight, but what I had to do was learn how to take care of other people. How to be an invulnerable parental stand-in. I...I never learned to have relationships. Really, until I started working with the Huckleberry County Ranching Association, I didn't even know how to deal with other people. Other adults. I have Damien, the one friend I've had since childhood, and otherwise... I wave to everyone in town. I do a good job of looking like I have it all together."

"But you're carrying so much on your own."

He nodded.

Quinn's heart squeezed. And she wanted to get closer to him. Wanted to lean on him. She and Levi both agreed on one thing. You couldn't depend on other people. You had to stand on your own feet. But she wanted to lean on him, and she didn't know what she was supposed to do with that. Because she knew better. Because he knew better. They both did.

"You want to stay the night?"

She dropped her fork into her macaroni salad. "Yeah," she said.

"Your sisters won't be mad at you?"

She grimaced. "Not *mad* at me. They might have questions. But I'll answer them tomorrow."

Tomorrow. Tomorrow would be a fine time to answer questions.

They finished eating in relative silence, and she grabbed her phone, just firing off a quick text to Fia.

I won't be home tonight.

Why?

I'm staying with Levi.

You're staying overnight at Levi's?

Yes.

There were dots. And dots again. They came and went, and came back. It was clear that Fia had no idea how to respond to this. That was fine. Quinn didn't really know how to respond, either. But it was happening.

We'll talk tomorrow, Quinn typed in, and hit Send.

Okay.

She helped Levi clear up the firepit area, and they did their minimal dishes. It was strange, to be so domestic with him. And wonderful, too. Her knee-jerk response was to want to pull away from it, but that was what she'd been doing every time they got angry with each other, every time they fought. Every time she got pointy.

Maybe the secret to being sticky, and a little more like honey, was to not turn herself into a blade at every opportunity. But rather to just leave herself open to the moment. Maybe that was it.

So she resisted the urge to get pointy. And she just enjoyed it, being with him. Afterward they went upstairs, and he laid her down on the bed, and he stripped her slowly. And when he made love to her, he teased her, tortured her. Kept it slow, kept it at his pace.

"You can't just have book learning, Quinn. It's not enough. You need someone with hands-on experience to teach you."

By the time they were finished, she was gasping for air. Clinging to him.

And when she was spent, she crawled beneath the covers and waited for him to come to her. She looked around the room, and one of the things that surprised her the most was the bookshelf in the corner.

She got up and padded over to the bookcase naked, looking at the spines.

"My mom and dad's," he said. "I moved them all from the small house when we brought them here. My mom liked to read."

"It's a good library," Quinn said.

He shrugged. "Kind of ironic. Got left a bunch of books."

"It's not ironic. It's just perfect. You love books. Audiobooks, you told me."

"It isn't the same thing."

"Yes, it is. It's absolutely the same thing. You love stories. It doesn't matter what format you take them in."

She grabbed a copy of *Pride and Prejudice* from the shelf and looked it over. It was a hardcover with gold letters. Beautiful.

"Have you read this one?"

"No."

"I'll read it to you."

He got that same funny look on his face, boyish, only this time a little bit skeptical. "You want to read it to me?"

"Yes," she said. "Let me."

"Okay."

She took the book over to the bed and got in it, partly beneath the covers, sitting against the pillow, leaning against the headboard. He joined her in bed, and she opened the book and started to read. She wasn't sure how they shifted, but eventually, Levi was lying across her lap, his eyes closed. She held the book over him with one hand, and with the other, she pushed her fingers through his hair as she read about Elizabeth Bennet sparring with Mr. Darcy.

"Sounds familiar," he murmured.

"Yeah, just a little bit," she said.

"I like it." He paused. "I like being able to hear something my mom read. Thank you."

She finished the chapter, even though the letters were blurry because her eyes had filled with tears she was trying not to show him, and put the book down. And then they both got beneath the covers, and he pulled her into his arms.

Quinn was sleepy, but she knew she wouldn't just be falling asleep. Because she wanted to live in this moment for as long as possible. In the sticky, sweet honey of it all. With Levi Granger, of all people. And maybe separately, it had been said that both of them were a little bit difficult. But together, right now, everything felt wonderful.

CHAPTER TWENTY-TWO

LEVI MADE HER BREAKFAST, which was very nice, but did not ease the fact that she had to do the walk of shame back to the farmhouse now.

"Am I going to have to worry about your sister showing up to my house with a shotgun?"

Quinn would've loved to laugh and say no. Because it was a ridiculous image. To him, maybe. To her, it seemed all too possible.

"I'll try to stop her from showing up with a shotgun," she said. "I don't actually know what her policy is on all of this. By the time we found out that Alaina was pregnant—" His expression shifted, just slightly, but she could see genuine *horror* there. "Not that that's the same. But by the time we all found out that Alaina was having a baby, the guy had gone. And Gus had already thrown his hat into the ring and offered to marry her. So. Fia never really got to grab her shotgun. I'm not saying that she won't."

"Right," he said.

"Thanks for breakfast. And the sex." She stretched up on her toes and kissed his mouth, and then he wrapped his arm around her waist and looked her dead in the eyes.

"It wasn't just sex. You know that, right?"

She felt warm. And she didn't know why he was saying that to her. Because he'd said that he didn't want anything. And the mention of pregnancy had terrified him; she could see it in the look on his face.

And yet… Then he did things like this. Except maybe there was ground between a fling—which she had already decided this could never be—and marriage and the like, and he wanted to make sure that she knew that even if it wasn't everything, it was different.

"I know," she said softly.

"Thanks for reading to me."

And there was a wealth of words in that simple statement. Because her reading to him no longer felt like something condescending. He took it the way that she meant it. That she had found a way to fit around him, around his life, and was just enjoying the ways they were different, the ways she could help him and the ways he could help her.

"I'll…I'll see you later?"

"You know where I live. I haven't been able to get rid of you for a few weeks now, and suddenly you're worried that you're not going to see me?"

No. Suddenly she was worried about how badly he wanted her there, and whether or not she was overstepping, because her feelings were involved.

Oh, boy, were they ever involved.

"See you later."

She bolstered herself on the drive back home with a fortifying breath, with the windows down.

She was grateful that she'd been with Levi a few times before Fia had found out, but it still felt new and raw and not like something she wanted to share, but this was what happened when you lived in your sisters' pockets.

She didn't play any music or anything as she drove. She just replayed the events of the night before, reinforcing that this was right. That they were right.

That everything they did, everything they were, was special.

How strange. She had wanted to find this, this softness inside her, and hadn't been able to. And now she didn't know how to get rid of it.

She was honey. Gooey and sticky and soft, and utterly lost.

She couldn't find pointy with anything she was.

She pulled up to the house and saw her sister Alaina's car in the driveway.

Great. They were ganging up on her.

She sighed and walked up the front steps, into the quaint little house. Fia was seated at the kitchen table with a large cup of coffee. Rory was standing at the cheerful yellow stove with a ruffly apron on and was cooking pancakes. Alaina was standing next to the high chair, where the baby was, and was also wearing an apron, holding a bowl where she was macerating some strawberries.

"So there you are," said Alaina. "We thought you might need some food to get your strength back up after the night you had."

"I ate. Thank you. He made breakfast."

They all stared at her.

"I'm not sure why you all think this is your business."

"Because you…"

"Nothing," she said. "I nothing. I was away at college for four years. None of you know what I did there. None of you had any idea when I stayed out all night."

"Did you?"

This came from Fia, who looked entirely too sharp and perceptive.

"None of your business."

"Okay, so let's say that you led a wild life at college. You have not led a wild life since returning, and Levi Granger is our neighbor, and he's eleven years older than you."

Quinn snorted. "Suddenly, you know so much about Levi, when, before, you didn't really seem to."

"It's convenient that way, sister brain."

"I'm fine," said Quinn. "I like him. I like him a lot."

"Listen," said Alaina. "We can all agree, he's hot as shit." Everybody looked at Alaina. "*What?* I'm married. I'm not dead. Also, my husband is more years older than me than that. So."

"You," said Fia, "got yourself in trouble…"

"I *got myself in trouble*? Is this the 1950s?"

"No, it was just different," said Fia. "Gus made his intentions very clear. In fact, his whole intent was to marry you."

"I know," said Alaina. "And to never have sex with me. Because he's an idiot. But thankfully, I brought him around to the idea."

"Goodness," said Rory.

"Oh, chill out, virgin," said Alaina.

Rory frowned. "Rude."

"I'm rude," said Alaina, shrugging. "At least, sometimes. But my point is, it's not really anybody's business what Quinn is doing or with who. And it's not fair to treat her like she's a child just because he's older. He's *hot*, and it's obvious why any woman would want to sleep with him regardless of age. She's not a child."

"Thank you," said Quinn.

Even though she knew that Alaina being her advocate was dubious at best. Seeing as Alaina had made some questionable decisions along the road to happiness.

Alaina was deliriously happy now. Yeah, she'd kissed a frog. An epic frog who had abandoned her when she was pregnant, but she'd found the right man after that. There was nothing that had made her ruined or kept her from happiness, and while Quinn didn't think she could do the being-married-and-having-children thing, the point was, whatever happened with Levi, there would be happiness on the other side.

Sure, there was Fia. Who was bitter and wretched and had never gotten over Landry. Or whatever. But that didn't mean it would be Quinn's fate.

She and Levi had been honest with each other.

Who knew what Fia had expected from Landry?

"So yeah, I'm sleeping with him, since you are being so nosy," she said. "But I don't actually want to fall in love and get married. I don't want to have kids. No offense, Alaina."

"Why would I be offended that you don't want my life? I don't care."

She really did love her younger sister.

"Good. I'm not saying there's anything wrong with it. I'm just saying…it's not for me. At least, not yet." Except she felt a tugging in her heart that made her feel like maybe that was a lie. Because she was softer now, changing. And she really hated the idea that somehow sex with Levi had changed her fundamentally. Because she had always rejected the idea that you weren't a woman until a man made you one, because it was ridiculous. Because virginity was totally a social construct and…

It hadn't really felt like one in bed with the two of them, when society wasn't around.

But then, she had also always known that sex wasn't a handshake. It wasn't that she judged people for doing it casually—she didn't—it was that for her she had always known it never could be wholly casual.

And how could it be with Levi? Her interactions with him had been thorny and difficult from the beginning. Complicated. So clearly anything naked with him was going to be complicated.

"It's just a lot," said Fia.

"I didn't say it *wasn't* a lot. It is a lot. He's a lot. But he's worth it. I like him. I mean, I really like him. As a human being, quite apart from the sex."

"Is it electric?" Rory asked, sounding dreamy.

She felt shy, and her face got hot.

"It is…*personal.* Very personal."

"That's not fair," said Rory.

"If you want details," said Alaina, "I am happy to share. Because Gus is amazing." She sniffed. "And I actually have something to compare him to. Because he isn't the only man I've had sex with."

"We get it," said Quinn.

"Is Levi the only…?" Alaina asked.

"Maybe," said Quinn. "But also not your business. And you should all know that he didn't seduce me, I seduced him, and you can't get mad at him, and also don't go to his house with a gun, Fia."

"Why would I do that?" Fia asked.

"I don't know," said Quinn. "You're a loose cannon."

Fia smiled. "I *am* a loose cannon—it's true. And a badass."

"Yes, yes," Quinn said, rolling her eyes.

"But you're happy," said Fia. "Like you're good. You don't feel coerced and you don't feel…"

"I said that. You don't need to be a hen about it. I'm not going to get broken up over it. He has been very open and honest with me, and I've been very open and honest with him. It's going to be fine."

And she ignored the slightly ominous feeling that bloomed at the center of her breast as she said that. There was no reason for it to be ominous. There was nothing ominous about it.

"We get started stocking the store today," said Fia.

"You should come to Levi's. And see the road. Drive on it."

"All right. You gotta do a little bit of work on that."

"Maybe Levi will help," said Quinn. "Because, you know, he likes me now."

"Well, that is a great reason to sleep with him."

Quinn rolled her eyes. "I did not whore myself out for a backhoe and access to his road."

"That would make *you* kind of a backhoe," said Alaina.

"*Rude.* Anyway. I will talk to Levi about maybe excavating that little bit that we need to finish up the road to the place."

"Perfect. Let's all go over now."

"Let me give him a warning," said Quinn.

"You must really like him," said Fia. "Because since when are you ever interested in giving somebody a warning?"

Well, Quinn couldn't really say. But she did know

that she didn't want Levi to be wholly ambushed by her sisters. And so, she did send a cautionary text.

When they all showed up, she could feel her sisters giving him a much more thorough examination than was appropriate.

"Good to see you," said Fia.

"You, too," said Levi.

"We were actually wondering if we could pay you to finish digging out the road to the farm store. We can hire somebody to do it, but that will mean bringing somebody else onto your land," Quinn said, looking at both Levi and Fia as she spoke.

"That's kind of the whole point of the road, isn't it?" Levi asked.

"Yes, it is. But I do have maybe a suggestion. That you might route the road slightly differently around certain spots."

"That's not a bad idea," he said.

She was so careful to not overshare his story. He'd told her things that he simply didn't talk about with other people, and she didn't want to go blabbing it to all the land. Even if all the land was just her sisters.

"My parents' graves are out there," he said, and that broke the seal on some of what she'd been holding back. "So yes, it might be nice to split the road at some point and build up a wall or a hedge around that so that my family is still able to use that part privately."

"We will pay for that," said Fia.

"It isn't going to cost me anything. I have the equipment to do it."

"It doesn't matter. It's your labor, and you should be compensated. We have the budget."

"I'll tell you what. Why don't you wait and give me

a little bit out of the profits? It's my understanding that you've been having to dip into the community funds for this project, and that there's a little bit of tension because of that."

Fia looked at Quinn, and then at Levi. "That would actually be wonderful, but you don't have to do that."

"It's a time expense, not an up-front expense, and I can definitely shoulder that. I appreciate you wanting to be fair. But I am satisfied that this is fair."

"Thank you, Levi," said Fia.

And Quinn knew that, whatever else happened, Fia at least could see in that moment what Quinn saw. That Levi was solid and steady and good. That he was the kind of man who looked out for his own.

And right now, he was treating Quinn like she was his own.

That thought made something hot and needy bloom in her stomach. She hadn't belonged to anybody in a long time.

And maybe she never really had. Not in that glorious, unconditional way that your parents should feel like you belonged to them.

She felt guilty, because it wasn't like her mother was awful. And her father hadn't been awful all the time. It was just in the end it had been unraveling, and he'd wanted to go, and maybe, just maybe, he had driven a wedge between the two of them so that the leaving would be easier. It wasn't. It never could be.

Oh, it really never could be.

There was nothing easy about leaving. And nothing good about it. And it made it difficult for her to remember the decent things in her childhood.

It had made her spiky and pointy and unpleasant.

And maybe all she had needed was a little bit of belonging to get back to being soft.

Maybe it was Levi, Levi himself, not the sex, but the way that he cared, that was softening her. Healing some of those old wounds. Giving her a chance to let down her guard.

Both of them had made such strong statements against vulnerability, but she was beginning to think that there just had to be a little bit of vulnerability to get you through life.

"What if we drove over to the store now?" Levi suggested.

"I'll ride with you," said Quinn.

CHAPTER TWENTY-THREE

WHEN ALL THE Sullivan sisters had shown up at his property, he hadn't quite known what to do with it. It was a whole lot of feminine fluttering, red hair and floral dresses.

And they all knew that he was sleeping with their sister, so they'd been giving him shiny, evil eyes every chance they got.

But it had all gone smoothly enough, and now he was invited to the store.

When they got into the truck, Levi reached across the space and took her hand in his. He was not quite sure what had led to that compulsion, and yet he felt it.

To just be closer to her.

He led the way down the dirt road that took them to the edge of his property.

Even though there was no road dug between the two properties now, it was drivable, across the flat field.

He could see the building that would house the farm store in the distance, and took them straight there. It was a quick and easy drive, much more so than if they were to go through the center of their land.

He could definitely see why they wanted to use it.

The building had been painted a slate gray with stark white accents. It looked like something his sisters would want to stop at and spend the afternoon poring through the different items on the shelves.

He could clearly see what sort of person would be coming to this place, and he had to give them that it was pretty darn smart.

"It's looking great," he said.

"It is," said Quinn. "I've been so consumed with trying to convince you to let us use the road that I haven't actually been out here for the last couple of weeks. They made a lot more progress. Gus has put in a lot of hours on the place. Honestly, my sister marrying into the McCloud family has been one of the more helpful things. We suddenly have access to a lot more labor that's just a favor and not an official thing that's going to cost us."

"Yeah. I imagine that is nice."

"Thank you. Thank you for being so good."

He shook his head. "I don't know that I'm actually all that good."

He had to be. For all these years. And somehow, he never quite knew if it was him, or just something he had to do. Maybe that wouldn't make sense to a lot of people, but he felt it all the same.

He'd wanted to go out and be a rodeo-riding ne'er-do-well who drank in corrals and lived kind of a hard life.

He had.

He'd fallen into a domestic life. He hadn't really had a choice. He didn't know what the hell that said about him.

"I told you," he said. "I'm done taking care of people."

"But here you are, taking care of us."

He huffed. "Not really."

He let go of her hand and turned the wheel on the truck sharply, pulling in front of the building.

They got out and walked inside.

It was clean and bright with different tables set up for displays. There was a stack of little signs in the corner, and the one on the top said Veggies.

So he imagined these were going to be placed all around when they got the displays up.

"We're going to be able to open next week," said Fia. "I mean, I don't want to put that much pressure on you to get the road done."

"It'll take me two days," he said. "I can start tomorrow if you want."

"Yes," said Fia. "That would be great. I'll start advertising for our soft open in two weeks, and then in three weeks we'll have a big party. We'll invite the whole town. And we will give everyone in town a chance to have items featured in the store."

"We really do care about the town," said Quinn. "We care about whether or not the town is thriving. If they aren't, then our own success doesn't mean as much. This is our home."

And he felt really humbled by that, in this moment, because he could see it to be true.

Because actually every step of the way, even if she hadn't done it with all diplomacy all the time, Quinn had only ever been trying to do the best thing for everybody. She had never behaved in a selfish way. Not even once. And he had been so lost in his own shit, and so determined to compare her to her father, that he just hadn't fully given her the credit that she deserved.

And that was on him.

He might have to wonder whether or not he was naturally a decent human being. The truth was, his father had been that man. Steady and good and wonderful, loving his wife so much that it had put him into the ground to lose her.

Levi had just been living in the aftermath of it. Trying to fill his shoes.

Quinn had been raised by a man who didn't seem to care about anybody but himself. A man who had abandoned his family, his ranch. A man who was alive and well, but never seemed to speak to his children.

Yet here these women were, in their community, doing good work, trying to keep their ranch going, trying to pull their weight.

Quinn had even taken the time to make sure that she offered him something in exchange for the use of his land. She hadn't just been fair, she'd been kind.

And he hadn't recognized it because he had associated her with her dad. He had associated her enthusiasm with him.

And he stopped right then and there in the store and turned to her. "I'm sorry, Quinn. I really am. For assuming the worst about you like I did. All of you, actually. Because you've never done anything, personally, to indicate that you didn't care about the community. I was hanging on to some old resentment, and I let that cloud how I approached this."

"It's okay. I think that your concerns about whether or not we bypass the town were valid," said Quinn. "But I am glad that we were able to come up with this as a solution. I get shortsighted, Levi. I'm not perfect. I get very entrenched in what I want, and I don't always consider all of the consequences."

"But you're coming from a good place. And I see that now."

She smiled, and it made his chest feel like it was expanding.

"Do you need any help getting the store set up?"

"I think we've got that covered," said Fia. "But if you can do the road, then the rest should take care of itself."

"I can do that," he said.

CHAPTER TWENTY-FOUR

HE GOT THE road dug out as quickly as possible, and Quinn was fairly busy over the next few weeks setting up the store.

And he took every opportunity possible to stop in and see about the progress.

It was coming together beautifully.

They had fresh-cut flowers and beautiful-looking produce. They had hazelnuts and almonds and walnuts, all taken from the farm.

They had meat from the Kings and the Garretts. But they had taken chicken and lamb from some other places that were local, and pork, as well.

And there was a little display in the corner of processed foods, John's stock, and it aesthetically did not go with the store at all, but if anybody passed through and they wanted a bag of chips, they could buy that, and the money would go back to John.

The care and thoughtfulness that the sisters had taken to include the community really was something.

He was...*proud* of Quinn.

He couldn't deny that.

The grand opening was coming up quick, and more often than not, Quinn slept at his place.

That was strange, too.

He had been domestic all of his life, but not with a

woman. And somehow, it felt different. Different from
the life he had been shoved into at eighteen. A life he
hadn't been certain he had the ability to keep going.

Yes, it felt pretty damn different.

Being with Quinn in the house that he had built was
something entirely different from being with his siblings in a house that his parents had built and decorated
and put together.

The new house, which, of course, they'd been in now
for a few years, was something that he and his siblings
had designed together, but mainly, it had been something that he wanted, because he'd known that he would
be the one that stayed.

It felt…chosen. This life. Waking up with Quinn
every morning and going to bed with her every night.

Well, almost every night.

She'd worked late at the farm store last night and
hadn't come to his place. She did remind him sometimes
that she had to go and get new clothes, even though he
had insisted she did not need to wear clothes when she
was at his house.

The house felt empty now, and not in a good way.

What a strange thing. He had been looking forward
to the emptiness. It was something he'd felt like he'd
earned, and yet now he didn't enjoy it all that much. Because not only did it mean his siblings were gone, but
that Quinn was, as well.

He picked up the phone and called Damien without
thinking, as he sat there at the kitchen table all by himself with his cup of coffee.

"Hey," he said.

"Hey, yourself."

"Is Jessie there?"

"Yeah."

"Do you think either of you would like to come down here for the grand opening of the Sullivan sisters' farm store?"

"What?" Damien asked.

"The Sullivan sisters are opening up a farm store…"

"I got that, but are you there to spray-paint it with invectives? Because you aren't really a huge fan of the Sullivan family."

And this was the problem with not being the kind of guy who shared what was going on in his life. His best friend was confused, and rightfully so.

"Well, it's just that she's started up this farm store and I agreed to let them use my land to take the cars through, and I dug a road and…" He realized there was still no context, and his explanation didn't make any sense.

"Yeah, I'm confused," said Damien. "Who is *she*? And why does she matter?"

"I…I'm in kind of a relationship with Quinn Sullivan."

"You're in a relationship?" The scream that came through the phone was his sister Jessie, and indicated that Damien had in fact had him on speakerphone.

"Not anything permanent—don't go getting sentimental. But I got to know her, and I just thought it would be good if people come out and support the opening of the store. Because now I support the opening of the store. You know, by extension of being in a…relationship."

"Holy hell," said Damien. "Honey, go outside and look and see if there's a pig flying in the sky."

"Knock it off," said Levi. "I let you off easy when I

found that you were sleeping with my sister, so maybe don't be a huge jerk to me now."

"No one's being a jerk," said Damien. "I'm just surprised. It's unlike you, all of this. *Any* of it."

Yeah. It was. But so what? Yeah, it was unlike him. And *so what*.

Why couldn't he be unlike himself?

Maybe he wasn't actually being unlike himself.

Maybe this was what life would have been like for him if he hadn't been raising kids for years and years.

Nobody'd ever thought of that, he bet.

"I'm happy for you, Levi," Jessie said softly. "We worry about you."

"You don't need to worry about me," he said. "I spent all those years taking care of you, and now that you've moved out, you suddenly worry about me? It doesn't make any sense."

"That's just it. You spent all those years taking care of us. While we got to grow and change and do whatever we wanted. While we got to grieve. And when did you, Levi?"

That really did suck all the breath from his lungs. And every word from his soul. He couldn't speak. He felt frozen with it. "I'm fine. I don't need to do that."

"I don't believe you," she said. "I think you do. And I think that we've all been waiting to see if you were going to collapse without us here. Or entrench and become the meanest old man in the history of the world."

"I'm *thirty-six*. Your fiancé is thirty-six also."

"It's a state of mind," said Damien.

"Yeah, thank you. Fuck off."

"I'm not trying to offend you," she said. "But you were able to take care of other people and not really…"

"I did what I had to do. And I had my own feelings. Believe me."

Except he knew she was close to truths he'd identified a long time ago. But what did it matter? He didn't know what to do about it.

He'd had to keep running.

It was all he knew how to do.

"I know you did," said Jessie softly. "And a lot of distractions, too. And you made it so that we never suffered. But I just wonder who did that for you. Who took care of you. Nobody, and I think we want to rectify that."

"Don't worry about me," he said. "I'm good."

"Do you love her?"

That question hit him square in the chest.

He couldn't say no. In these past weeks, he'd been a strange, bittersweet happy he hadn't even known existed.

Quinn brought a softness and a sharpness into his life that he hadn't known he was missing.

She was funny and quick. She had a temper, but she was also cute, and she turned red when he called her *carrot*. And he really did care about the girl a whole hell of a lot.

But love…

Love wasn't in the cards for him, simply because it couldn't be.

Because love made him think of his father. Stumbling around for months, gray and lifeless, and nothing like he used to be. A man whose soul had gone out of him when his other half left the earth.

And then he could remember, clearly, the day his father had gone to the ground out in the field.

It made his own chest ache to even think about it.

He had often thought he had his father's heart. He'd been to see several doctors, cardiologists, who'd said that what his father had was not hereditary. Not a genetic heart condition or anything like that. The widower phenomenon was real. The stress that grief put on your heart was something many people couldn't get past. It was common, Levi had found out, for spouses to die the same year as each other.

But he had his dad's heart. For the land, for his family.

He had his dad's heart.

"She's a great woman," said Levi. "Let's just leave it at that. I enjoy spending time with her, and I care about her and her store. So can you come?"

"Yes," said Jessie. "We'll be there."

"Good."

QUINN BROUGHT A big duffel bag full of clothes over to Levi's the night before the grand opening of the farm store.

She planned on having him help her choose dresses, which was kind of a funny thing, because normally she would have done that with her sisters, but she wanted his opinion.

One of the most charming things about Levi was that he actually really liked to watch her try on clothes. She had a feeling it was because she got naked in between, but he seemed completely captivated by every new outfit she put on.

It made her smile a little bit just thinking about it. When she got there, she was shocked to come into the kitchen and find Levi there pulling a roast out of the oven.

"What are you doing?"

"Cooking. For you. You've been working so damned hard."

"I have been. But this is like Sunday dinner." –

"Yeah. Well. I thought it might be good to have the leftovers. Jessie and Damien are going to stay the night down in the cabin tomorrow."

"Really?" She felt instantly nervous at the idea of meeting his other sister.

"Yeah. They're coming for the store opening."

She just stopped and stared at him. Levi Granger. *Her...*

She didn't know what he was to her. Her lover. Undeniably.

But he felt like more than that. She crossed the space and put her hand on his face, stretched up on her toes and kissed him on the lips.

"You are wonderful," she said.

"Thanks," he said.

"Today we got all the artisan stuff into the store, and it looks amazing. Clay pots and handmade baskets, trivets made out of marble and wood. Glorious. Everything is all set up, and I am so excited. We've baked so many pies, and they're gorgeous. I'm really sorry I didn't bring you one. I should have. I'll get one from the store tomorrow."

He waved a hand as if he was chasing her apology out of the air. "You don't need to be wasting your pies on me."

"It *isn't* a waste. You deserve it."

"Do I, carrot?"

"Yes. You do." She tapped her chin. "I need to come up with an appropriate corresponding nickname for you."

"No, you don't," he said.

"I do. My darling radish."

He grinned, albeit reluctantly. "I'm *not* your radish."

"Rutabaga."

"Nope."

"Turnip."

"My masculinity is shriveling."

She frowned. "Eggplant?"

"I mean…"

She laughed. They were ridiculous sometimes, and she never really had a person she could be wholly ridiculous with. At least, not in her memory. Not recently. She just… She was really working overtime to not think what she was beginning to feel, because she was afraid that when she thought it, she was going to say it. And she was afraid that once she said it she was going to disrupt this. She did not want to disrupt this. Because it mattered far too much to her. It mattered far more than anything.

They got plates out and set them on the table, and she loved that they were using real plates, real silverware. Because it felt official. Not like a picnic or like easy cleanup for guests. It felt like maybe they shared this place. Like it was their kitchen.

The idea of that made her heart squeeze, made her stomach go tight.

She chatted more about the farm store while they ate, and she could see that something was on his mind. She could read him now. As easy as anything. "What's going on?"

"Oh, nothing."

"Levi," she said. "I know it isn't nothing."

"It was something that my sister said," he said.

"What?"

"I haven't told anyone this," he said, the words coming rough. "Because I was never going to tell the story to my siblings, and I've never been close enough to anyone else to tell it, not even Damien."

"Tell me," she said.

"I saw my dad die. I saw him go down in the middle of the field, holding his chest, but he didn't… He didn't cry out in pain or fear or anything like that. He just went straight down. And I ran to him, and he looked up at me, but he didn't really see me. He was looking past me. And he just said her name. Two, three times. And that was it. I called for help, but he was beyond resuscitation by the time they got there. It was a massive heart attack. The kind that just takes you. And they figure it was because of the stress. The stress of his loss. A broken heart. That's what I figured. That's what I know. He didn't want to stay."

She didn't have any protection left. Not any. Not from that truth. Not from the raw admission that had just come out of his mouth.

"You saw your dad die."

He nodded. "Yeah. And, you know, I think it's right. Because he watched her go, and somebody needed to bear witness. To him. What he lost. To his light going out." He was quiet for a long moment. "His light went out when she died, though. That was when it changed. Forever. It changed forever." He coughed, like it was a replacement for a sob. "I couldn't ever talk to anyone about it. But I want you to know. I want you to understand."

He looked up at her. "I had to go on," he said. "For everybody, I had to go on. I wasn't perfect. I was a little bit messed up, and I made mistakes because of it. But I tried. I had to. I couldn't… I couldn't let my own heart give out. I had too much left to take care of."

"Levi, you are incredible. You have done so much to make everybody as okay as you possibly can and you…" She realized that while he had told her the story, he hadn't actually said what his sister had said to make him think of it.

"What did your sister say to you?"

"I asked her why they all acted like they needed to take care of me. She said I never had any time to grieve. Because I was too busy taking care of them. But what she doesn't understand is that taking care of them helped keep me together. It was a good thing. But if there's one thing I maybe needed to get out, it was that. So, thank you. Thank you for letting me tell you."

She reached across the table and put her hand over his. "Of course. Whatever you need. I'm here. Whatever you need to say, whatever you need… Whatever you need, Levi."

"Thank you."

She didn't know why she was the one that he confided in. Why they were the ones that seemed to fit each other. Or maybe her instincts had been better at fourteen than she'd realized. That was pretty funny. The idea that maybe… Just maybe her dad had been so wrong about her, even then. It almost made her want to laugh.

Instead, she helped Levi clean the kitchen up, and then they went up to bed. And when he made love to her, fierce and hot, it took everything in her to not say what was burning in her chest.

I love you.

She really did love him.

And she had tried so hard not to.

But maybe that was the lesson.

You couldn't live life protected.

You had to let yourself be broken open. Or you could never be everything that you could be.

Tomorrow, the farm store would open, and she and Levi weren't talking anymore about the inevitability of the end of all this.

Maybe it wouldn't end. But maybe it would.

Or maybe she was going to have to figure out how to fight, not just sharp and pointy, but soft.

And with everything that she had. With everything she was.

Everything he had shown her she could be.

Because she was Quinn Sullivan, every part of her. Not just controlled, motivated and perfectly held together.

She was Quinn Sullivan. Brave and afraid, determined. Confident but willing to listen. She was Quinn Sullivan. Every single part of her. And it made her feel both stronger and weaker than ever before.

And that, she figured, was just how she knew she was on the right path.

CHAPTER TWENTY-FIVE

SHE WORE A white dress to the farm store opening, because Levi had made his love of it perfectly clear that
morning when he had pushed it up around her hips and
licked her until she unraveled, and now she was wearing it, standing next to her sisters, feeling every inch
like the innocent white was a *lie*, and enjoying that
down to her socks.

Which Levi had also managed to make sexual.

Everyone had come out for the grand opening. Some
of the ranch hands from Four Corners who played in a
band were there doing live music. The Kings had even
shown up, as had the McClouds and the Garretts, all
of their respective partners and much of their extended
families.

The town of Pyrite Falls had come out for them. In
spite of everything.

They had worked so hard to patch everything up,
and she was beginning to think that they might've actually done so. They had built bridges because of Levi.
Because he had shown them their blind spots so effectively.

She really appreciated that about him. He was intense, and uncompromising, but there were reasons
for it. His own experiences had made him a staunch
defender of everyone who might need defending, in

spite of what he said about wanting to be done taking care of people. The way he'd advocated for the smaller ranches at the town hall meeting was evidence that he was a caregiver through and through. His care for others didn't hold him back, either. It was the fuel for all of his intensity. And it had helped them accomplish a hell of a lot.

"This is it," said Fia. "We're doing it. Opening the store."

"We are," she said. "It's amazing."

And then the band started playing, and Fia, who had not wanted to give a speech of any kind, grandly opened the doors.

The crowd that flooded in was enthusiastic, and pretty soon they had a line to the register that wrapped through the store and outside.

It wouldn't be like this every day, she knew that, but it was a wonderful embrace. A welcome that was beyond any of their expectations.

And when the influencer crowd showed up, Rory was filled with glee. So many girls with long, loose curls and hats taking perfectly framed photographs of every corner of the store.

"This is it," said Rory. "Perfect."

"Well, your keen eye for merchandising certainly helped with that," said Fia. "Because I don't know about any of this stuff, and I don't care about it."

"You will, when they all discover your store because of these pictures. Yeah, then you will."

Quinn went to Levi's side then, because there was a woman and another tall, good-looking man standing near him, and she assumed that that was Jessie and Damien.

"Hi," said Quinn.

"Damien, Jessie," said Levi, wrapping his arm around her waist. "This is Quinn."

He just introduced her by her first name, which honestly felt more intimate. And he had his arm around her.

"Very nice to meet you, Quinn," said Jessie. "The store looks beautiful."

"I love it. Do you think there's any chance you might want to carry my wine label in here?" Damien asked.

"Yes," she said. "We don't have wine yet."

"If I could get some of your baked goods to carry in the tasting room, that would be amazing. I don't know how easy it is for you to bake and transport many pies."

"I would love that," said Quinn. "That would be a great advertisement for the store."

"Exactly what I was thinking," said Damien.

And Quinn decided she liked him a lot. But more than that, she was lost in the way that Levi had brought her over, the way that he touched her, the way that he was being openly possessive of her in this space.

In front of God and everybody.

They worked in the store, selling things until it turned dusky.

And when they were finished, Fia was buzzing. Gus was still there, sitting in the corner playing with Alaina's hair, holding their baby in his other arm.

Fia was practically lying across the counter, and Rory was sitting in the corner, her book on her lap. Quinn had a man with her. And Levi had stayed.

"That was incredible," said Fia. "We need to get some food trucks to come park out here sometimes. Or maybe we can make soup and bread. That would be perfect. I need some really good soup recipes, and then we can have them on hot plates ready to go."

"You're already thinking of expanding?" said Levi.

"After success like that, we have to. If people could also have a little bit of lunch here…"

"Well, what would Becky think about that?" Alaina asked.

"Nobody is entitled to being the only game in town," said Levi. "As much as I support every local business, I support this one, too, and everyone ought to."

"You've changed your tune," said Gus.

Levi shrugged. "Yeah. I have."

Gus arched a brow. "Good."

The funny thing was, Levi's house was even closer to the farm store by way of the road access than their own house was. She smiled thinking about that as they drove back to his place for the night. She felt slightly disloyal, wondering if she should have gone back with her sisters, especially because Damien and Jessie were staying over anyway, albeit in a different structure.

But she wanted to be with Levi. The realization— or rather, her admittance—of how much she loved him had shifted something in her, and she wanted to be with him. She needed to be with him.

They went back to the house and went inside. Jessie and Damien came in for a while, and Damien shared his wine with all of them. They ate some baked goods from the farm store and had some local cheeses. And when it was over, she and Levi settled into their new routine of cleaning up the kitchen. He filled the sink with soapy water, and she got an apron and a dishcloth.

He had handed her the last of the wineglasses, and she held it, wiping the dish towel over the whole thing, watching as it started to shine.

This was an old dream. Or maybe one that had never gotten a chance to fully form.

And here she was now. With him. Living this kind of life she'd thought she was too wounded to have.

Men could leave. It could destroy you. But you could also live like this. With someone who supported you, cared for you. Accepted you.

Called you *carrot*.

The reward seemed so much greater than the risk.

"I love you."

She hadn't meant to say it then. Over a sink full of soapy water, and with the dishes still to be put away. She hadn't meant to say it this soon. She maybe hadn't meant to say it at all. But there had been talk of things being finished after the farm store opened, and she still didn't know where he stood on that.

So it seemed… It seemed fair…more than fair…that she put her cards on the table now. Because why not. Why not?

Well, there were so many reasons why not. But she could lose him no matter what. And she had changed. These last weeks had changed her.

"I didn't really mean to say it like this. But I do."

"Quinn," he said. "We…we talked about this."

There was no anger in his voice, and she had expected anger. Because she heard anger from him so many times. He had been so angry at her at first, and maybe this would make him mad. Make him shout.

"I know," she said. "I know we talked about it. I do. But I love you anyway."

"Quinn… Didn't you hear me? The other night. The story that I told you. When I watched my father die of a broken heart."

And there was something desperate in his voice, and something unbearably sad. Something that made her feel sorry. Like maybe she was doing something to him that she shouldn't be doing. He wasn't doing her the courtesy of being angry. She knew how to be soft now. She knew how. And she would be whatever he needed now. Soft or a fighter. Or maybe both all at once. Because she didn't have to be one thing. Because she didn't have to close herself down and cut herself off, and break herself into smaller and smaller pieces.

"Of course I heard you. And I care, about all of it. Everything that you said. It broke my heart. You should never have had to go through that. But I still love you. Because...because you are the most wonderful man, for taking care of everyone. Absolutely everyone. You deserve to be taken care of. You deserve for me to be here, loving you. And you don't need to do anything. You don't need to say anything."

He shook his head. "Quinn. You deserve somebody who isn't used up. You deserve a man who didn't...get turned into both the oldest and most immature man all at the same time, because that's what I am. I am somehow eighty years old, with no desire to have more kids or more time at home. I want to retire. And I'm also... I don't know how to do this. I never got a chance, and I'm too tired."

"I've been with you for weeks now, and nothing about you is used up. Nothing about you is done. You are the most incredible man that I have ever known. I was raised by a man who didn't know how to stay. I was raised by a man who took advantage of you, Levi. And you... You are just such a wonderful example of what somebody can be when they love selflessly. And

I don't believe that you're used up. I don't believe that you don't have anything left, but until you can find it, why don't you just let me love you. Let me have this."

"Because. Quinn…" And he looked devastated. She had been willing to take his anger. She had half expected it. But she hadn't expected him to look broken. "I have been responsible for people…"

She shook her head. "That isn't it. That isn't what's wrong. You *like* being responsible for people. You like taking care of them. Yes, you threw me in a pond, but you never actually kicked me off of your land. You explained things to me. And you *helped* us."

He looked at her, his blue eyes shattered. "I've always wondered. Which one of me is the real me. I will never know the answer to the question, Quinn, because I never got to be the version of myself that I dreamed I would be. I wanted to show people. That I was great. That I wasn't lazy. And yes, I've done something here, but it wasn't the glory that I wanted. But I don't feel unfulfilled."

"You did show them. You showed them all, and better yet, you lived gloriously. And I think that this is you. What did you think you would do when your glory days were over, Levi? Did you think you would come back here?"

"Well, yes. I did. Because I figured this place was my legacy."

"That's who you are. The man who wanted to come back here. And it would never have been when your glory days were over. Because these are glory days. You have built this ranch. You have fought through so many obstacles. The community should've taken care of you, and they didn't. An adult that you should've been able to trust took advantage of you. You are bruised. And it is understandable. You have every right to be distrustful. Of the world, of everything. And isn't Four Corners lucky that you're in the community now? That Brian Sullivan is gone? Aren't they lucky in this town that they have you to look out for them? And if some kid was ever in the position that you were, you would come alongside them and you wouldn't let them suffer. Just like you didn't let me suffer. Even though you wanted to. Even though you wanted to be angry, and you said angry things, you didn't abandon me, because that's not who you are. You didn't trick me. You didn't take advantage of me."

"I just can't," he said. "Dammit, Quinn, you have no idea how much I wish I could. If I could love a woman, it would be you." He walked toward her and cupped her face, his eyes desperate. "No one else has even come close. If I could imagine having this life, it would be with you. But in my head all I see is dropping dead out in that field in a couple of years. I fucking can't handle that. It's the unknown. I just can't."

It wasn't people he was afraid of being vulnerable to. It was the world. It was himself. It was his own heart.

She could see it in his eyes.

And she was…broken for him. For them, yes, but mostly for him.

Because Quinn had had her share of trials. The abandonment of her parents really hurt, and it had shaped her. Changed her. There was no way around that. But his life had been a different kind of hurt. The devastation and scarring that he had endured, the way that he had been used. Every time he had shown a little bit of trust in another person… She didn't know how to get past all of that. She didn't know how to fix him. She didn't know how to help him. Because there was no way to do it. No easy way.

Not when it was just that simple thing of getting over grief, of getting over loss, of getting over betrayal.

The fear of death and brokenness.

These were not things that people could do. They couldn't. It wasn't easy. And there was no real answer to any of it. She knew that. She knew that she couldn't be angry at him. Because they were Quinn and Levi in those first days, and that moment that she had yelled at him outside of the bar and said that he was being stupid.

He wasn't being stupid. The world was dangerous. And he was right to be afraid, and everything in his experience had taught him that that was true.

She loved him, but he may never be able to love her, because life had shown him that love was pain. And why would he ever see it as anything else?

She wanted to fight, but she didn't even know how.

"I could... I could protect you," she said.

"Shit. No. Quinn. You are not... You are not supposed to protect me."

"Someone should have," she said, the anger that burned in her breast now at the world, at her father, and everyone who had ever failed her. And him. "Somebody should take care of you because all you have done is take care of other people, and they don't even deserve it. Nobody deserves how good you are. Nobody."

"Quinn, I will never regret my life. Ever. But it is what it is."

"I love you."

"I know, carrot," he said, his voice rough. "I believe you. Dammit, I believe you. I wish..." He moved his hand across her bottom lip, and she closed her eyes. "Oh, Quinn. For a while there, things felt magical. Not the kind of thing that I've ever experienced before. I'm never going to know how *Pride and Prejudice* ends."

That broke her. Split her in half. It cracked her soul, and everything she was.

He didn't want to break up with her. But he didn't want to care for her. And he had valid reasons for that. She couldn't argue against them.

She just couldn't.

"What am I going to do? What am I going to do without you to hold me every night?" she asked, through her tears.

Dammit, the tears. Why was this happening?

You can't let it make you angry. He's hurt. He's not trying to hurt you.

He's not your dad.

"You are a smart cookie. You're gonna figure it out. And you are going to be just fine. You don't need me, Quinn. You have done so much without me. You got those scholarships, and you put yourself through school. You stood strong in the face of all the criticism your dad ever leveled at you. You're the greatest and best woman that I have ever known. That I ever will know. And you don't fucking need me. I am just a sad guy who's old before his time, out in a shack in the woods."

"This is not a shack," she said, almost laughing through her tears.

"It doesn't matter. The principle of the thing. I'm just a guy. You're something special. You were right. To come in and tell me that you were better than me, smarter than me. Look at what you did. The life that you imagined was not a life that was put in front of you, and you got that farm store opened. You went toe-to-toe with me, and you refused to back down, and that is all you. It is all you. You are determined, and brilliant, and a hard worker. You understand ranching. Deep in your bones. You talk about it the way that I feel about it. I've never known anybody who could put words to the things that are just in me. But you do it. You gave me words for myself. For what I think. You fixed my office. You made me feel like this isn't insurmountable. You're so smart you made it so that I could live without you here." And that, too, was soft, spoken like it was the highest of compliments, but it made her want to weep.

He wasn't being angry. He was heartbroken. And so was she. And she hadn't expected that. In all the scenarios of what might happen when she imagined telling him that she loved him, this was not it. This regretful, horrible goodbye. Where he said nothing but wonderful things. Nice things. Where he said everything but *I love you*.

Everything but *stay with me forever*.

"But I don't want to leave you," she said.

"Later, maybe a lot later, but later, Quinn, you are going to be glad that you left. Because you are gonna go find everything that you want. You did it once before. Hell, you've done it more than once. You have pushed on over and over again, and you will do it again. I will never be the thing that keeps you from having it all. Please don't make me into that. Don't tempt me past what I can handle."

"Okay. But I want you to know something, not because I want you to regret anything. I don't. I really don't. But I want you to know that over there across the field, working in that store, is a woman who loves you. Sending me away won't make it so that I don't love you. Because I just do. With everything that I am. And everything that I ever will be. I don't know what I'm going to go on to do. I know that I'll love you every minute that I do it. I was wrong, Levi. It's okay to need somebody else. I have never felt so alive as I have needing you. And I would break my heart a thousand times, over and over and over again, for this. For you. Because you're worth it. And I just want you to know that."

And she kissed him, because he was so close. And that kiss was devastating.

It didn't stop.

And then he had her backed up against the wall, kissing her like a man on fire.

And he carried her up the stairs, stripping her white dress off, and laid her down on the bed.

His movements were feverish and hot, like the kisses that he trailed down her body.

But she wasn't going to let him have all the control. If this was goodbye, she was going to say it her way.

She stripped his shirt off, his pants. Licked her way down his sculpted chest, all the way down to his heart and arousal. She wrapped her hand around him and licked him, before taking him in deep.

She loved this.

Just like she loved all of him. She loved pleasuring him. Tasting him. She loved being his. And she would surrender to that tonight.

She loved the feel of him pushing his fingers through her hair, pulling hard, coming up against the edge of his control.

And when she found it, he moved her away, growling as he laid her down on the bed and pressed himself against her.

And then he entered her in one swift thrust, his movements broken. And he said her name, over and over again. Like a prayer. Like a spell. Like maybe there was enough magic between them to fix all of this brokenness.

Maybe. Just maybe.

And they found their release together, a thundering crescendo that made her want to weep. Because, in the end, she was bereft of him.

But she was too spent to move. And so was he. So they fell asleep, in his bed, not touching, with space between them. She woke up with a start at 2:00 a.m. And then she slowly climbed out from beneath the covers and grabbed her things, dressed and went out to her car.

And then she began to drive home, alone. With no idea of what the future would hold.

CHAPTER TWENTY-SIX

WHEN LEVI WOKE UP, he was in bed naked. And Quinn was gone.

Quinn.

His heart throbbed.

It hurt so bad. It hurt to breathe.

She was gone. And the sun was beginning to push its way up behind the mountains, casting gray light on the land.

Quinn was gone. He had sent her away. She loved him, and he couldn't… He didn't want to. He didn't want to love her back.

Because people died, and you couldn't hold on to love forever. Because, in the end, loving someone too much could kill you.

He clutched his chest. He was close to it now. He was sure of it.

You didn't get a chance to grieve.

Without thinking, he put his jeans on, didn't bother with the shirt or anything else, and stumbled down the stairs, out the front door to his truck. He got behind the wheel and drove out toward his parents' graves.

There they were. Silent and steady as ever. His touchstone, in so many ways, because he didn't have their physical presence. He'd always felt like they could hear him, and maybe that was a lot of bullshit, but there was only so much harsh reality he could take. Only so much.

There they were. Next to each other. There they were, their names carved in stone. It was a testament. To their love.

He dropped to his knees there, right in front of their graves. A rock bit through the denim of his jeans, into his skin. He didn't care.

And a rush of certainty so intense that it couldn't be denied flooded him.

This was love.

And it was worth the pain.

He would love her like he'd never lose her, and if he did, it would've been worth all the years he had.

And if that loss sent him to his grave…it was worth it.

He'd avoided this all of his life because he never understood it. His father had been at peace because it was all right. Because he had love. Real love. The best love, and he was going toward it that day in the field.

And Levi had been afraid of it. But not now. Not now. And he knew that his parents still loved. Even now. Because he felt it. In everything he did. It had made him who he was. How had he ever questioned it? It was love that had made him into the man that could stay. That wanted to. That took care of those kids. And it was love that brought him here now. He wouldn't let go of loving his parents, no matter what. So why would he let go of Quinn? There was no point in preserving himself, not if he didn't have her.

Then it was like the floodgates opened. And for the first time, sorrow, joy, understanding, acceptance. Here on his land, a place where his blood soaked the dirt, the tears began to soak it, too, because he finally understood. He finally grieved.

And in that grief was love.

It was like all those lost years came to him then. Came through Quinn. Who didn't need him to be perfect or invulnerable. Who saw the dyslexia and everything else. Who saw the man, the boy and all the things in between and loved him anyway.

He knew that very few people would understand this, but he was facing down his fear. And the knowledge that the best kind of life would be one where he knew that at the end of all things, when he lay down and went back to this land, her headstone would be beside his.

That would be the sign of a good life. A real life. That was what was real.

The sun was starting to come up in earnest now, the sky going from pink to a lighter blue, and he knew that he had to go.

He had to find Quinn.

He wiped his face and walked back to his truck. And then he drove to Sullivan's Point.

Toward his heart. Toward his soul.

Toward his future.

The fulfillment of all the life he ever needed to live.

QUINN WAS SITTING listlessly at the kitchen table, next to a giant stack of pancakes that Rory had made for her desperately.

"It's okay, Rory."

"It's not okay. It's not okay."

"I'm going to gut him," said Fia.

"Please don't," said Quinn. "I'm sad. But he has been through hell. I'm not angry at him for this." She was just brokenhearted. There was a difference. And she still had hope. She despised that part of herself. Why wasn't she hopeless? Destitute. It made no sense. Because he had made himself clear.

And she had never once seen an instance where true love conquered anything.

Well, not in her life, anyway.

"He's being an idiot," said Fia.

"Right. Because you're so emotionally healthy, Fia. You literally hate a man that you've barely spoken to for years. You never date. If you got laid in the past decade I would be shocked. So maybe take your umbrage down a peg."

Great. She hadn't gotten angry at him, but now she was being petulant at her sister. But she felt defensive of Levi.

"I'm sorry," said Quinn. "I'll leave…"

"Your pancakes," said Rory, slapping the top of the stack with her spatula.

"You're bossy," said Quinn.

"You need it," said Fia.

She sighed heavily and started to put some pancakes on her plate, when she heard the sound of tires on the gravel.

Her heart stopped.

"Don't you dare," said Fia, going to the window.

"Is it him?" Rory asked.

"Yes," said Fia. "Let me at him." She picked the butter knife up off the counter.

"No," said Quinn. "Let me. Please. Just let me."

She got up and walked out to the front porch. And as soon as he got out of the truck, she knew.

His eyes were red, and he hadn't bothered to hide that.

He looked different. She could finally see the change on his face that she had felt inside.

Softening.

"Quinn," he said. "I love you."

She jumped down off the porch, skipping all three steps, and flew into his arms. He kissed her, deep and hard and long, and she clung to him.

"I love you," she said against his mouth.

"I realized... Quinn, I realized that I need you. And that if it breaks my heart, it is worth it. Because you are worth everything. Every potential cost. All the risk. I would gladly break myself into pieces for you. I get it now. My parents. Everything. I don't care that I've been hurt. I don't care that there are bad people out there. There's also you. I don't need just anybody. I need one person. And that's you. Nothing scares me. Not anymore. Because when I put everything through my Quinn-colored glasses, I can see that all I want, what I really want, is to have you. No matter what."

"Levi, that's...really and honestly the best thing anyone has ever said to me."

"I bet they didn't teach you this in college." He kissed her.

"No," she said, breathless, when they parted. "They didn't. Neither of us were as smart as we thought we were when this all started."

He laughed. Long and genuine. "No, carrot. We weren't. And I love you. You and your little cotton socks."

"You have a real thing with my socks."

"I have a real thing with you."

She sighed, joy filling her chest, her lungs. "They end up together."

"What?"

"You told me that now you wouldn't know how *Pride and Prejudice* ended. But I just wanted you to know, they end up together."

He smiled, and she remembered that moment, staring into his blue eyes at his house that first day she had come. When she had wanted to move nearer to him, but she hadn't. This time, she did.

"Of course they end up together. It's the only way."

"That's right. It is."

They kissed again, lingering out there in the early morning light. They would have so many days like this. They would work together, and eat dinner together, and go to bed together.

And it was just the most beautiful, hopeful thing she'd ever dared dream.

She'd felt like she'd lost her dreams when she was a kid. A kid who dreamed of Levi and life in a city, of something bright and glittering.

This was all the glittering she needed.

Right here.

With him.

He sighed heavily. "I expect I need to go inside and apologize to your sisters."

"Yeah. Probably. But on the bright side, there are pancakes."

"That sounds just about perfect."

So they walked up the steps together, hand in hand, and sat down around the breakfast table, around Rory's heartbreak pancakes, together.

Quinn Sullivan had always been book-smart. But she had never been in love before. And if she'd learned one thing from Levi, it was that smart could mean so many things. The way you saw the land, the way you saw people. The way that you loved.

And just like that, she realized she didn't need to define herself that way anymore. Because she was everything. But most of all, she was in love.

* * * * *